Falling

Emma Kavanagh

W F HOWES LTD

This large print edition published in 2014 by
W F Howes Ltd
Unit 4, Rearsby Business Park, Gaddesby Lane,
Rearsby, Leicester LE7 4YH

1 3 5 7 9 10 8 6 4 2

First published in the United Kingdom in 2014
by Century

A CIP catalogue record for this book is available
from the British Library

ISBN 978 1 47125 980 7

Typeset by Palimpsest Book Production Limited,
Falkirk, Stirlingshire

Printed and bound in Great Britain
by TJ International Ltd, Padstow, Cornwall

For my Mum and Dad, who told me that I could.
For Matthew, who made me believe it.
And for Daniel, so that he may know
that all things are possible.

CHAPTER 1

Cecilia: Thursday 15 March, 6.08 p.m.

A shrieking of wind, screeching of metal as the plane ripped itself apart, the wicked cold tearing at her throat. Cecilia Williams gripped the seat, fingers burning with pain. She tried to close her mouth, but the sound prised it open, stealing her breath. A giant's hand pinned her to the bulkhead, tumbling, tumbling, so that she couldn't remember which was the floor and which was the ceiling.

She couldn't see the people. Just black night air where there should have been a plane, space where there should have been seats. She squeezed her eyes shut. If she leaned this way, then it could almost be like she was sleeping.

They nearly hadn't taken off at all. It had been touch and go. The air had thickened days ago, grey clouds massing as temperatures plummeted far below the March average. Then the snow, thick and bulbous. It came down in thick flurries, wrapping itself around Cardiff airport, climbing into mountainous drifts. Flights cancelled one after the other. There had been no reason to believe that this one would be any different. Except that it would be, because it had to be. Cecilia had sat in the crew room, sipping harsh black coffee, beads of sweat breaking out beneath her blunt-cut fridge as a potted ficus wilted and slowly began to die in the fierce heat charging from the radiators. She had pulled at the turquoise polyester jacket, letting it drop to the floor beside her. She hated that uniform. Saw the other flight attendants looking at the crumpled pile. Drank her coffee. She wouldn't wear it again.

'Gonna cancel it, you think?' The co-pilot looked at her, running knuckled fingers through curtained hair. Concentration-camp thin, all teeth and nostrils. He was new, coming in as she was going out. Cecilia didn't know his name, didn't really see the point in learning it, not now. She had handed her notice in. This would be her final flight. She stared out of the window, watched the falling snow. She didn't answer.

'They'll cancel,' the co-pilot mumbled, almost like he was whispering a prayer. 'They'll cancel.'

The pilot, Oliver Blake, glanced up at him, then back down. Staring at the ground. Jaw tight.

Made everyone tetchy, a night like this.

The plane kept tumbling, over, over. Seemed to be no end to it. There were things she should be doing as the wind whipped past her, the ground rushing closer. Her arms wanted to fold themselves over her head, mouth to scream brace. But she couldn't move her arms and she couldn't move her mouth and the rest of her just didn't care. It would be over soon, anyway.

They had waited in the crew room, roll-on cases lining the wall in a chain gang. Cecilia's at the end, bigger than the rest. She blew on her coffee. Her graduation certificate. She hadn't brought it. It was in a frame, displayed in the study that they used to hang laundry. She should have brought it. But then the interview wasn't for another month. Ground crew. She would be based out of London again, if she got the job. There would be a lot of applicants, would always be a lot of applicants for a job like that. But she had worked there before, and she knew people, and hopefully that would be enough. It didn't really matter about the certificate; she would have to speak to Tom again. Eventually.

'We'll never fly tonight. No chance.' The co-pilot was working his jaw, teeth grinding against the hum of the heating.

Cecilia had never thought she would want to go back to the chaos and the London smog and the pillar-box-red uniforms. Never thought that at thirty years old she would pack up her life, walk out on her husband, her almost-three-year-old son. Something stuck in her throat, choking her almost. She had looked out of the window at the snow and tried not to think about that.

She wondered if Tom knew that she had left, if he had found the closet door hanging open, all of her most prized belongings gone. She should have left a note. Should have done that at least.

Then the crew room phone rang, and they all looked up. Oliver pushed himself to his feet, trudging as though through a snowdrift.

Watching. Waiting.

He hung up the phone, turning back.

'We're on.'

She hadn't kissed her son goodbye. She should have kissed him goodbye.

Then it was all hurry, hurry, hurry. She had grabbed her bags, a quick slick of lipstick even though her fingers were shaking, pulled her skirt straight, then click, clack, click, out into the terminal. Passengers' heads bobbed up like meerkats, the whisper running through the terminal in a bow wave behind them. Cecilia raised her chin and looked straight ahead.

Suddenly there was no time. It was a narrow window. There was more snow coming in. We go now or we don't go. And Cecilia very much wanted to go.

'Hello, hi, welcome, straight to the back, please.' A pasted smile, gesturing with French-tipped nails along the line of the plane. She bit her lip as they shuffled their way in, buffeting one against the other with their thick anoraks, all clumsy in heavy gloves. 'If you could move out of the aisle, please.' Smiling, smiling. 'Let me help you with that.' She moved alongside the Jude Law man with his Armani shirt, open at the collar, reached up to angle the carry-on luggage into the overhead bin, not looking at the thin-lipped, flat-eyed woman who stood beside him.

Then the doors were shut and they were moving, and all eyes were on her as she pirouetted through the safety briefing. Smiling. Always smiling.

Trying not to smell the smoke rising from the bridges that she had burnt behind her.

They were taxiing, building pressure pinning her to her seat. Cecilia turned her head, watching pinprick lights against the dark night sky. Sighing. She had straightened her hair three times today. Teasing the fringe that curled from the damp of the snow, pulling at it with fingers that trembled, ever so slightly, knowing that it would do no good. But doing it anyway, because it was better than thinking. Anything was better than that. Then the lift. Littered lights giving way to black sea. A turn, climbing, climbing.

Cecilia leaned back in her seat. Was staring off into space when her gaze was pulled by the sense of being stared at. The little girl was three, four maybe. Chocolate streaked across the tip of her nose, solemn jaw moving up and down. She was twisted around in her chair watching the flight attendant. She was beautiful. Dark eyes. Like Ben's.

Cecilia looked away.

They were climbing, up through clouds. The plane shimmied, but she was looking at her reflection again, where the mascara had smudged. And now she was thinking about Ben's smell, his velvet skin, the way he slept with his mouth ever so slightly open, snoring a little boy snore. She felt sick.

A murmur rippled through the cabin, washing up at her feet, and she glanced up, looking because she was waiting for something, anything, so that she didn't have to think about the little boy she had left behind. The girl had turned around, curling into her mother as they leafed through the pages of a book. But there were others, glancing back at her. Cecilia tugged her shirt straight. An attractive girl, maybe twenty, maybe a little more, looking at her, overlarge hoop earrings swinging, and it was like she wanted to say something, but she didn't and, biting her lip, she dropped her gaze back into her lap where her hands twisted one inside the other.

Then the plane bucked. The murmur replaced with a 'whoa' of riders on a roller-coaster. Cecilia flung out her hand, bracing herself against the window.

'It's only crosswinds. Nothing to worry about.' Her words were lost in the groaning of engines. But she said them again, whispering to herself.

The engines whirred, singing in an unfamiliar key. The girl with the hoop earrings was looking at her again, eyes wide, willing her to say something. Another buck. A high-pitched whining she hadn't heard before. There was nothing beyond the windows. A sea of grey cotton breaking into darkness.

The engine was straining, a dog pulling at its leash, and now they seemed to be tilting, not climbing now but pointing upwards, steep, steeper than she had ever seen it. A solitary bottle of Dr Pepper had shaken itself loose from somewhere. It rolled down the aisle, rattling, bouncing, all eyes watching as it drifted to a stop at her feet. Then the chaos of noise vanished into a deafening silence.

And she knew.

She hadn't said goodbye to her son. She had stood on the threshold, where the murky blue glow of Ben's *Toy Story* nightlight met the darkness of the hallway, and watched him sleep with his arms thrown up over his head, the way he had slept ever since he was a tiny baby. And she had turned and walked away.

Someone screamed. Then they were falling.

CHAPTER 2

Tom: Thursday 15 March, 6.16 p.m.

Tom's feet skated on black ice and for a moment he hung in the air, shoes scrabbling for purchase on the steep incline. He slid, past gluttonous wheelie bins, through the puddle of yellow light that spilled from the street lamp, back into the darkness of the alleyway, a narrow artery littered with used syringes and disco balls of silver foil, air choked with the spiky scent of urine and rot. Then ice gave way to glistening tarmac, feet settling on to solid ground again.

The heroin-thin figure was just ahead, plunging through banked-up snow, skin blue on drug-tracked arms. Callum Alun Jones had been out of prison for a little over a month. The iced wind pulled at his breath, throwing it back towards Tom, dousing him in sweet alcohol, the musk of cigarettes. This time Callum's victim had been eighty-seven years old – a survivor of the Normandy campaign, an English teacher. A tremulously thin man with a shock of white hair who had buried his wife and his youngest daughter within a year of one another, and who had spent the last six months clinging grimly to a life that had all but defeated him. He'd been sleeping when Callum had broken into his tiny terraced house, had woken suddenly, roused by something that he couldn't identify. Had found the drug addict in his kitchen, seen Callum's rats-tail fingers closing around his dead wife's wedding ring, and then the fists that rained down on him until everything turned red. The man had woken in the hospital two days later, face grey and eyes empty, finally defeated.

Tom had held the old man's hand as he wept, and had thought that there were days when this was the worst job in the world. He had been in the force for fifteen years. Eight in uniform, pounding pavements in the lashing rain, drain-pipe drizzles plopping from the rim of his helmet on to his fluorescent jacket. Then CID. A detective, just like his father. He tried not to think about that. His mother said that was why he had never gone for promotion, why sitting at detective constable was enough for him. Not because he didn't think he was capable of reaching the dizzying heights of detective chief inspector, but because if he did then he would truly be his father's son. And anything was better than that.

Fifteen years. Fifteen years in which Tom had seen more than a dozen dead bodies, smelled death more times than he would have thought possible.

9

He remembered the last time he had arrested Callum Jones, spared a moment as he danced through patches of ice to wonder how long it would be until he was arresting him again. A never-ending carousel.

Tom breathed in the bitter cold air, skidding on ice-rink tarmac. Thought of his son that morning, eyes still heavy with sleep. No idea that his mother had gone.

'You're going to go to Grandma's today. Okay, Ben?'

His son had studied him, the light from the rising sun throwing shadows on to a face creased into a little-boy frown. Then a smile that could break your heart. ''Kay, Daddy.' Baby-fat fingers reaching up carefully, hovering over the slick aubergine skin. 'Show Gaga my owie.' Clumsy, the fingers brushed the bruise, and his rosebud lips pulled down, face creased. 'Ow, Daddy.'

'I know, bud. You're okay. Gaga will kiss it better.' And he'd tucked the toddler's windmilling arms into thick padded sleeves, and tried not to think about what would come next. Watching his son's chubby fingers spreading themselves wide, the frown as he examined them, like he'd never seen them before. Suddenly fascinating. Tried to ignore the words that circled his head, vultures above a carcass. *Your mother has left us. She's not coming back.*

Callum was inches ahead now, running ragged on the steep incline. Tom dug his feet hard into

10

the slush, gritting his teeth, the cold whipping at his lungs as he ran. He could see Callum's arms, pumping back and forth beneath his T-shirt. Callum's girlfriend had stood there on the doorstep of their council flat, biting her lower lip as she cradled her track-covered arms and tried to disappear into the flocked wallpaper. She had watched as her boyfriend – the one who loved her and who had beaten her hard enough to kill the drug-addled baby growing inside her – pushed past the arresting officers and into the snowbound night.

They were plunging down the hill, the cold catching at Tom's throat, running so fast it seemed that they were falling. Sound of cars, getting louder, and then the alleyway opened up, spitting them on to the curve of a main road, traffic thin and moving slowly in the slush. Past the skeleton of a phone box, all jagged glass edges, glittering in orange street lighting. The snow was thinner here, mounds thinning into furrows of slush. Callum raced onwards, not glancing left or right, past the wide-eyed shop windows where late shoppers peered over displays, out into the road, an almost terminal slip in the car-tracked snow, then regaining his balance and diving on past the Co-op. Tom veered around slush, breathing easy, compact body primed by years of running.

A beam of light and the slam of a car door.

Tom glanced sideways at his partner, Dan. 'Took your time.'

'Got fucking lost. Ended up in a bastard funeral procession.'

'At least you're clearly not the Grim Reaper. Not got the figure for it.'

'Whatever, skinny arse. You going to catch this little shit, or what?'

'Shall we?'

Tom had woken that morning to the sound of the front door. It always stuck in the cold. It had pulled him from a dream into a moment of disorientation, and he lay blinking into the darkness. Then the growl of an engine, settling back into a steady grumble, swaddled in snow. He wondered distantly just where it was that Cecilia was going this early in the morning. She wasn't due to fly until that night. The rhythm of the engine climbed, wheels crunching on the snow. But then did it really matter when you came right down to it? He listened to the car until he could hear it no more, then lay for a while in the silence. He didn't know what made him get up. How it was that he just suddenly knew. He pushed back the duvet, bare feet on thick carpet, and padded down the hall, to the room that had become known as Cecilia's room. He pushed the door, that feeling in his stomach of treading where he wasn't supposed to go. Snapped on the light. The curtains were closed. The bed was made, duvet pulled tight across the box frame. He stood there for a moment. It looked like a guest room again. The book was gone. The one she had been reading, the one whose title he had never bothered to learn. And the picture of Ben in its knotted silver frame that had sat on the bedside table. That was gone too. He crossed the room, slowly pulled open the wardrobe door. Ran his fingers over the few clothes that remained. They smelled of his wife. He stood there, staring at the gaping hole, the naked metal hangers. And knew. His marriage was over.

He had gone back to bed, footsteps slow. She was supposed to watch Ben today. That was what she had said. But it was probably for the best, after yesterday. He hadn't been able to sleep, though, had stared at the ceiling for an hour, maybe more. The bedroom door had creaked, a little after six, and Tom had listened to the tread of little-boy feet on carpet, hiding a smile as a soft voice whispered, ''Kay, Daddy. Back to sleep. I stay here now.' The heart-stopping warmth of his son creeping under the duvet, huddling against him. Tom cuddled him in, painfully aware that it didn't even occur to Ben to wonder where his mother was.

Callum turned sharply, into the road, past the primary school – closed, thank God – then a sharp left into the alleyway that snaked by the steepled building. Snow climbed into peaks, hiding the detritus that lay beneath. But it was dark. That was why he didn't see the leaking downpipe and the lake of ice that had spread out across the narrow alleyway.

In fairness, Tom didn't see it either. What he saw

was Callum's legs stretched in a giant leap over a protruding bank of snow, sailing through the air in a balletic moment of elegance that Tom doubted his sad little life had ever seen before. Then that moment when everything goes wrong, as his right foot made contact with the ground, expecting a solid surface, somewhere safe to land, arms wind-milling as his body realised before his brain did that there was no safety here and that the solid ground had warped into a sheet of ice. Then his left foot, landing because it had no choice, desperately trying to make the situation better but only making it worse. And then both feet giving up the game, as they slid out from under him and he dropped like a stone, skinny arse landing on the frozen ground with a sickening thud.

Tom skidded to a halt, keeping his feet on firm ground, before reaching out, hands encompassing the bone-thin wrists. 'Come on.' He hoisted him up. 'Callum Alun Jones, I am arresting you for assault and burglary . . .'

'Little fucker, little fucker, little fucker . . .' Tom didn't look round, didn't need to, to know that Dan was skidding, arms flailing wildly from a body more designed for rugby than slalom. 'Stand still, you little shit. I swear to God, I'm going to . . .' then a pause, as ice and breathlessness tore his partner's words from his mouth.

Tom snapped handcuffs on to the addict's wrists, the narrow figure writhing as Tom read him his rights, kicking out at Tom's shins.

'Fuck you, wanker.' Callum's voice sounded like sandpaper.

Tom wrapped him in a tight grasp. 'Yeah, yeah.'

Callum twisted, pulling his head back. Tom should have seen it coming. He'd been here often enough. Shouldn't have come as a surprise. But he was off his game today, not paying the attention he should, and the gob of murky fluid hit him square in the face.

'Little shit.' Dan grabbed hold of Callum, pushing his shoulder into the ground. 'Fucking little shit.'

Tom wiped his face with his sleeve. 'Forget it, mate. He's a twat.' Pulling him bodily to his feet. 'Come on, wide boy. Walk.'

Snow had begun to fall again in thick flakes, and in spite of himself Tom wondered if Cecilia would be flying today. Took a second to reflect on the irony of running away from your husband and son only to be grounded by a late spring snowfall. The wind had whipped up, bitterly cold, swirling torrents of snow into miniature tornadoes. They walked slowly, heads down. Callum had stopped struggling, was trudging beside them now, cuffed hands folded behind his back as he muttered to himself about his human rights. It would be a tough night to fly.

They were in the car, Callum tucked into the back, shivering wildly without the adrenalin to keep him warm.

Dan turned the key, the engine sparking to life. 'Bloody weather.'

15

'Yeah.'

'Supposed to be like this for a while.'

'So they say.'

'You, ah, you hear about Madeleine?'

Tom watched the snow tumbling by his window. 'Yeah.'

'May, the baby's due.'

'Yeah.'

'Said she'll be sticking around in CID with us. They've got her doing light duties.' Dan eased the car out on to the slick roadway. 'You guys talk much now?'

Since he had told her he was leaving her. Since he had broken her heart and his own in the process.

'A bit. Not much.' Tom reached, twisting the volume button until another voice drowned out Dan and the memory of what could have been. The newsreader's tone was serious. Tom was going to change the channel, his hand moving, but then something fluttered at his subconscious, so that his hand hung in mid-air, stayed by something that he didn't recognise. Then the words.

Aeroplane crash.

CHAPTER 3

Jim: Thursday 15 March, 6.25 p.m.

It was the darkness. That was his first warning that there was something wrong.

Jim had pulled up outside his daughter's house, driving carefully, muttering to himself. Ridiculous weather. Cold would decimate his daffodils, yellow trumpet heads bowing under the weight of the snow. He had pushed open the car door, carefully hoisting the plate from the passenger seat. Had ducked his head, pulling his chin in to the neck of his thick jacket. Snowflakes crept down the back of his neck. He knew that Libby wouldn't be home. She would be at work, was afternoons today, but it would be here for her when she returned. *She's too skinny, that girl.* Esther had been making cookies, narrow arms fearsome as she pounded together sugar and butter. *I swear she's disappearing.*

Jim had hurried down the path, thinking that it was slick, that perhaps he would salt it before he left. Had swerved to one side, to where the snow was thicker, the grip firmer, because that was the last thing he needed now, falling in the snow like some decrepit. Breaking a damn hip. Thirty years on the police force and winding up a snow-bound corpse on a housing estate, delivering pork chops to his youngest. It was unsettling enough, this retirement thing, without the indignity of that. That was when he had realised that there was no line of light creeping its way between the closed curtains. He had stopped, right there in the snow. Had frowned.

It wasn't like Libby.

Libby hated the darkness, always had, even when she was a little girl; needed the reassurance of knowing that there was life there, no monsters under the bed. Would leave the living room light on day and night, even though he had nagged her about wasting electricity, teasing her that no police officer should be afraid of the dark, even an unwarranted Police Community Support Officer, a bobby on the beat with a scant eight months on the force. But not tonight. Tonight the house was black.

He slipped the key into the lock, pushing open the door, and slowly reached, flicking on the light.

The room was as it should be. Everything in its place. The cat blinked at him, curled into the sofa with its plumped cushions. A tiny creature, white and black, little pink nose and two black smudges across its eyes that gave the impression of a boxer down on his luck. With a long stretch it jumped down, letting loose a miaow too big for its little body; began weaving its way around Jim's legs.

'Hey, Charlie.'

Jim crouched down, scanning the room as the cat curled itself into him. It was tidy, everything tucked away as it always was. Apart from the coat, flung across the arm of the sofa. Jim's pulse quickened.

Miaow.

Libby's work coat. The one she had worn when she came home on her first day in uniform. A Police Community Support Officer. Almost like her daddy. There was a plan – there was always a plan. Serve her time, learn everything there was to learn, and when they started recruiting again, apply to be a police constable. Then, when she had gained enough experience, start the climb, to sergeant, then inspector, then super. Just like her daddy. He reached down, fingering the lapel of the coat.

Miaow.

Jim pushed himself up. The kitchen door was closed. She never closed the door, because then the cat couldn't get to its food, and she doted on that damn cat, ever since she'd found it curled up in the brambles that ran alongside the railway tracks, a tiny, shivering bundle of fur. Bringing it home and letting it eat her out of house and home, sleeping on her bed and following her around like they were joined at the hip. He eased the handle down, snapping on the light.

The surfaces had been wiped down, chairs tucked snug beneath the kitchen table, floor mopped. The cat's bowl was empty. Charlie ran to it, pushing his head against it. A look back at Jim, a loud miaow.

Jim stood there for a moment, trying to identify the unease. A quick look up, eye caught by movement beyond the window, but it was just the falling snow. He slid the bowl on to the kitchen table. The cat was twisting around him, knotting itself around his legs.

'All right. Let's get you some food.'

Jim crouched down, levering open the narrow cupboard that stood alongside the fridge. He would ring her, just to check, and she'd laugh at him, would say that he was getting soft in his old age. But he would ring anyway. After all, he was a father. That was what you did.

Then the cat leapt at him, tiny frame landing on his folded knees. Light, hardly any weight at all, but enough to startle him. Jim swayed, knocked off balance, grabbing at the side of the cupboard to save himself. To stop himself from falling.

'Charlie!'

He laughed, insides fizzing from the almost fall. Was just thinking about how quickly everything could change. He let go of the cupboard. Then he saw the blood.

CHAPTER 4

Freya: Thursday 15 March, 6.36 p.m.

Freya moved the paint across the thick paper, quick strokes, flick, flick, before it dried and became unwieldy. Sunflower yellow. She swirled the brush in greying water, a quick shake, then a swipe of ochre. The light in the kitchen was warm, the colour of corn. Not ideal for painting, but she didn't mind. She allowed the brush to trace the curve. She liked it like this, the warmth from the oven, the rippling Beethoven, her mother's movements unselfconscious, for a little while at least.

'That's beautiful.'

Freya glanced up, smiled. Her mother was in her off-duty clothes today, loose jeans, a jumper that hung so that it disguised her hips, her narrow frame. Her long, narrow hands – her paws, she called them – naked, her wedding ring sitting waiting in the little cup on the windowsill. The barest touch of make-up. *Just enough so I don't scare the postman.* A laugh like dancing raindrops and then a quick turn away from the mirror. She rarely looked at herself for longer than she had to.

'Thank you.' Freya looked back down, scanning the page.

'Although . . .' a sizzle as ice-white onions hit hot oil, 'surely you must be able to find something more interesting to paint.'

'I like painting you, Mum.' Freya let the brush sit loose in her fingers, the rough grain from years of moments like these scratching against her skin. Her mother was beautiful, so Freya had always thought at least. Slim, and warm as fresh-baked bread.

They had the same nose, her mother and her. The same little upturn at the end. The same eyes, fir-tree green. That was where the resemblance ended, at least as far as Freya was concerned. Where her mother was narrow and delicate, Freya was tall and curved. *You get that from your father's side*. She had her father's cheekbones. And sometimes, just occasionally, her father's temper.

Her mother tipped minced beef into the pan, little red curls screeching with the heat. Freya loved these rare moments. The house quiet and warm, the snow a silent marching army beyond the windows. Low music and the sweet smell of onions. She surveyed the page. She didn't paint much, not any more, time so often gobbled up by research for the psychology PhD that she had nearly finished, and by her friends. But they were all locked up tight by the snow now. She wondered if for them too it came as a relief, a moment to breathe and stop and just paint.

'I wonder if your father's taken off yet?' Her mother was leaning, looking out into the snow. 'It's an awful night to fly.'

'I know.' Freya dabbed at the ochre, soft, soft, just feathering the edges.

'He probably hasn't. I mean, they've been grounding flights all week.' Her mother glanced at the clock. 'I expect we'll hear from him soon.'

'What time are Grandma and Grampa coming?' The trip had been planned for months, a pilgrimage to Cowbridge from St Ives. Freya's mother had suggested that they postpone it, just by a week or so, given the weather, the problems that would inevitably follow. But her grandmother had scoffed. They had plans, she had said. They would be coming. Even though the traffic would be bad and Gramps' driving awful and her grandmother would complain about every stop from Polperro to Cardiff. Then they would arrive and the house would pulse with an unspecified tension, her father's teeth gritted, her mother's voice climbing an octave with each passing day.

Freya's mother looked at the clock again. 'They called. About an hour ago. I thought it was your father, actually, you know, saying he was coming home. But it wasn't. Grandma said they were around about Bristol.' She glanced across her shoulder at Freya, a small smile. 'Said the way your grandfather is driving they should be here by Christmas.'

Freya grinned, brushing hair from her face with the back of her hand. Liquid sunshine, her mother called it, when she stroked her daughter's hair, forgetting for a moment that she wasn't a child any more, twenty-three years slipping away in the blink of an eye. Freya had always thought it was more the colour of buttered popcorn, a burnished yellow flecked with hints of brown. A colour caught her eye, a flash of red paint, and she grimaced. She should have worn an apron. Now her skinny jeans were speckled with measle spots.

'So you never told me . . .'

'Huh?' Freya wasn't looking at her mother, scratching at the paint with her nail.

'Last night. How did it go?'

'Oh. You know.'

'You know, good?'

'Well, yeah. I mean, yeah, it was okay. It was just a couple of us. Zoe and Rena and a couple of others. But it was nice. We had a laugh.'

'And Luke?'

Freya looked up from the paint, fixing her mother with a level stare, lips twitching with an almost smile.

'I'm just saying. Was he there?'

'Yes, Mum.'

'He seems like a nice boy.'

Freya laughed, leaning back in the chair. 'Mum. He's thirty-two.'

Her mother smiled, sweeping the meat around the pan. 'Love, believe me, when you're my age, that will make him a boy.'

Freya shook her head. 'Because you're that old?'

Her mother sighed heavily, looking out of the window into the snow. 'Feels like it some days.' She shook her head, glancing back at Freya. 'So are you interested in him?'

Freya dipped the brush back into the jar. The colours were a little too dark, and she sprinkled water across the painting, sunshine through the rain. Could feel her cheeks flushing. 'I don't know. I don't think so.'

'Well, you'll meet somebody. Give it time.' Another sigh. 'I do hope your father isn't flying in this.'

Freya looked up. Her mother was staring out of the window again, fingering the petals of the tumbledown lilies that Freya's father bought her every Friday. *Flowers for my flower.* But they were browning now, pink petals curling inwards, turning sepia at the edges. The sickly-sweet smell jarred against the cooking meat.

'You were late in last night.' Freya said.

Her mother didn't turn, looked down, spoon scraping at the bottom of the pan. 'I know. Got caught up. Talking. You know how it is.'

The kitchen door creaked open, grinding against the tiles. Richard's hair was damp, dark, brushed back from his angled-cheekboned face. Long enough that it had grown into loose curls.

25

Baby-bird dark eyes, narrow frame hidden in an Abercrombie & Fitch T-shirt, lean muscled arms bare. A man's body for such a little boy. Her brother was beautiful. Not just a big sister's love; he was genuinely beautiful, with his chocolate-brown eyes, long dark lashes, his tall, strong frame and his wide mouth that looked made for smiling.

'Hey, kiddo.'

He looked tired, drawn. Freya pushed a kitchen chair back and he slumped down into it.

'You okay?' Freya asked.

'Yeah. Didn't sleep very well last night.'

Freya watched him, resisting the urge to reach out and smooth down the hair that stuck out at odd angles. *He's seventeen now. Can't keep treating him like a child.* Even though he was her baby brother, ever since the day they brought him home from the hospital, buried within white wool, his dark eyes watching her like they knew, even then, that she would always protect him.

'Where's Dad?' Richard asked.

'He's working. Glasgow.' Her mother glanced up at the snow again, as if by the force of her gaze she could make it stop. 'Unless he's been cancelled. He hasn't called, though.'

'Is he back tonight?' asked Freya.

'Ah . . . tomorrow? Evening, I think. But with this weather . . . we'll just have to see.' She stirred the pan, metal spoon scratching against the stainless-steel rim. 'Maybe he hasn't taken off. He probably hasn't. They wouldn't let him fly in this. He'll probably call soon.'

Richard nodded, his long, narrow fingers reaching for the television remote. There was a burst of sound, and Freya looked over her shoulder at the television, blinking to remember that there was a world outside.

And there it was. Fire and metal and snow.

And Freya knew.

CHAPTER 5

Cecilia: Thursday 15 March, 6.39 p.m.

The pain swallowed her, not just her left arm, which seemed to belong in its entirety to someone else, but climbing towards her shoulder, radiating around her back, her neck. Hands shook, knees begged to be allowed to fold, and the cold snow looked so inviting.

'Away, now.'

The girl tried to struggle, but didn't try very hard, so weak she could barely stand. 'My mother.' She clawed at Cecilia's blouse, charred black. So young, a teenager, but just barely. 'Please. My mum.'

It was hard to make out her words, gobbled down in amongst the growl of fire, creaking metal. Acrid smoke scraped at her throat. The battered aft section of the turboprop jutted out from a bed of trees, vertical stabiliser reaching up into the grey sky. Sparking electrical arcs crackled, melting the snow down to bare earth.

Cecilia wrapped the girl in her good arm, pulling her bodily down the sloping ground, away from

28

the trees and the burning carcass of the plane. 'Come on.' Wading through the deep snow, to where the smoke is lighter, and they can breathe. Pulling her, because she still wants to turn back.

There were others, gathered in a knot in the snow. Her throat searing from the shouting. *Everybody off. Get away from the plane. Leave everything. Everybody off.* And when they wouldn't move, frozen in their seats, not dead yet but feeling like it, dragging them bodily from the sparking wreckage, the pain gripping her arm threatening to drown her. Screaming at them, *get away, get back.* She pushed them down the hill into the field, away from the trees, out into the wide expanse of snow where there is no shelter and no warmth, and where they will have so little time, but what else can she do? Dragging them together, cursing British reserve, because now it may be only body heat that will keep them alive.

'Just wait. They'll come. Just wait here.' Having no idea whether she was lying or not.

Moving all the time, because there's a role to play, an explanation for why she has survived. And if she keeps moving, then she won't have time to think about baby-soft skin, and the scrape of brick against her bare back, and the sensation of falling.

'Can you keep her with you?'

The woman wasn't looking at Cecilia, arms wrapped around her knees, staring at the wreckage of the plane.

'Hey.' Cecilia nudged the woman with her foot,

only then realising that her leg was bleeding. 'I need you to watch her.'

The woman looked up at her, like she didn't understand what she was saying, then looked at the young girl, who was crying now, back at Cecilia. Nodded. Reached up a hand, pulled the girl down to her side, and wrapped her arms around her, sighing like it was a relief.

Cecilia looked down the hill, a gentle curve peppered with copses of trees. And there, where the mountainside gave way to the village, an orange glow and flashing blue lights and the distant wail of sirens.

There was a roaring in her ears, and they were falling again; the scream of metal, the plane breaking in two. She stared at the lights, and then turned away, just couldn't look at it any more. All that death. Seemed like there was no room in her head for it. Turning back to her little group, the ones who had survived.

It took Cecilia a moment to make out the figure in the snow. It wasn't that far away, a couple of hundred yards maybe. For a moment, she thought it was a snow bank, mounded beneath a solitary oak. Then she saw it move, realised it wasn't.

'Wait here.'

She plunged through the snow, towards the mound. The old woman had curled in on herself, tucked together like a snail, knees pulled to her chest, shoulders dropped low, wrapped in snow. Cecilia sank to her knees beside her. The woman was staring upwards, towards the naked branches of the tree hanging protectively over her, her breath shallow, face an inner-city grey.

'Hello. I'm Cecilia.' She watched her, waiting for movement, for something. 'What's your name?'

Blue lips, slightly parted, breathing like she'd run a marathon. It was like there was a time delay between them. After a few more seconds, she turned, movement awkward. 'Mrs Collins.' A moment, and she thought about this some more. 'Maisie.'

'Are you hurt, Maisie?'

'I . . . I don't know. I'm so cold. Very cold.'

Cecilia took hold of the old lady's hand, fingers blue, stiff. A deep red trickle seeped its way beneath tightly bound grey curls, staining them crimson, blusher scarecrow red on death-white cheeks.

'Are they coming? Is someone coming to get us?'

'Yes. We just have to wait.'

'I don't know, love.' The words were little more than a whisper. 'It's awful cold.'

'Where were you heading?' Cecilia forced a smile into her voice.

The old woman nodded, snow falling from her. 'Glasgow. My daughter.' Teeth clenched, words squeezed from between them, a whistle on the inhale. 'Moved there when she got married. Stupid man. Always knew it wouldn't last.' A cough, body shuddering so that the snow shifted around her. 'Can't tell them, though, can you? Got to let them

31

find out themselves. Two little girls now. Ernie loves them.' Looking up at Cecilia, and then straining, trying to move her head. 'Ernie. I forgot. Where is he?'

Cecilia didn't bother looking around, just folded the old woman's hand tighter into her own. 'He'll be around here somewhere.'

Another cough, and what might have passed for a laugh if you were gullible. 'Always wandering off. Nuisance man. Never stays put.'

'So, how long you going for?' asked Cecilia. 'To your daughter's, I mean.' The ashen face was draining, skin melting into snow, and she had stopped looking at Cecilia, was gazing upwards again, somewhere above her head. 'Be lovely for you to see her.' Cecilia jiggled the old woman's hand in her own, sliding her fingers down her wrist. Smiling. Always smiling.

'Mmmm . . . suppose.'

Cecilia had come home late on Sunday. Had thought that Ben would already be in bed. Instead she had found him in the kitchen with Tom, small hands thick with azure-blue paint. 'Look, Mummy.' He had waved towards the blue handprints on the stark white paper laid out across the kitchen table. 'I did it, look.' She had known that she should smile, clap her hands. But her head was still too full of the phone call. Heather's voice. *Did you hear? They found Eddie dead. Tragic. Just tragic.* But then of course, Heather didn't know. Why would she know? Cecilia had never told her.

Cecilia had never told anyone. And anyway, you had to say something nice, didn't you, when someone died? Even if they had wandering hands and eyes that seemed to be already dead. So she hadn't smiled at her son when he waved his paint-covered fingers at her, pointing at his work with his little chest puffed out. Instead she had looked at the paint, and the spread newspaper, and the little fingers that surely wouldn't come clean without a bath, when all she wanted to do was curl up into a ball and cry tumbling tears of relief. So she had shaken her head. Had sighed. Had watched her son's smile falter and fade away.

'Be lovely,' Cecilia said to Maisie. 'You'll have a great time.'

The old woman didn't answer.

'Maisie? Come on. Maisie?'

CHAPTER 6

Jim: Thursday 15 March, 7.20 p.m.

'Your daughter's how old? Twenty-five?' The man-child detective gave him a look, the kind you give a kid who has mixed up her words. 'Yeah. That's not something we'd be getting involved in.' A ping, and he pulled a phone from his pocket, scrolling down the screen with his thumb. His shirt was creased, tie pulled loose, knot too tight, hanging askew. He hadn't polished his shoes. Didn't look like he had ever polished his shoes.

Jim's hands shook. He'd washed them, once, twice, seemed like a hundred times, but he could still see the blood there. The cat had been purring. Jim had stared at the blood. Had to think, had to calm down, had to think. Because if he could, then he could figure this out. There would be an answer, something simple, and then there would be a flooding relief, a deep sigh, maybe even a laugh, his heart still pounding. He'd hang his head, sick with relief. Go home and tell Esther, and they would laugh at his fear. Then it would settle down into some dim and distant corner of his memory, where it would stay for ever – the day he thought he'd lost his only daughter.

'Is Nate about?'

The boy didn't look up, still staring at his phone. 'Mmm?'

'The DI. Nate Maxwell. He about?' They'd joined together. Stood shoulder to shoulder as rocks and petrol canisters rained down on them in the Bristol St Paul's riots, when they'd been pulled in on mutual aid. Played more rounds of golf than Jim could count.

The kid looked up then, nostrils flaring. 'I'm the senior officer on tonight.'

You've got to be kidding me. Jim rubbed his face, turning slightly.

He had stood in the empty house, and it was like he was frozen, somewhere in a no-man's-land where he couldn't just be a father, because if he was a father then he would lose it, just lose it, but he wasn't a policeman any more. Stood there feeling fat and old and useless.

He had pulled his mobile phone out of his pocket.

There would be an explanation. Libby would answer the phone with her sing-song 'hello', and she would laugh when he told her where he was and what he had found. She would tell him a story, something that he hadn't thought of.

And then everything would be all right.

It took a moment before he realised what it was

that he was hearing, why suddenly the kitchen was full of sound. It took a moment before the sounds coalesced in his head into the ringing of his daughter's mobile phone.

And he knew then, beyond any shadow of a doubt, that nothing would ever be right again.

Libby's mobile lay on the floor, half hidden beneath the Formica kitchen table.

Funny how such a small thing can tell you everything that you need to know. When it's your daughter, who you know inside and out, who you have cradled and fed and loved and watched as she grows into the most remarkable young woman you have ever seen. When you and her brother have teased her a hundred times about that mobile phone that she is never, ever without.

'Look, mate, she's a big girl. If it'd been a couple of days, well, okay, but a couple of hours . . . Sorry, but my hands are tied.' Sipping his coffee, because he could. This was nothing to him.

'She didn't show up to work this morning.'

He'd rung her sergeant. Nice kid, had worked under Jim in his last few years of service.

'Ceri. It's Jim Hanover.'

'Hiya, boss. How you doing?'

'Ceri.' No time for small talk. 'Sorry to bother you. I'm actually looking for Libby.' Quick false laugh, because then perhaps his heart would stop beating so hard. 'Silly sod left her phone at home.'

There was silence on the line, and Jim found himself praying for maybe the first time in twenty years. Because he knew what silences like that meant.

Then, 'Ah, boss, the um . . . look, thing is, I've been trying to get hold of her myself. She never turned up for work this morning.'

He'd closed his eyes, and the world had swirled around him, opportunity for an easy answer dimming to an ember.

Jim had hoped that Nate, the DI, would be there. He had blown into the station, Irene on the front desk who he'd known for ever – who'd bought his kids Christmas presents, whose flat tyre he'd changed – buzzing him through, seeing the look on his face and asking no questions. If Nate had been there it would have been okay. Because Nate knew him, knew that there was no way Jim would be there if he didn't have to be. That Jim Hanover didn't piss about. Instead there was this child, with his unpolished shoes, the phone that never left his fingers. Looking up as Jim entered the CID office, a barely disguised sigh of impatience. Staring as Jim had stood there, spilling the story about his daughter's empty house and the jacket and the phone and the blood, all the while playing on his phone, the occasional 'uh huh', even though it was obvious he wasn't listening.

The kid scratched his ear with a pencil. 'Well, what about family? Friends? Anyone spoken to her?'

Jim should have called his son, Ethan. Maybe

he'd have heard from her. Although privately Jim doubted it, given what had happened. Couldn't see Libby confiding her deepest secrets to her elder brother. Not the way things were between them now.

'No, I . . . Look, I just know that something's wrong.' Could hear it, how vapid it sounded, could see how he must look to this boy with the world laid out at his feet, no wedding ring, no pictures of kids on his desk. *A daft old git who can't let go of the police force.*

'Tell you what, I'll make a note. Anything comes up, I'll give you a shout. But to be honest, mate, best bet is to head off home. She'll show up.'

'Look, kid, something's happened. She's a police officer, for God's sake. She hasn't shown up to work. That doesn't mean anything?'

'Sounds like an issue for Professional Standards to me.'

'Oh for fuck's . . . I did this job long enough. You really think I'd be here if I didn't know there was an issue?'

His face had flattened out. He was losing him. 'Look, please . . .' The word tasted uncomfortable in his mouth. 'Please. She is reliable. She is dedicated. She has never missed a day. She is never without her phone. And the blood . . .'

Then there was a look on the detective's face, the dawning realisation that he should have been listening, that playing on his phone as Jim talked – the empty house and Jim's missing daughter and the smear of blood tumbling from Jim's lips – was perhaps a bad idea. He leaned back, pushed himself upright, nodding now, like he had been listening all along. Like he hadn't missed it.

'Tell me more about the blood.'

CHAPTER 7

Tom: Thursday 15 March, 8.45 p.m.

They flocked together, sheep in a pen, the artificially warm hospital air alive with panicked bleats. Pawing at one another, each one more fearful than the next. Waiting.

'I'm so sorry, look, I know you are worried, and this is so awful, but if you could be patient . . .' Sing-song voice almost lost in the sea of sound. The receptionist leaned across the desk, hands narrow, with black-painted nails. She looked too young to be dealing with all this grief.

The man was elderly, although perhaps older now than he had been that morning. He clung to the desk edge. Tom watched him as he swayed.

'Look, love, I know it's not down to you. But it's our daughter. She's . . . our only little girl. Just look on your computer there . . . look . . . you must have something. Please. There must be something . . .'

He was crying. Tom couldn't see his face, just the back of his greying head. But his voice was thick with tears. Tom found himself looking down

40

at his own hands. They were broad, nails bitten to the quick, the platinum wedding ring scarred and scratched. They were steady.

He had been only dimly aware of the drive: houses flashing past, the bright glowing lights of Swansea central police station, Dan jumping from the car almost before it had stopped. Shouting to him to wait, do not move. Pulling the handcuffed man – was there a prisoner? He seemed to remember that there had been – from the back seat. And Tom sitting there and sitting there and knowing that it was finally over. Then Dan flying out of the station again, alone this time, jumping into the driver's seat, not a word, and then they were flying, screeching out into honking traffic.

Winding on lean roads beneath steep mountains, through the villages that got more and more tired. Drained of coal, drained of life. The sleeping giant stretched across the Cribarth ridges, bathed in snow. His father had always pointed, directing his son's gaze towards the mountaintop. *See that? People say that he'll wake up one day, when people need him most.* He never had, though, no matter how much Tom had needed him. He stared at the mountains, half expecting to see colossal arms breaking free. But nothing, just dead rock and snow. They were fenced in, when you thought about it, ringed by precipitous heights so that no matter how high you flew, you still couldn't escape. The shadows turned the snow grey, the gullies giving way to mountain streams frozen solid. Then the black expanse of reservoir. A stripped-bare landscape, skeletal trees, nothing to hide behind.

Then there was the smoke, the reddened glow of fire. The tiny village of Talgarth, narrow streets choked with police cars, fire engines. Knots of people, wrapped in inappropriate clothes, staring up towards the flames. The air hummed with sirens. Ambulances, laid out like bishops in chess, waiting for the right time. Because surely someone had survived.

The car stopped, pulled up short by police cordons, and Tom was out of the door, running. Ducking under the narrow tape that twisted in the breeze. Cold air replaced by heat, the crackle of flames. 'Keep Out' signs screaming at the throng of people that pumped into the abandoned lunatic asylum. This was where the plane had hit, although there was little evidence that there had ever been a plane. Apart from the destruction. The main building of the asylum now a blazing pile of bricks and glass and metal. Wooden joists and the boards that had once tried in vain to keep the curious out now kindling for fire, clock tower supine on the weed-infested drive. Fire destroying what madness couldn't.

Tom stopped, pulled up short because there was simply nowhere further to run. Eyes searching for form, anything that you could point to and say, 'That, I recognise that.' There was no cockpit, no seats, no wings. No jump seat. He ran his gaze up the mountainside, along the trail of fire. How could this have happened? Was it the snow, the whipping wind? Ice?

How does a plane just fall from the sky?

He leaned forward, hands on his knees, chest screaming with cold. Breathe. Think.

'Tom.' Dan's arm was around his shoulder, thick biceps steering him away. He was saying something, words lost to the roar of the fire and the thrumming of blood through his head.

And all Tom could think about was Ben. He was two. He was only two. How could this be right? How could this be the way life was? Two years old and losing his mother twice in one day. And even though his thoughts seemed to have fragmented into a thousand pieces, already in his head Tom was planning the lie. How his mother had adored him. How she would have done anything for him. How tragic it was that she had been snatched away, because she would never, ever have left him willingly.

'Tom.'

He felt himself being pivoted, away from the gawking onlookers, the firemen with their futile hoses, the paramedics with nothing to do. Felt Dan's dinner-plate hands on his shoulders, forcing him to look at him.

'Did you hear me? Tom?'

Shaking his head.

'The plane split. They said there's another site.

A couple of miles away. They say there are survivors.'

The hospital smelt of fear. Fear and antiseptic and sweat.

They had found the survivors in a field, halfway up the mountain, the tail of the plane blazing like a beacon. Had taken them to the hospital. Morriston. *Oh, so you just came from Swansea? You'll know the way then.* Back to the car, trying to push away a growing sense of the ridiculous. Back along the iced winding roads, going too fast.

The queue stretched out to the doors of the hospital waiting area and beyond. Dense heat, of overcoats and scarves and bodies, punctured by a bitter cold as the doors slid open and closed. The crowds behind him and beside him and in front of him, all with a single goal. That window and that desk and that hapless receptionist with alarm written plain across her face. Beneath the voices, the steady background hum of crying.

Ben had gone to bed already, Tom's mother's voice a whisper, taut as piano wire on the phone. *He doesn't know anything. Don't worry about him. You just go and see . . .* Hadn't said what he was to see. Likely that neither of them knew where to go from here.

'Isn't there anyone you could ask?' The man was crying openly now, not even trying to hide it any more.

'I'm so sorry. I'm really, really sorry. Look, have a seat. Just until we find out some more.'

Then it was Tom's turn. He stared at the receptionist, eighteen if she was a day, looking for all the world like she wanted to cry too. Knowing what he had to say. *My wife. Is she alive?* But then stuck on the words, because this right here couldn't possibly be his life.

'Sir?'

'Cecilia Allison.' But it wasn't, was it? She had never taken his name. 'Sorry.' His voice was shaking. 'Cecilia Williams. She's a stewardess.'

There was dejection on the receptionist's face, shaking her head but typing the name in anyway because that was her job. Then suddenly sitting up straighter. A smile of dazzling relief.

'She's here.' A laugh, as if she couldn't believe it. 'She's here.'

People looking at him, faces ugly with jealousy that it was him who got the prize; he who couldn't even be bothered to shake or to cry. Then he was walking through the crowds, them parting for him like the Red Sea for Moses, and the doors to the treatment area were swinging open. And the noise. The noise was deafening here, as nurses ran from cubicle to cubicle, all with that same look of focus. Cries of pain and a scrabbling scream as someone realised that they'd survived alone. And there, right at the back, in amongst a knot of people coated in bruises and blood, there she was.

He should have run to her. Should have called out to her at least.

But she looked up anyway, as if she already knew. And her body began to move, a half-turn, as if it still wasn't too late, as if she could still run if she really tried. Then she stopped, and looked at him.

Tom pushed through the survivors, towards his waiting wife, and tried not to see her look of despair.

CHAPTER 8

Freya: Thursday 15 March, 10.19 p.m.

They had left the television on. Hadn't been able to bring themselves to turn it off, not whilst helicopters circled above leaping flames, orange sprinkled with flashes of blue. Freya watched it, couldn't seem to pull her eyes away from it. Without thinking, she sipped the tea, so sweet that her teeth stung, sinuses humming. It scalded her lips.

They were waiting. After all, what was there left to do but wait? Freya had called the airline, once, twice, her fingernails dredging into the phone as it chirped, engaged, again and again. Her mother was at the table now, slumped into the chair like all the bones had simply vanished from her body, her head resting on her hands, a puddle of tears gathering on the tabletop beneath the shadow of her hair. Richard beside her, so close it seemed that he would crawl into her lap if only she would allow him. He hadn't spoken. Not since the television flared to life, the screen lighting up with fire and snow. He just stared.

'It's stopped snowing.' Freya's grandmother was drying dishes, rubbing a tea towel around and around and around the outside of a mixing bowl that had once reached the stage of dry and was now on its way back to wet. Her brow furrowed, as if in concentration, eyes red-rimmed. 'Well, for now. They say we'll be like this for days yet. So much for spring. My flowers have had it.'

It could not have been more than moments after the world had changed that her grandparents arrived. She remembered that it was before her mother sank into the chair, a puppet whose strings had been cut. Before Richard began to cry. They had been hanging there, in that world between the past and the future, when the front door had swung open. And their breath had caught, and even though none of them said it, they were all thinking the same thing. That they were wrong and he was home.

Then her grandparents, sweeping in like a breath of Siberian air, the argument that they had been having about something she couldn't possibly remember now still fresh on their lips. Halting in the doorway, as if the fear hit them head on, buffeting them so that they had forgotten the latest affront to their patience, the snow and the long car ride. Their gazes trickling towards the television. Faces changing with the knowing.

Freya's grandfather sat beside her, hands folded. Ignoring his own mug of over-stewed tea.

'You know they still haven't gritted our road.

I'm going to write a letter. Ridiculous. Someone'll have to die . . .' Her grandmother stopped, stumbling on the word so that it came out as little more than a squeak. A deep breath. '. . . before they get around to it. Then they'll be gritting it in the middle of August.' She pulled out a chair, tea towel clutched tight between her fingers. Her lips were trembling now.

'Betty.' Her grandfather's voice was thick, dense with years of smoking roll-ups. He'd given up, years ago now, but still when Freya thought of him, it was that smell that she thought of.

'What?'

'This tea tastes like battery acid.'

Freya's grandmother rolled her eyes, lips pursing like she wanted to say something but, just this once, had decided to refrain. Freya bit her own lip, pushing down a flush of anger. Wanted to tell them to shut up. Wanted to shout: *Look at the television. Don't you understand what's happening here?* But she drank her tea instead, watching her mother across the rim of her cup. She seemed to be slumping lower, sinking into the hard wooden chair. She hadn't said anything, not a word since the television had flashed to life, changing their world.

'Mum? Why don't you go on up to bed?' Freya leaned across the table, fingers stroking the soft skin on her mother's arm. 'Just for a little while. We'll wake you when . . . we'll wake you when we have some news.'

49

It seemed like her mother didn't hear her at first, that her words couldn't penetrate this hell into which she had descended. Then eventually she looked up. Freya started. Her mother had aged fifteen years. There were lines that Freya had never seen before; her gaze was dead, skin as white as the snow that lay thick on the ground beyond the windows. Her lips moved, a child testing her first words. Then she seemed to give up, speech more than she could possibly handle. Her gaze dropped and she shook her head.

'You know, you can't be sure he was on that flight,' Freya's grandmother offered. 'I mean, they change the crews around all the time. You know what these airlines are like. He's off one minute, he's working the next. Always getting called away. He'll have been on a different flight. I'm sure of it.' Looking down, studying the red chequered cloth. 'I'm sure of it.' This last a whisper.

Freya also looked down, studying her fingernails, chipped saffron paint colouring the edges, and tried her best not to think about yesterday, about her father standing in the snow, the tension that pulsed across his shoulders. The look when he saw her, desperation edging into fear.

'I'm telling you,' Freya's grandmother had twisted the tea towel into a tight spiral, 'he'll be fine.'

'I'll try the airline again.' Her grandfather's chair scraped against the floor, nails down a chalkboard. 'Someone must know.'

They watched him leave, closing the door softly behind him.

'It's awful.' Her grandmother was watching the television, shaking her head. 'Just awful. Those poor people.' As if she hadn't realised that 'those poor people' was them; as if it was just one more news cycle of murder and flooding and genocide. Tragic, but not really real.

Richard moved his hands so that they covered his ears. His hair had flopped forward over his eyes. The lights of the television danced on the loose curls, and his fingers dug in, tugging, again and again.

And in what seemed like seconds, the kitchen door was opening again, slowly this time, and Freya's grandfather was there. Only he wasn't looking at any of them and his steady fingers were trembling. Freya knew it without him saying it, could see it in his eyes, in the downturn of his lips. She reached out, taking tight hold of her baby brother's hand.

'Grampa?' Richard was looking at him, and it was like he was pleading. *Say it isn't so.*

Then her grandfather reached out, took hold of her mother's shoulder. And she was looking up at him, eyes pleading, large tears leaking from the corners of her eyes.

Freya's grandfather shook his head. 'I'm so sorry.' His voice cracked. 'I'm so, so sorry.'

It seemed that time stopped in the kitchen. That they hung there, the world no longer spinning.

51

Then a sound, her mother, a low moan creeping from her, the sound of an animal caught in a trap. Her grandmother gasping, the news punching her in her narrow stomach. Her grandfather had moved, had wrapped his arms around her mother's shoulders as she shook. Richard, rearing back, pushing the chair away so that it tumbled, hitting the tiled floor with a clatter, shoving his way past his grandfather. And Freya frozen. Because this wasn't real. None of this could possibly be real.

CHAPTER 9

Cecilia was alone when she awoke. Unimaginable that she could have slept, and it seemed to her now that what she had experienced could not possibly have been sleep. Sleep made you think of rest, a gentle sinking into an easier state, not that plunging over the cliff edge, a black hole of unconsciousness. There had been dreams, if you could call them that. Rather piecemeal snatches of sound, flashes of light that danced on the edge of her vision, and that pain that wrapped itself around her arm, wrenching at the socket, hauling her up towards wakefulness before the painkillers gripped her again, tugging her back down into the roar of the engines and the heat from the fire.

She lay, staring at the ceiling. Not so different from every other night. Just different dreams.

Her mouth seemed to be full of cotton wool, head thick. She blinked, once, twice. There were the magnolia walls, the Degas reproduction that she had chosen that Tom hated. It seemed like there should be fire. There was the thick duvet over cotton sheets, but her body shivered as though it was snow. There were sounds, right at the edge of her consciousness, a voice, familiar, strained. Cecilia turned her head, away from the sound, but it was still there.

The sky was a dull cotton today, snow falling in a relentless drone. She gazed out of the window at the grey sky, and the grey rooftops, and thought of plunging towards the ground. There were other voices, further away, laughter, childish shrieks and dull thuds. She thought of the scream of metal.

'She's sleeping now.'

Cecilia closed her eyes again. It seemed so loud, that voice. Disproportionately loud, like the roaring of engines. Perhaps she could sleep again. Or pass out. Whichever.

'No. There's no way I can today.'

It seemed to be getting closer, looming larger the further under the duvet she sank, tightening around her. Her head throbbed.

'Yeah, I know. No, Ben's with my mother.'

Ben. Her eyes fluttered open. She wanted to see him. Now. It was a sudden need, like the pull for breath at the bottom of a swimming pool. Had to see him. Her tiny baby, born earlier than he should have been so that he came out little bigger than a bag of sugar. Too small for her to hold, even if she had wanted to, even if she hadn't been too

54

ripped apart, too addled with drugs to care. The nurses had taken her to see him, wheeling her in an overlarge chair that looked to be of Soviet design. This minuscule creature, with the wires and the tubes, buried behind glass. They had encouraged her forward, in voices that promised Christmas and spring flowers, glancing at one another in satisfaction when she had finally rested her fingertips on the glass of the incubator. Then the baby had turned, and, although now it seemed that she must have imagined it, looked straight at her, and something had swelled up on the inside, a terror that they had got the wrong woman. They were standing there, smiling, thinking that it would be okay, that she would be able to take care of him, give him everything he needed. Didn't they know that she couldn't even take care of herself? They hadn't understood when she had wanted to leave.

'Yeah, I know. No . . . no, I didn't tell him about the crash.'

And Tom. So damned capable. So much a father, right from the start, even with the tubes and the wires and this thing that looked barely human. Talking softly through the Plexiglas walls, as if there was someone to hear him. And then it seemed that he had heard, because in what felt like a moment he was two years old, and it was his father he ran to when he fell to the ground because walking was still an imprecise affair. His father who made him smile so wide that it seemed his face would split apart. Whilst she floated, still stuck behind Plexiglas.

Would Ben have noticed if she had never come back? Cecilia felt tears building. She already knew the answer.

'I know, boss, but it's a really bad time. I feel like my place is here.'

Tom seemed to be just outside the door now. She wondered if he was listening, waiting for her to make a sound. He had a smoker's voice, a deep throaty bass, even though he'd never touched a cigarette in his life. She remembered that voice, how it sounded through tinny telephone lines, distant and surprised that she'd called him. Three years ago. After she had left him, assumed she would never see him again. After all, they weren't much, were they? A little casual affair, dipping her toes back into the water. And then, after it had drifted to its inevitable conclusion, she had left, retreated home, back to her parents' in the leafy outskirts of Hay-on-Wye, even though she had sworn she would never go back to that house choked full of silent hostility and jagged edges. But she had nowhere else to go. She had sworn that she was laying off relationships. No more pointless dating, killing time with men that left her feeling empty inside. Then had come the nausea and the backache and the little blue line on the unremarkable white stick. And she had called him, because she didn't know what else to do. There had been a ripple in his voice, forced politeness because he just was that kind of man, and she had known that he had missed her no more than she had missed him. Her hand had hovered for a moment. He didn't want her. She didn't want him. What was the point? But then the memories had crowded in on her, and she had felt a shiver of fear, and almost without her meaning them to, the word had tumbled out. *Pregnant.* Feeling like she was falling down the rabbit hole and knowing that she was sealing her fate, that uttering that word would make it so. The stunned silence as he figures out what he needs to do next, then the soft sigh as he realises that he is as trapped as she is now, and the quiet 'It'll be okay. We'll figure it out.'

For a moment, she had almost believed him.

It had all tumbled away from her then. She'd told her parents, words digging into her throat. Her mother resting her head in her hands. *You'll have to get married. It's the right thing to do.* Cecilia shaking her head, but doing it without conviction. *I'm telling you. Motherhood is tough. You don't want to do this alone. A screaming baby. Enough to push anyone to the edge. You know how it was for me. If he's willing . . .* her mother had shrugged . . . *you tie him down. You won't be able to do it on your own, Cece. It's not in your nature.* And then, before she could turn around it seemed, she was married, in a civil ceremony in a scuffed registry office, her parents and Tom's mother the only witnesses.

The air had been clogged, a stupefying July day, heat pressing down on her chest so that she couldn't breathe. Everything in her pulling her backwards, telling her to run, because this isn't the life she wants. But her mother's fingers are wrapped around her arm, whispering something about cold feet being natural, and there's a wall of pressure at her back, so that she can't turn around either. And then they were married, and it was too late. They went for a meal afterwards, in a little bistro that no one really liked. Her father had drunk too much, not looking at her, or anyone else, concentrating steadily on the bottom of his wine glass, her mother laughing too loudly, like she thinks if she makes enough noise she can distract from her husband. Then when they were done, she had hugged Cecilia, whispering about how she had done the right thing, because otherwise, what would people have thought?

It was three months later that her parents announced they were getting a divorce. A late-night phone call from her father, slurring his words. *That slut. Having an affair. Moving to Glasgow with her fucking boyfriend.* Cecilia had cried, whether from frustration or anger or childish despair she wasn't sure.

She buried her head in the pillow. But it didn't help. The walls still crept closer, licked with flames, and the sheets still smelled of petrol and death. She pushed back the bedding, movements too quick so that her arm jarred and pain shot through her. She wanted to be sick.

'I'm sorry, boss. I know. It's just . . .'

It took three lifetime-long strides to cross the bedroom. One herculean wrench to pull open the door.

Tom looked like he hadn't slept. He started when he saw her, like he was seeing a ghost, and for a brief moment Cecilia wondered if that was exactly what she was. But her arm still throbbed and her head still spun and surely that didn't happen if you were already dead. His chestnut hair stood upright the way it did after a long day, when he'd run his fingers through it too many times. He wasn't someone that she had ever really considered to be good-looking; rather, if she was being generous, on the more attractive side of average. He looked like he'd lost weight since she'd seen him last. Was that even possible in the day that she had been gone? She leaned against the door frame, eyes fighting to close again, to slip back. 'It's okay.' Her voice came out rough, stale from lack of use. 'Go.'

'Sorry, boss, just a sec.' He cupped the mouth-piece with his hand. His wedding ring glinting in the winter sunlight. 'They've found a woman's body. Some guy walking his dog in Swansea called it in. It's okay, I've already said I'm not going in.'

'Go.'

'I . . .'

'It'll be better. I'd rather.'

She didn't see him nod, even though she knew he would have. Didn't see his shoulders slump in that way they did when he had tried and she had shoved him away. Just heard him say, 'Boss? I'm on my way.'

CHAPTER 10

Jim: Friday 16 March, 9.28 a.m.

Jim had remained at the station late into the night, arms folded tight across his chest, pacing worn-out linoleum as the kid rang DI Nate Maxwell, the DI rang someone else, and suddenly the office flooded with people. Because that was what happened when there was a problem with one of your own. The air filled with hurried voices, the clacking of computer keys, the clunk of phones hitting cradles. People that he didn't recognise hurried past him, pulling on thick coats over dark suits. Going to look for his daughter.

Jim's stomach knotted, like it had that time in Sainsbury's when she was five, when he'd turned around and she was gone and a spasm of fear had gripped him from the inside and he'd run down aisles until he found her, tiny hands reaching upwards, helping herself to the pick-and-mix. Any minute now. Any minute now the phone would ring or a radio would spark to life, and the people he didn't know would look up, faces relieved.

They'd say, 'Mr Hanover. Your daughter's on the phone.' Then they'd laugh at what they had all thought, and his insides would unclench, just like that day with the pick-and-mix.

It was midnight before the DI came, Nate Maxwell's eyes searching the office for Jim, and for an instant they were in the pub again, or on the golf course, anywhere but here. Nate had been out on the streets, looking, even though it wasn't really his job. Had laid his big burly hands on Jim's tight-tensed shoulders. 'Go home, Jim. Nothing you can do here.'

Jim had known that he was right, knew that Esther would be waiting for him. His wife would have spent the evening ironing. She did everyone's – his, Ethan's, Libby's – said she enjoyed it, that she found it relaxing. Then when she was done she would sit down with a treat, a small glass of Baileys – just the one – and by now she would be a little bit giggly. Jim had thought that he might be sick. He'd called her: *I've bumped into a couple of the boys. Going to pop to the pub for a pint. You know, quick drink. You mind?* Esther laughing and saying that it was like the old days, not to expect her to peel him off the kitchen floor when he'd had too many. And he'd laughed along with her, the sound ripping a hole in his gut, and prayed and prayed and prayed that he would never have to make her feel what he felt. Because surely if he waited long enough, it would all be all right. Then he would tell her. When he had Libby safe in his arms. When everything was okay. He'd tell her then.

'Come on. I'll drive you.' Nate had put an arm around his shoulder, steering Jim towards the door, and suddenly he was too tired to resist any more, was being led downstairs and out to the parking lot, through the snow, into an unmarked car, and driven home, all the while gazing out of the window as if he actually expected to see her on the side of the road.

Esther had been in bed by the time he got in, back turned to him, breathing soft. He had slipped into bed and stared at the ceiling and waited.

Any moment and then the phone will ring and it will all be okay.

Then it was morning, a grey, unyielding morning, and the phone still hadn't rung. He lay there whilst Esther stirred, listening to the pattern of her breathing change, to her stretching, throwing back the covers and slipping her feet into the slippers that Libby had bought her last Christmas. Listened to her padding from the bedroom, movements cautious because she didn't want to wake him.

Then Jim had prayed. He had prayed like he hadn't done since he was a boy, when he believed that prayers could come true.

The television was on in the kitchen, the air sweet with the smell of freshly made Welsh cakes. He poured himself coffee, watching as Esther deftly worked the dough, flicking tawny-coloured hair from her eyes with flour-covered fingers.

'This is awful.' She nodded at the television, where the screen glowed with orange flames. 'Did you hear about the plane?'

Jim sipped the coffee, grimacing. It was too bitter. He hadn't added his usual sugars. It just didn't seem right. 'No.' Because there was no world outside. There was nobody beyond his family and his life and his missing daughter.

'Terrible. Those poor people.'

He felt sick.

'Did you speak to Ethan?' Esther flopped dough on to the floured kitchen counter.

'Huh?' Jim wasn't listening, was staring down into his coffee.

'Ethan. Did you call him?'

'Um, no. No. Not yet.'

'You should. I think he's really down. You know, what with everything.' Esther pulled the rolling pin from the drawer. 'I don't know. It's such a shame. Poor boy tried so hard.'

'Yeah.' Jim nodded, but no matter how hard he tried, he just couldn't think about his son, his career disappointments, not when his daughter was missing.

Esther was pushing down on the dough, twirling the rolling pin in her hands, turning the ball into a flattened sheet, when the doorbell rang. She started, looking up with that empty look of inno-cent surprise. 'Who's that now?'

Jim didn't move. He couldn't seem to drag himself from the kitchen table, couldn't seem to make his legs move. Watched Esther wiping her hands, leaving white streaks on her dark apron. He wasn't breathing, couldn't possibly, because his heart had stopped and the air frozen in his lungs. Heard the creak of the front door. Knew what was about to come.

There was a low bass mutter, then Esther again, voice bubbling over with suppressed laughter. Like champagne, he'd always thought. Then there were footsteps, heavy on the carpeted floor, and Esther, still smiling because she simply hasn't realised that this is the moment their world will end.

'Jim, look who it is. Come on, have a seat, Nate. Coffee? I've got fresh Welsh cakes.'

The kitchen smelled of sugar and cinnamon and coffee. Esther clinking, reaching for the good mugs. And Nate, his face locked into that look, the one that Jim had worn a hundred times before.

He couldn't watch any more, just dropped his head and closed his eyes, like a child diving under the quilt to hide from a bogeyman.

'Why don't you come and sit down, Esther?' It was there in Nate's voice too, soft, sad, thick with the warning of what would come next. She must have heard it, because she suddenly stopped moving, the instincts of a policeman's wife, one who had finally relaxed her guard after thirty years of worrying, suddenly alert again.

'What's going on? Jim?'

He couldn't look up. If he looked up, then she would know. Her world would crumble, and he would have crumbled it. He just reached out, gripping her hand tight.

'Jim?'

'It's our Libby, Ess.' He looked up then, wrapping his hand tighter around her shaking fingers. 'He's here about Libby.' He lifted his chin and looked at Nate, gaze steady, although it seemed that the world swirled around him. 'What is it, Nate?'

'What do you mean? What's wrong with Libby?' Her voice was tighter now, fighting back panic, and she spun her gaze from him to Nate and back again.

But Nate was looking at Jim and Jim was looking back, and in that moment he knew that it was over.

CHAPTER 11

Tom: Friday 16 March, 10.48 a.m.

They sat on chairs, tables. Tom sat on his desk, leaning his back against the wall, one hand wrapped around his knee. He'd given Maddie his chair. He stared at the whiteboard, trying desperately not to notice the smell of her perfume, the rounded curve of her belly. She was rubbing her belly, over and over again, sunlight sparking against her diamond wedding ring, head bowed so that her hair fell across her eyes. Tom knew that she was doing it so that she wouldn't have to look up, wouldn't have to see the picture of a dead Police Community Support Officer tacked to the whiteboard.

'It'll be better. I'd rather.' Cecilia had leaned against the spare-room door, hadn't looked at him as he cradled the phone in his fingers. A bruise had flourished now, wrapping itself around his wife's right eye. Tom had hung there, dangling in indecision. He should stay. It would only be right. But then she didn't want him there, she needed some time to herself, and hadn't she been through enough already without him forcing himself on her? He had tried to smile, had pushed back the words that clambered over his tongue. *You left us. You left your son.* Instead he had nodded. He would go to work. Pretending to himself that it was for her, to give her some space. Pretending that it wasn't because he couldn't look at her. Trying not to think about the fact that she still hadn't asked about her son.

Tom had showered quickly, dressing in his usual suit, a dark tie, his shoulders unfurling. Had dawdled on the landing for a moment, then, with a small sigh, had pushed open the bedroom door. Checking to make sure she was all right before he went to work, like a good husband. Her back was turned to him, quilt pulled high. He had felt a bubble of relief, then turned, hurrying down the stairs, glancing at his watch. It would be a late one. That was just the way it was with murders.

He shifted on the desk. A patch of sunlight had worked its way through dense clouds, was burning through the office window into his back. He concentrated on that, on the sweat that was starting to work its way between his shoulder blades. Tried not to look at Maddie, the tear rolling down her cheek.

He had been on his way into work, driving along the M4, taking it easy, because the snow was still banked up along the carriageway, outer lane

68

unusable to all but the stupid. Thinking about the incident room, the actions to come, flicking through radio stations, changing the channel, when a newsreader with a heavy voice coloured the car with orange flames, tearing metal and deep red blood. Was listening to Florence and the Machine when the phone rang.

'You coming in?' Dan's voice tumbled in a bundle of others.

'Just passing Junction 38.'

'Oh, right. Things okay? You know, at home?' His tone was cautious, the kind one uses when someone is sick or bereaved.

Tom knew that Dan was thinking about the long wait in the hospital car park, the two figures crossing towards him, Tom's arm, awkward across his wife's shoulders, her body stiff. The seemingly endless drive home, car choked with a toxic silence. That look, the one when Tom was getting out of the car, when he'd ducked his head back in to thank him. The look that said Dan knew more than Tom was prepared to admit.

'Cecilia's tired. She needs to rest. It'll be better if I'm not there.'

'Yeah. Probably.'

'I was going to stay, but she . . . Better off in work. Out of the way.'

'Yeah. Yeah. Let her sleep. Do her good.'

A heavy silence.

'You in already?' asked Tom.

'Yeah. Fucking 'mare, mate.'

Eased out into the middle lane, past a car doing thirty. 'What's going on?'

'You know who it is, right? The vic?'

'Who?'

'Libby Hanover. The PCSO.'

Tom stared at the picture on the whiteboard, the woman young, fresh, dark hair pulled back into a low bun. He had spoken to her, once, twice maybe. Nothing of note, the exchange of pleasantries in a hallway. Maddie knew her, though. Maddie knew everyone, just the way she was. Would tuck a new PCSO under her wing, show her around so that she recognised people, would feel welcome even in the areas where her authorities would never extend, like CID. He remembered her bringing Libby in, explaining how they worked, their investigations, giving Tom a swift kick on the ankle when he hadn't turned fast enough. He remembered smiling at Maddie, trying desperately not to think about the last time he kissed her.

'People, listen up.' The DI looked stripped bare, eyes red, skin pale; couldn't have slept much, if at all. He had pulled his tie loose, slipped his jacket off so that circular sweat stains were visible beneath his armpits. 'Dog-walker found a body this morning at 8.15 a.m. Located along the banks of the river Tawe, just outside of Clydach. Uniform attended and positively identified the body as that of Libby Hanover.' A pause, a gulp of air, and

70

Tom looked down at his fingernails, studying the edges where they had been bitten to the quick. 'Ah, um, family have been informed.' The DI was studying the papers in his hands. Tom was prepared to bet that he had every piece of information on those pages memorised. 'For those of you who do not know her, Libby is . . .' Another breath. 'Was one of ours. A Police Community Support Officer with eight months' service. A good girl.'

There was a noise, a soft moan from Maddie, and Tom reached out, gripped her shoulder. For her benefit or for his, he was not sure.

'Her father, Jim Hanover, is a retired superintendent, and a good friend. Libby, she lived alone, single, twenty-five years old. The condition of the body – Scenes of Crime are with her now. They say she was fully clothed, dressed in her uniform, no obvious evidence of sexual assault, but we'll have to wait for the PM to be sure.'

Tom raised a finger. 'Boss?' he said quietly. 'The murder site?'

'Yeah, Jim, her dad, notified us that she was missing late last night. His concerns were raised when he found blood in her kitchen, so obviously we're looking at that as a possible murder scene. Again, Scenes of Crime are there as we speak. Jim said that when he arrived, the front door was locked as normal. We've examined that door, windows, all locked up nice and secure.'

71

Tom shifted, running through a house he'd never seen. *She let her killer in.*

'Obviously we're considering that Libby may have let her murderer in. It's possible that they had a key. Equally possible that after they . . . they killed her . . . they *took* a key, locking up behind them to throw the investigation. Now . . .' The DI slapped another photograph on to the whiteboard. A kitchen. 'As you can see, someone's been cleaning. If the kitchen was the murder site, someone has worked very hard to make sure that it doesn't look that way. The only obvious blood spatter was at the side of one of the cabinets. Out of the way, so it looks like they missed it.

'Have a look for your names on the board. I've got you split into teams. Outside action team, you're going door-to-door. Somebody must have seen something. We'll brief again at the end of the day.'

There was a flurry of movement, the office filling with the scraping of chairs. Maddie wiped her hands across her eyes, glancing back at Tom with a watery smile.

'You okay?' Tom asked. Could still feel the wool of her sweater beneath his fingers.

She nodded, slowly. 'Not much choice, is there?' Her hands circled her belly, and for a moment he thought that she was about to say something. Then she shrugged. 'I'll see you later.' She turned, slipping into the mass of bodies, leaving him sitting there, watching her go.

He'd thought about leaving Cecilia. Of course he had. Sometimes, when Maddie laughed, or just brushed past him with that rush of perfume that was utterly and entirely her, the thought would occur to him that he could leave. But then he would remember his father, the black bin bags lined up neatly alongside the front door. Stooping down in front of Tom, eight years old. *You know this isn't about you? You know that, right?* Trying to tousle his hair, Tom jolting backwards as if he had been stung. That look in his father's eyes, like the time he had cut his finger, slicing the top clean off with the carving knife. *It just isn't working, your mother and me. It's not about you.* Then stay. His father grimacing. *It wouldn't be right. I'd be living a lie, Tom. I can't live like that.* So Tom stayed, and watched as the world moved on without him.

'Tom.' The DI moved through the crowd towards him. He looked worse up close.

Tom took a breath, smoothing out his expression. Pushed himself up to standing. 'Hey, boss.'

'Tom, I need you to do something for me.'

'Of course.'

'Jim. He . . . he'd be more comfortable if he had a CID liaison there. A fellow detective. He's met with the Family Liaison Officer, but, you know, he's a detective at heart. Could you . . .'

Tom nodded. 'Sure. I'm assuming you'll need someone to take statements anyway?'

'Yeah, yeah, of course. Just, you know, also hold their hands a bit. Okay?'

Tom watched his boss, thinking about the crime scene. The locked doors and a young woman dead. Thinking that in all likelihood she had been killed by someone she had allowed in. Wondered to himself if she had been killed by someone she loved.

'Sure. No problem, boss. I'll go see the family.'

CHAPTER 12

Freya: Friday 16 March, 11.21 a.m.

'Another cup of tea?'

'I'm okay, Grandma.'

'Coffee? There's coffee here. It's not, well, I mean, it's instant, but you don't have . . . ah . . . no. It is Nescafé. Nice cup of coffee?'

'No thanks.'

Freya rubbed at her eyes. The kitchen was grey, sky outside heavy with unshed snow. She had put the light on, a brief burst of colour in a black and white world. Her grandmother had turned it off again. It's daytime. We don't need the lights on. The world was fuzzy on the edges, colours leaching across one another as if someone had dragged at them with a wet brush. But that could be just her eyes, weighted down with the need for sleep.

'Looks like snow again. Look. They said it wouldn't. It's supposed to be gone by now.'

The paint was still on Freya's nails, unkempt patches of colour. She hadn't showered, hadn't dressed. Sat at the kitchen table in purple checked pyjamas, baby-soft brushed cotton. Her hair pulled up into a rough topknot that her grandmother's gaze kept trickling back to, lips pursing.

'What about your mother? Would she want tea, you think? I could bring her a cup.'

Freya shook her head, watching the sky outside the kitchen window, thickening, the entire world doused in sepia tones. 'She didn't sleep much. Leave her. Let her sleep while she can.'

It had taken a moment, after her grandfather had come back, after the world had split into a thousand pieces. Her mother staring at him, the enormity of his words too much for her to take in all at once. Then it had happened, the truth breaking through the shell of denial, the light blinding. And she had crumbled. Freya had grabbed for her, catching her under the arms before she hit the floor, biting her lip as a wail pierced the air, a sound she had never heard from her mother before, one that ate at the inside of her, that would chase itself around in her dreams when she finally managed to sleep. Her mother had clawed at her, begging her to say that it wasn't true. That he wasn't dead.

Freya had wanted to lie to her, had wanted it so much that it made her bones ache. But instead she had hugged her mother close, feeling her shudder with grief.

They had carried her to bed, Freya and her

grandfather, lifting her up, limp between them. Freya had lain down beside her, wrapping her arms around her whilst she cried and cried and cried.

'Do you have bacon?'

'Huh?'

'Bacon. I found the sausages, but I don't see bacon. Your grandfather likes bacon. Do you have any?'

'I don't know, Grandma.'

Her grandmother sighed, frying pan hitting burner with a clank. 'Have to be sausages, then. Do you want to clean the mushrooms or will I?'

Freya didn't answer, shaking her head as the kitchen filled with the sizzle of oil, the smell of a breakfast that no one would eat. There had been thirteen survivors. Thirteen. Out of seventy-four. The turboprop had torn in two, tail severed against the slope of the mountain. That was what had saved them, being pulled from the body of the plane, tossed into snow. Everyone else had died, eaten by fire. No bodies found. The television was dark now. Her grandmother had snapped it off, muttering something about how knowing too much would do nobody any good.

It had been a little after 4 a.m. when her mother had finally fallen into a restless sleep. Freya must have slept as well, for a while at least. Had vague recollections of kaleidoscope dreams, of fire and rushing wind, her mother's scream. Each one pierced with the distant sound of her brother sobbing.

'How many sausages for you? One or two?'

She should be crying. That was what a normal daughter would do. She should be breaking her heart that he was gone, the man who taught her to ride a bike, who put her to bed at night, who came to her school plays and her graduation. Freya picked at the cuff of her pyjamas. But he hadn't done any of those things.

'Freya? I'm speaking to you.'

'I'll have eight, please, Grandma.'

Her grandmother tsked, throwing two sausages into the pan, oil splattering against the tiled wall.

She tried to muster it up, the sense of loss. A catastrophic reshaping of her world. But she couldn't find it. Just this vague sense of a murky figure – a shape behind a newspaper, a back walking out of the door – gone. She had experimented with self-delusion, telling herself that she was trying to be strong, looking out for her mother and her brother. But it hadn't worked, wouldn't stick. Because even though he was gone, and you were supposed to rework it now, tidying up history to favour the dead, there was still that chasm there, the one that had always sat so neatly between herself and her father. In her darker moments, as she listened to her family grieve, she had found herself wondering just who it was they were grieving for.

'Come on. Breakfast. I've done you an egg as well.' Her grandmother set the plate down in front of her, harder than was strictly necessary. Two thick sausages. Quartered mushrooms. An egg, glistening yellow with oil. The yolk had been broken.

Freya stared at it. Sometimes you had to lie. That was what her mother said. To protect people's feelings, to keep things nice and calm. *You're too honest. It must be something to do with the psychology, all this stuff about talking everything through. People don't always deal well with that. You have to learn when to fib.*

'It's snowing again. I told you.' Her grandmother paused, the crinkle of vertical blinds. 'Now what do they want?'

'Who?'

'There's reporters out in the front garden. Look. They've got a camera.'

Sometimes you had to lie. Because your mother needed you to, so that she could grieve for someone who never really existed. Because your brother needed you to, and wasn't he still little more than a child? And so what if what you remembered was different from what everyone else said they remembered? Because all that mattered now was protecting these two people who had been through so much. And wasn't that worth a little lie?

'I'm telling you. It's disgusting. These people. Going round asking questions that they've got no right to ask. No right at all. I'll close the blinds. Disgusting. Should leave well enough alone, if you ask me.'

Freya stood, pushing back the chair with a scrape.

CHAPTER 13

Cecilia: Friday 16 March, 11.22 a.m.

Cecilia squeezed the concealer tube with her right hand. Biscuit cream pooling on to the index finger of her damaged left hand. It shook with the effort. Touching her fingers together, although it hurt. Only then did she look up. The eye was swollen, almost hidden by the dark blue bruise. She dabbed the concealer and tried to make herself believe that it was working.

Ben. She could get Ben. That was what she would do. This house, it was too quiet, too dead. The walls, each one more fucking beige than the next, and even though she'd wanted that, had insisted upon it at the time when Tom had wanted something warmer, something more homely, they closed in on her now. The heating had gone off, air frigid. Her skin prickled, perhaps from the cold, yet still she was suffocating.

She circled the eye, or where the eye used to be. Rubbing her finger back in the concealer, concealer on to the bruise. She had tried to put mascara on, but her eye had watered too much,

81

had left her with dark streaks trailing down her cheek.

She would go and get Ben. That's what normal people did, wasn't it? When they had almost died. They held their children. That's what she would do. Patting the eye with pressed powder. Standing back from the mirror and squinting. Then looking away and wanting to cry. She would go and get him. She could be that, just this once, a normal mother.

Like the other mother. Working her way on to the plane, bundled against the cold. *Hi. Welcome aboard. Straight on to the back, please.* What had she said to her? The girl, three, maybe four, jet-black hair in a pageboy cut, fringe grazing hazelnut-brown eyes. She had worn a pink coat, hadn't wanted to let go of her mother's hand, even though the aisle was too narrow, and they had to pirouette awkwardly. She had a Tiny Tears doll tucked under her arm. They had sat in the fifth row from the back. Against the window.

Cecilia remembered counting the few rows that remained, her head spinning, her arm throbbing, pulling the prostrate into what was left of the aisle, stumbling through jagged edges, tumbling into snow. Four rows from the back. Then nothing but snow.

She pulled cream blusher from the Lancôme bag, smoothing it across death-grey cheeks. Her arm was throbbing, swamping her with pulses of pain. She'd swallowed a couple of painkillers, the ones they had given her from the hospital. *They're strong, mind,* they'd warned her. But her arm still throbbed, and now her head swam, tongue feeling thick and unwieldy.

They were reading a book, the mother and the child and the Tiny Tears doll, as she checked seat belts and closed lockers and adjusted tray tables. They were reading *The Gruffalo*. The little girl had laughed as her mother did the voices, burying her face in the child's cheek with a low growl and a giggle. Like they had done this a thousand times. Like they would do it a thousand times more.

She should go and get Ben. She should bring him home. Then it would just be the two of them. Here. Alone.

Cecilia sank down on to the bottom step and leaned her head against the banister. That was what any normal mother would do. The silence was deafening, tearing at her insides. It sounded like engines and rushing wind. She could pull Ben towards her, holding him tight, forget all about the fact that she was running away, that she had left, that she had taken everything that mattered to her. That she had left him. Because she was here, wasn't she? She had survived when she shouldn't have, because she had chosen the jump seat four rows in the right direction, because the plane hadn't gone down two seconds earlier or two seconds later. Just because. And there must be a reason, because otherwise why would she live and the good mother and her little girl die?

Cecilia pushed herself up again, sticking her chin out and trying to slow her breathing. Twisting a tube of lipstick. Red rose. Smoothed it on to lips that were too dry. He would be glad to see her. Wouldn't he? She was his mother, after all. He would look at her, his face lighter simply because she was there, and this time he wouldn't turn away, wouldn't bury his head in his father's leg, eyes turned sideways towards her, unsure of her. This time she would know what to say to him, know what he needed, simply because she was his mother. And when she looked at him, she wouldn't see the other one. This time she would just see him.

That was when she remembered, spinning on her heel so that her arm seared and her lipstick smudged. Cold gripped her, from inside to out. She stepped forward. Stepped back. Then stood there, because there was nowhere else to go. The picture, the unformed foetus, was gone, like everything else she had valued enough to take.

Closing her eyes, resting her head against the cool of the mirror.

You take what matters when you run away from home. You take what you will need, the things that make life bearable. You take your secrets.

84

She was trembling, trying to breathe. It would be okay. Breathe. Think of Ben. It'll be okay. Because she had to have survived for a reason, and he's her son and she's his mother, and this time he'll be enough and she'll be enough.

CHAPTER 14

Tom: Friday 16 March, 11.27 a.m.

The snow covered Libby, tucked in beneath her frozen silver chin. Her head was cushioned by bracken and leaves, chestnut hair fanning out into a halo. Her lips were pressed lightly together into a kiss. Eyes open, navy blue. Seemed that she was staring at him. But then Tom moved, and the illusion shifted, a trick of the light, gaze becoming vacant again. Dead.

They stood on the path, looking down towards the river, the body. A bitter cold wind had crept up, whipping at their white protective suits. The DI a broad-shouldered snowman beside him, his arms folded tight across his chest. Down below, through the snaking embankment of bracken and brambles, white-clad scenes-of-crime investigators moved around the body. They stepped slowly, cautiously, every inch taking more time than would have seemed possible, because one wrong step now and the forensic evidence is gone and they can't get it back.

'I, uh, thanks. For, you know.' DI Maxwell's voice

tripped on the wind so that Tom had to strain to hear. He wasn't looking at Tom, was staring down the bank to where Libby lay. Seemed almost impossible from this distance that she could be real.

'Not a problem, boss.' Tom had been heading to the car, mind full of crime scenes and blood spatter and the secrets that lie within the heart of all families. Had pulled up short. The DI had been standing beside his car, his face pale, gaze long. *Okay, boss?* Looking up like he hadn't heard him pull in. *Yeah, bad morning. You know. Libby.* A heavy sigh. *Going to the scene now.* Tom had tucked his car keys into his pocket. *Mind if I tag along?*

He stared down the bank at the body. There were leaves in her hair, twigs. It was matted, pulled at, as if something had tried to make a nest there. A curtain of blood, swathing her left ear, crawling down her chin, and he wondered if it had been a blow to the head that had killed her. Her left arm was flung out, white shirt hidden against the snow.

The forensic team inched around her, struggling to erect the protective tent on the precipitous bank, pure snow churning to mud. The whine, flash and click, the CSI lowering the camera, her face grim.

'Jesus.' DI Nate Maxwell's voice was soft, barely audible.

'Yeah.'

It wasn't a great place to dump a body. She would be found. In an hour or a day, hard to say in weather like this. But it seemed that they had made little attempt to hide it. More like they had made a nest for her, had lain her where she would be comfortable rather than leaving her on ice-hard ground.

Tom watched Libby, thought again that Libby was watching him. She looked like Cecilia. A little. Or maybe she didn't. Maybe it was the snow and the blood and the death making him think of his wife. They had the same lips, full, wishful. Hair that waved, thick. Cecilia was darker. Or maybe this was just what happened when you went to a murder the day after your wife died and then didn't.

The CSI was leaning in closer now, zooming in on Libby's face. *Click. Snap. This way. Beautiful.*

A line of disturbance ran through the bracken, just to Libby's left. Where someone would have walked, climbing their way down the embankment. Tom leaned over, chin out, assessing. Tough climb with a body. Especially when you could have dropped it, pushed her off the side, achieved pretty much the same result. But that hadn't happened; someone had struggled down the bank. They had carried her to where she would rest.

'How long before they get her out of here?' he asked.

The DI shook his head. 'They're saying twenty-four hours. Maybe more.'

Tom stared at Libby. Thinking that Death doesn't

always come where he's expected. That sometimes your world shifts, and your brain begins to work, and already, without you even meaning to, it's reordering your life, moving parts to fill up the sudden vacuum. And then, just as suddenly, stability reasserts itself, and everything goes back to just the way it was before, and you're left feeling just a little bit out of time, like maybe you woke up in the wrong universe today. But it's only because Death changed his mind. He visited somebody else instead.

The DI cleared his throat. Shook his head. 'Sorry, Tom. Tough one, this.'

Tom still didn't look at him, could hear the ragged edges to his voice, so let his gaze travel down the steep bank to the river, a knot of ice. 'Yeah. Different when it's someone you know.'

The DI nodded, slowly, stubble grazing against his shirt collar. 'Her father, good friend of mine. Jim, you know Jim?'

'By reputation. I've heard good things about him.' Tom glanced down at his feet, almost invisible, the white suit buried in the snow. Not looking at Libby. Someone's daughter now. And now, instead of Cecilia, he's seeing Ben. 'My father. He knew him.'

'Of course. He would have done. I . . . I was there. This morning. Had to, ah . . .' DI Maxwell gestured towards Libby, still not looking at her. 'Had to break the news.'

Tom nodded, that sudden sickening thought of

a heavy knock on the door. What it would be like to hear someone form those words. *Your child is dead.* Shaking his head, trying to concentrate.

He looked at where Libby lay, the way her body had been half hidden, brambles haphazardly uprooted, arranged across her torso, her legs. Falling snow doing the rest. The river ran past, sluggish, banks capped with ice. An inch or two away from her toes.

'You see him much?' The DI had folded his arms across his chest, feet scuffling at the snow.

'Boss?'

'Your dad. Get to see him often?'

Tom shook his head. 'No. Not much.'

He scanned up from the body towards the bank, turning, eyes running along the cycle path, back down to the river Tawe, watching as the current carried along a stick. Its own private game of Pooh sticks. Thinking about the walk he had made when they arrived at the crime scene. Leaving the car on a patch of roughened ground. Through the outer cordon. Up an incline almost overgrown with brambles, weeds. Watching the river flow past them, down towards the distant sea.

'Have the search teams done the river yet?'

The DI was looking past him, still down at Libby. 'Huh? No. They're just starting at the outer cordon. Why?'

'Do you mind if we . . .' Tom gestured back along the way they'd come. 'I'd like to have a quick look.'

The DI sighed, nodded. One last look at Libby, a last shake of his head. 'No. Come on.'

They walked, heads down into the wind. Tom blinked, eyes watering with the pressure of it, but he wasn't paying attention to that. His eyes were fixed on the river itself.

'What are you thinking?' the DI asked.

'Just, the river. She's right by it. I just wanted to see . . .' Tom stopped, leaning over the edge of the embankment. 'Do you . . . you see that, right?'

The DI squinted, frowning. 'I see something.' He pulled out his radio. 'I need a search officer here, now.'

They waited as a white-clothed figure worked its way along the path. The man stopped short of them, waited patiently as Tom pointed out the dark patch hooked on to the bank just above the flowing water. Began making his way down the bank.

They stood, staring after him.

'Your missus okay?' asked the DI.

'Boss?'

'Cecilia. Terrible thing, that crash. Terrible. The village . . . I mean, they're all reeling. You don't expect it, in a place like that.' He shook his head. 'Or any place.'

'Yeah.'

'You were lucky, mind. Really damn lucky.'

The world shifts, and you think it's going to land one way, and then it spins, and it lands another. Now your world is left just where it was, and somebody else's crumbles instead.

'Yeah.'

'So she's doing okay?'

'Yeah, thanks, boss. She's doing well. Really well.' Tom watched the search officer in his white suit leaning down towards the river, one hand grasping a branch, the other fishing around in the frigid water.

'Very, very lucky. Thank God, eh?'

Tom didn't answer. Was watching the search officer study the dark object. Saw him slip out a plastic evidence bag, placing whatever it was inside, and begin the climb back up the slope. Tom felt his heart beat a little faster.

'Well, you were right.' The officer's voice came out uneven as he struggled for breath. 'It's a glove. Large.' He held out the evidence bag. A winter Thinsulate glove, dark grey, almost black. 'And look.' He turned the evidence bag over in his hands. Across what would have been the palm sat a fat ring of blood.

CHAPTER 15

Freya: Friday 16 March, 11.28 a.m.

Freya pulled open the door, cold air rushing in, wrapping itself around her ankles. The snow was falling heavily now, drowning the world in a bitter white.

The two men stood at the end of the drive. They hadn't seen her yet, were leaning in towards one another, deep in conversation.

Freya wondered if her mother was still sleeping, if she was escaping the worst of the dreams. Hoped that her brother remained in bed. They didn't need this, not on top of everything else.

'Excuse me.' Words came out, sharper than she had intended. She cleared her throat. 'Hello?'

The shorter man, the younger one, turned, painting on a too-ready smile.

'Hello?' He was walking towards her, wide stride on the snow-bound drive. 'Mrs Blake?' Doubtful, scanning her up and down, taking in the pyjamas, the lack of make-up. Her youth.

'No. I'm her daughter. Freya.'

He smiled, simpered almost. Had a soft look, flesh

93

moulded from dough, dark hair swept severely aside, grey at the edges. 'Of course. Of course. How are you, Freya?' Face contorted, going for sympathy; failing. 'I'm sorry, silly question. It's a terrible time.'

'Yes. It is. Can I help you with something?'

The other man was there now, a slower walk up the drive, breathing like a freight train. Camera forcing creases into the shoulder of his leather jacket. He smelled of stale cigarettes. Freya looked down the lens, red light blinking.

'Oh, just . . . we just wanted to see how you were doing.' His head was canted to one side. 'How *are* you all coping?'

'Okay, I guess.' Freya folded her arms across her chest, snow seeping through her cream slippers, through thick woollen socks.

'I know, I know. It's an awful time.' Leaning in conspiratorially, washing Freya in a wave of musk. 'You have no idea how many people I've spoken to in situations like yours.'

'You mean plane crashes?'

'Well, ha, no, I mean awful, awful tragedies.' Puts his hand on her shoulder, leans in so close that she can see the row of black fillings that line his teeth. 'People make it. You would be amazed what people can survive.'

Her mother, her world crumbling beneath her. Her brother, face stripped bare with shock.

'I know this is such an intrusion, but I have to report on it. I mean, I know you understand, it's such an important news story, and I wanted to make absolutely sure I got my facts right.' His hand heavy on her shoulder, damp through the cotton. 'It's bad enough for you guys without the extra insult of factual errors.'

She could have turned, shut the door in his face, and she almost did. But then they would come back, and next time it would be Richard that they would speak to, or her mother. 'Okay. What do you want to know?'

'Captain Blake, he's forty-six, is that right?'

Freya nodded. 'He'll be forty-seven in January. I mean . . .' She stopped, for the first time the enormity of what happened hitting her. Breathe. 'His birthday is January the twenty-fifth.'

'All right.' He squeezed her shoulder, then his hand dropped, jotting quick notes in a pad. 'That's lovely. And can I ask, how long has he been a commercial pilot?'

'Um, I guess twenty years, maybe.'

'Gosh, so very experienced, then. How long has he been flying with JetCymru?'

'Four years nearly.'

'And before that AirBritain? That's right, isn't it? Long-distance, out of Heathrow, with them for a number of years?'

'Fifteen . . . yes.'

'Lovely. So, goodness, a very experienced pilot. But it would be fair to say that he has had problems over the years?'

Freya could feel it, her skin littered with pinpricks. 'Problems?'

'Problems. Difficulties. See, I spoke to someone in AirBritain who told us that he was quite well known for being difficult.'

You need to know when to lie. You need to know when to lie to yourself. But what happens when the rest of the world knows the truth? What happens to your lie then?

'Who said . . .'

'A source, I'm sorry, I can't expand on that, but I'm sure you can understand. See, what they said was that he was notorious within AirBritain, arrogant, that by the end no one wanted to work with him.'

Dad's coming home, Frey. He hates being away from us. He's going to leave London, get a job somewhere local. That way we can all be together. Her mother's eyes shining, face creased into a smile. *It'll be wonderful. He misses us all so much.*

'People are saying that he was known to be reckless, that he would do things that went against protocol. In fact he was disciplined for it. That's right, isn't it? Just before he left AirBritain? We have been told that was why he left. That it was a case of jumping before he was pushed.'

He wants to come home, Frey. So we can all be together.

'I . . .' Suddenly Freya was aware of the bitterness of the wind, pulling at her skin, the thick snow piling around her slippered feet.

'And at JetCymru? He's had problems there too, right? People saying that he has a bad attitude. Again, the word "reckless".'

Freya stepped back, closer to the house, suddenly feeling out of her depth. The red light still blinking. 'I have to go.'

'Now, Freya, you know I have to ask you this: what about yesterday? How did he seem to you? Tired? Upset, maybe?'

Red-rimmed eyes. A start when he sees his daughter, standing in the kitchen where he doesn't expect her to be. His hands, shaking, still cradling the phone.

'Had he been depressed?'

'Why?' Her voice seemed to be sticking, thick in her throat.

'People are talking, Freya. They are saying pilot error.'

She didn't want to be here now, had bitten off more than she could chew. She should have listened to her grandmother, should have stayed inside where it was warm and safe.

'Have you seen the crash site, Freya? We've been there. You should see it. It's a dreadful scene. Just dreadful. A lot of people dead. So many families devastated. And your father had something to do with that. So I have to ask you, Freya. What was going on with your father?'

CHAPTER 16

Tom: Saturday 17 March, 9.02 a.m.

Libby's father rested his hand against the wooden door, looked like he would fall without it. His stomach blossomed into a gut that hung over the band of his jeans, eyes red, face slack. He looked at Tom, and for a moment it seemed that he didn't see him.

'Super, DC Tom Allison . . .'

The man shook his head. 'It's not Superintendent any more. Just plain Jim now.' But his shoulders straightened a little, and his eyes came into focus, running over Tom. Pausing for a moment at his shoes. Tom had brushed the mud off them. Rubbed them over with a cloth. Jim nodded, a fractional movement of his head, then looked back up at Tom. 'Come on in.'

The hallway was wide and bright. Tom felt a pressure brushing against his leg, glanced down. The black and white cat looking up at him with overlarge eyes.

'Charlie. Sorry. My daughter's cat.'

Tom nodded. Looking at Jim's hands. They

hung limp at his sides, as if they weren't connected to him any more. Small, smaller than you would expect to see on a man with a reputation as a lion on the force. His wedding ring dug into his flesh, as if his finger had grown around it, pulling it into his skin. 'I . . . DI Maxwell, he said you might be more comfortable with someone from CID . . .'

'That's good of him, very good of him. Was CID a long time myself. Lifetime ago now.' He wasn't looking at Tom, gaze drifting off into the middle distance. Looked emptied out. The way one would expect a father to look after the death of his child.

Tom cleared his throat. 'It's a good job. Busy.' What else do you say when nothing matters any more? You talk about the stuff that never mattered anyway. Like the weather. Because that at least remains the same when everything around it has changed.

'Takes the heart of you. Have to love it otherwise it'd kill you. Tough for families, though. That's why I got out in the end. Wasn't seeing Essie, the kids. Said to myself, Jim, you're going to end up married to no one but the job. And the kids . . .' His voice sputtered, a failing candle, then went out.

Tom's stomach spasmed, the way it had in the hospital, the receptionist's voice trilling, 'She's here,' and the faces turning, looking at him with something akin to hatred, that he had got what they so desperately wanted. The feeling of a gift unjustly given.

A door opened, closed, slow footsteps. The mother walked in, every step painful to watch. Jim turned, and now there was a new kind of grief pulsing from him. He held out his hand.

'Essie, this is Tom.' Pulling his wife in, mother bird cradling young beneath its wing. 'Tom, my wife Esther.'

Tom smiled, and she nodded, face contorted like she's really trying to speak, but her mouth is stoppered up by sadness. Fingers wrapped themselves around her husband's shirt, and he stared at them. Hands again. It was like he'd become obsessed with them. Narrow, small. Trembling. They clung to her husband as though that was all that was keeping her from falling.

'Why don't you have a sleep?' Jim stroked her hair.

One beat. Two. Then she looked up at him like she'd only just realised he'd said something, eyes watching the shape of his lips. 'I . . . No . . . I'll stay. Just in case. You might . . .'

'If we need you, we'll call you.' Kissing her on the forehead.

Esther nodded, not looking at anyone now, sleepwalking towards the stairs, and up. They didn't say anything. Watched her go.

Jim cleared his throat, wiping his eyes with the back of his hand. 'Come into the kitchen, Tom. Let's talk in there.'

It smelled of sugar and cinammon and burnt pastry. A narrow man, tall, with an aquiline nose, blonde hair cut short, stood staring out of the kitchen window.

'Tom. This is my son, Ethan,' Jim said.

Tom nodded, a brief smile. Ethan looked to be close to his own age, early thirties maybe. He started, looked like he hadn't heard them coming. Tom held out a hand, and the other man shook it, briefly. His hands were large, solid.

Jim pulled a chair out from the kitchen table. 'Have a seat, Tom. Coffee? Eth? Grab us some coffee. Tom. I need to ask. Where are we with the investigation?' He leaned forward, splayed his fingers flat against the pine tabletop.

Tom hesitated, diplomacy vying with honesty. 'Well, we're doing everything . . .' His voice trailed off into nothing, caught up in Jim's stare. It was hard, face pulled tight as a drum. He recognised the look. It was the one he saw in the mirror. 'How much do you want to know?'

'Everything.' Jim's voice was different, all sharp edges and slick surfaces. A policeman's voice.

Better to be a policeman now, because being a father is just too damn hard.

Ethan set the mugs of coffee on the table, clumsy, the dark liquid slopping.

'Incident room is up and running. Got a good staff there. Senior Investigating Officer is DS Barker, new in from Avon and Somerset. He's got a good rep. The boys like him.'

'Do we know when . . .' Jim's voice trailed off,

too hard to put it into words. *When was my daughter murdered?*

'We're waiting on the pathologist.' Tom kept his voice even, trying to be the detective, trying not to think that it was no more than a day, two at the most; before the plane crash, after the plane crash. Such a short amount of time for the world to turn on its head.

'I . . . right.' Jim looked down, clearing his throat. 'And the scene?'

'Not bad. Mostly untouched. Snowfall wiped out any footprints, but Scenes of Crime are doing what they do.'

Tom sipped his coffee. Stoppering up his mouth. So that he wouldn't have to tell this man that his daughter was still lying on the riverbank, covered in little more than a tent. Scenes of Crime were hopeful that they would get her out today; that had been the message from this morning's briefing. Hopeful, not certain.

'The house?'

'Forensics are there now.' Turning his daughter's life upside down, searching through her private belongings in the hope of uncovering her deepest, darkest secrets. Like the condoms that she kept in the bedside cabinet even though she was supposedly single. The empty condom wrapper buried at the bottom of the bathroom bin. Tom wondered how much this man truly wanted to know about his child now that she was gone. 'House-to-house team are canvassing the

102

neighbours. We're hoping someone'll throw something up.'

Jim nodded, looked down at his hands as he sucked in a low breath. 'Was she raped?'

'Dad!' Ethan's expression was taut. 'Don't . . .'

Tom shook his head. Watching the brother. 'We don't think so. So far there's been no evidence of sexual assault.'

Jim released the breath, his shoulders slumping. 'Okay.'

Ethan turned, staring back out of the window into the still-falling snow.

CHAPTER 17

Cecilia: Saturday 17 March, 9.30 a.m.

Cecilia didn't know why she had come. She stood in the hospital lobby, surrounded by tight faces and torn bodies and broken hearts. She hadn't heard Tom come in last night, but then, there was a murder. That was the way it was when there was a murder. And what did it matter to her anyway? Ben had stayed with Tom's mother. She had rung Cecilia, thrusting Ben on to the phone to say good night to her, even though all the child wanted to do was watch television and be left alone. Cecilia had tried to make the noises that a mother should make. Had said good night, told her son that she loved him. Wondering if she was doing it right, what her mother-in-law would think.

She had woken a little after eight, sleep disturbed by the sound of the door slamming. She had got up and, for the first time in the longest of times, had hoped that it was Tom coming home, so that he would be there and she wouldn't have to be alone with the beige walls and the sounds of a screaming engine. But the house had been silent, driveway empty. She was alone.

She had tried to settle. Had showered as best she could with the pain in her arm. Had put on the television and tried to block out the sounds and the smell of jet fuel until she couldn't any more.

She hadn't known where she was going. Had got into her car and turned her key in the ignition, guiding it on to the motorway, doing eighty, car ploughing through slush like a ship through storm waves. She would go and get Ben. That was what she would do. And she was going to get Ben, she really was. But then the miles had fallen away behind her, and all she could see was herself standing in the hallway of her mother-in-law's house, with its ugly beige-flecked Anaglypta, holding out her arms to her son, stomach eating her from the inside, him turning away, choosing his grandmother over her. Her mother-in-law's face, faux sympathy tinged with triumph.

Driving past the junction. Foot flat to the floor. Then blue hospital signs, her finger flicking the indicator, plunging up the steep ramp of the slip road, and she doesn't know why. But she's thinking about the knot of people sitting huddled in the snow, and the way they looked at her like she had all the answers. A sharp left, not waiting at the roundabout even though there was a car coming, a Volvo that braked sharply, honking its horn.

It was quieter today than it had been yesterday. The crowds had thinned out. The information desk had been pushed back into the corner, tucked out of the way, as if that way one could pretend that it had all been a bad dream and a plane hadn't really fallen out of the sky. It was still manned. A single, solitary receptionist, foundation thick on her lined face, elbows resting on the table. She wore coral lipstick. Eyes heavy, like she had been there for ever. She watched the people, gaze tracking them, body folded in tight, willing them to keep walking.

Cecilia stood, too close to the sliding doors, so that they hung agape, a billowing breeze bringing with it a dusting of snow that turned the grey linoleum white, the desk feet away. It seemed that she couldn't move, her feet sunk into the ground, figures moving around her, in their pyjamas and suits and white coats, and it was like she was invisible. That fleeting sensation again, as though maybe she was already dead. Her gaze tracking the crowd, looking for someone to notice her. That was when she saw him. A young man, little more than a teenager; black hair, dark eyes, distantly familiar. He was leaning against a wall, a spike of tension running through his neck, looked like he'd been crying.

Cecilia stood a little straighter.

'Can I help you?' the receptionist asked.

Cecilia started.

The woman was watching her, had pulled her

mouth into a sympathetic smile. But it was in her eyes still, that look, that says that she wants Cecilia to say no, that she's fine thank you, so that she won't have to deal with it again today, won't have to break another heart.

'I . . .' The words stuck. *I want to see the people, the ones that I pulled out from the plane before it caught on fire.* But nothing seemed to be working the way it should, her lips moving, no sounds coming out, and her shoulders slumped. Her arm throbbed, and even though she didn't want to, she cradled it, looking now like just another victim. She glanced over her shoulder back towards where the boy had stood. Nothing there now but an empty space. She shook her head, her gaze sinking back to the woman with the bad make-up.

The woman's eyes ran over her, the bruise that was flowering yellow and blue on her cheek, the arm cradled in its sling. Then back up to her face, now with a new look.

And Cecilia wanted to cry.

'The people . . .' Her voice came out small and uneven.

'The ones on the plane?'

Suddenly the air was filled with the scream of engines and bitter cold wind. Cecilia blew out a breath, slow. 'Are they . . .?'

The woman looked down at the paperwork in front of her. Then back up. 'I'm sorry, my love, but they're gone.'

A sickening feeling, the sense of falling. 'Gone?'

'No, no. I don't mean . . . They've been released. They've gone home. Most of them were minor injuries. I . . .' Looking back down. 'Most of them.'

Cecilia stared at her, knew what it was that she was trying not to say. That the passengers either had minor injuries. Or they'd died. That there was no in-between.

'Here we go. There's a lady still here. Mrs Collins.'

Mrs Collins. Maisie. Skin so cold it seemed to sear, drifts of snow that climbed up her bare legs. 'Where?' Cecilia's hands were shaking, must be from the cold, and she tucked them into her coat.

The woman was looking at her like she wanted to cry or to hug her and Cecilia took a step back. Just in case. She was nearer the door now, close enough to feel the swish as it slid open, the cold blast of air. Could she smell burning?

'Maisie Collins. Ward . . . nine. If you go straight on past me, take a left and then up the stairs.'

She turned in the seat, gesturing along the corridor, then looked back at Cecilia, face locked into a sympathetic smile, and a look like she was expecting something further, confessions or tears or something. Cecilia tugged her coat tighter around her, began to walk. Didn't look back.

Maisie was gazing out of the window. Small, frail, lost inside the oversized hospital gown. Her face was blackened, lips twitching as if saying a rosary.

Cecilia stood at the entrance to the ward, feet sinking into deep, deep snow. Now there was definitely burning, the acrid smell scraping at her throat. She wanted to turn, but couldn't do that either, couldn't seem to do anything but stand there and stare at the tiny woman. And the tears that had begun to track down her cheeks. She looked grey. Like she was already dead.

Then Maisie gave a little sob, so quiet that you wouldn't hear it, not unless you were listening for it.

'Maisie?'

The old woman's head swivelled, unsteady, wobbling on a spring. There was a look there. Cecilia realised with horror that it was hope.

'Ernie?' A moment as Maisie focused. 'Is it Ernie? Have they found him?'

'I . . .'

'I'm sorry, love. I'm sorry. I thought that you were here to say that you'd found my Ernie. You aren't, are you? I'm sorry, pet. I'm awful worried about him, see. But then he's probably gone to another hospital. You know, rather than this one. Can't expect this one to take all the survivors in. NHS being what it is. That's what's happened, I'm sure. Don't you think?'

Cecilia couldn't seem to think what to say. But she moved forward, unstuck finally.

'Do I know you, pet? You look awful familiar. You a nurse, are you? So many of you about, I forgets who I've seen and who I haven't.'

'It was the mountain.' Fire, ice, snow. 'I was the flight attendant . . .'

Maisie squinted at her. 'You held my hand. When it was snowing. You held my hand, didn't you?'

Cecilia hesitated. Shattered cabin crackling with electrical wires hanging free, swinging. Barely able to breathe for the smell of jet fuel. The middle-aged man who sat, stock still, eyes wide, fingers gripping armrests that were no longer there. Pulling him bodily to his feet, back bowing under the weight of him. Knowing that she was about to die. She nodded.

'I remember. I remember you.' Maisie nodded, certain suddenly, then glanced down and back up, less certain now. 'My Ernie. You didn't see him, did you?' She looked past Cecilia. 'I can't find him.'

'I'm sorry, Maisie.' Cecilia sank into the chair at Maisie's bedside.

'Well now, always has been a one for wandering off. Sixty years. Sixty years next year we've been married. I was seventeen. Cute as a button, mind. Skinny. Skinny, skinny, skinny. And there was Ernie. He'd just left work. An engineer, he was. Happiest day of my life, that one was. Happiest day.'

Cecilia glanced down, twisting her own wedding ring. Remembering. She had only been back in Wales for a couple of weeks. She hadn't wanted to meet a man; that had been the last thing she'd wanted, in truth. Had run back across the Severn Bridge because it was safer, skin still crawling with the thought of Eddie. She wasn't sleeping. Couldn't sleep, because when she slept there were the dreams: fingers grasping at her, pulling, a sharp pain. Laura had invited her out: *Let's go for a quiet drink. It's time we caught up.* Cecilia hadn't wanted to go, couldn't face the thought of the crowded bar, the bodies pressing in on her, the eyes that seemed to undress her. But her mother had pushed. *You're turning into a hermit. Go. Staying in this house, day in, day out. People will be thinking you've had some kind of breakdown.* So she had gone. Laura hadn't said that she was bringing her husband; did they do everything together now? Was that how it worked? She hadn't said that her husband was bringing a friend.

'Love at first sight. That's what it was. Love at first sight. He was all dirty, oil on his hands, under his nails. And do you know? I thought he was the handsomest man I'd ever seen. Even with all the dirt.' Maisie laughed. 'Can you imagine?'

Her eyes had skirted across him. His narrow build. She liked broad shoulders. Chestnut-brown hair with a slight curl. She liked dark hair. She'd closed in on herself, boxed in like this. Had barely looked up from her drink.

'We were married six weeks later.' Maisie shook her head. 'You married, love?'

'Yes.' Cecilia's voice came out quiet. 'Tom. He's . . . he's a policeman.'

It was about a month from that meeting to the next and she had been as little prepared for that one as she had been for the first. She had locked her keys in the car, buried them inside plastic bags full of Tesco shopping. Stupid. Was standing in the rain in the car park, gentle drizzle gathering strength, a full-on storm threatening on the horizon. She was just about to cry when a quiet voice had said, 'Are you okay?'

Was it that she needed rescuing? Was that why she had turned with a smile he hadn't seen before, allowing him into her life, if not with open arms then at least with a tacit acceptance.

'Good man?'

Cecilia looked down at her ring. 'I guess. It . . . We have a little boy. We . . . It happened before. Before we married. I found out, that I was pregnant I mean. So, we just . . . we got married.'

Their fledgling relationship had made it to three months. Barely. Seemed like they had hardly scratched the surface of who the other was. Had gone to dinner and to the cinema and once to the theatre because it was something that Tom had thought she would enjoy. A distraction, a rough approximation of a relationship that lasted as long as it lasted and then simply ended because Cecilia stopped answering her phone and Tom stopped leaving messages.

Then the sickness had begun. An uncomfortable rumbling at first. The feeling like she was walking through clouds. And that little blue line that spun her world.

'Ah.' Maisie watched her. Seemed like she was seeing right through her. 'It's tough then. Tougher when you don't get the time to figure each other out first. Before the kids.'

'Yes. I . . . we, we've been trying.'

'Well, you do, love, don't you? That's what we all do. Try. There wouldn't be a marriage around if it weren't for people working hard at it. You can't love them every minute of every day. It is work, a lot of the time.' She peered at Cecilia. 'I've got a girl. My daughter, Caroline. She would be here. If she could. She's busy, you see. She'd be here otherwise. She said that on the phone. But with the kids, as well. Two little girls. Lovely little girls. Lovely.' Shook her head. 'Keep you busy, kids do.'

'Yes.'

'How old is your little one, pet?'

'Ben. He's two.'

Cecilia hadn't wanted the baby, couldn't have the baby; she knew before she *knew*. How could she have it, when every time she looked at it she would see the other one? And even if she had wanted it, she didn't deserve it. How could she, after what she had done? And kids picked up on that kind of thing, they knew when you had secrets, and they knew when you weren't good enough.

'It's . . . Sometimes it's like I just don't know how to do it. How to be a mother.' Cecilia could hear the words, said in her own voice, but they came from so far away. Surely wasn't possible that it could be her. 'I want to. Now, I mean. I didn't, back when I first knew, but now I want to so much. But . . .' A sound escaped her, more like a sob than anything else. 'I just don't know how to do it.'

It had all got away from her. Once she had told Tom, after that it had happened so fast. And then she couldn't get out of it, counting down the days on her calendar. Two weeks to make her mind up, one week, three days, then suddenly it was over, and not making the decision had made the decision and she was going to be a mother. Then she was getting married and moving into a house and getting bigger and bigger, and all the time this feeling was building in her. Horror. Like she wants to jump out of her own skin. Leave her body to this thing that has taken over her life.

'Oh my,' said Maisie, 'it's a tough job. And there are no guidebooks. And no one can ever prepare you for it.'

Cecilia had watched her son, had held him, had changed him and fed him. All the while with this feeling nestling in her stomach that he knew. His wide-open eyes staring at her, seeing right through the shiny made-up veneer, through to the fractured soul of her. And she knew that he could see it, that she was damaged and broken and that she had already failed one child and so would inevitably fail him as well. So it got easier and easier to hand him to Tom, let his oh-so-capable father do all the things that she was so afraid of getting wrong.

'The thing is, love, you've got to muddle through. And I think some people are naturally confident at motherhood, they just figure they'll pick it up. Then there's the rest of us, and for us it's scary. I tell you, even the most confident ones, they're just making it up. Same as we do. But for the kids, all that matters is the showing up. The being there, day after day. Even if you aren't perfect. Kids don't mind that. What matters to them is that you keep trying, just keep showing up.' Maisie shook her head, then looked past Cecilia towards the door. 'I don't know. It's a pity. That my Caroline can't come, I mean. But like I said, she's busy, and what with the girls and all . . .' She twisted the sheets in her hands. 'Anyway, I expect it won't be much longer now.'

'What won't?'

'Well, that they'll come and tell me that they've found my Ernie. He'll probably come himself. He'll insist. Very protective, is my Ernie. No. It won't be too much longer now.'

Cecilia sat for a moment. Then leaned forward and took Maisie's hand in her good hand. A deep breath, and a glance up, a swift smile. 'I'm sure you're right, Maisie,' she lied. 'I'm sure that he'll be here any time now.'

CHAPTER 18

Freya: Saturday 17 March, 9.33 a.m.

reya pulled a loose-fitting sweater over still-damp hair. Citrus green. She tugged her hair up into a bun, twisting loosely, looping it with an elastic band. Stooping down, pulling brown leather boots from the bottom of the wardrobe, stuffing her feet in, holding on to the wardrobe door for balance.

What was going on with your father?

She could still feel the reporter's breath on her neck, the soft-fleshed man's patent shoes clip-clopping behind her. Her slippers sliding on slush. Pressing her fingers against bitter cold wood, the warmth of the house hitting her in a wave. Pushing the door shut, cutting off the voices that still called her name.

What was going on with your father?

She'd slept fitfully. There had been dreams of crashing planes and snow on fire that jolted her awake, that allowed her to drift back into soft sleep, then yanked her back again. Had he made a mistake, some kind of terrible error that had

117

brought his plane tumbling into the mountains? Freya had lain staring at the ceiling, wanting so badly to believe that it was the plane, that in spite of all his faults, her father had fought hard, railed against some mechanical failure that had eventually proven too much for him. It would be the plane. He was a good pilot, in spite of what the dough-skinned reporter had said.

She had almost convinced herself, had almost allowed her eyes to settle closed. Then she had thought about the night before the flight, her father's car and her mother's little Fiesta missing from the drive when she had returned home, a little after eleven. Coming home to a house that felt wrong, cold and empty. Richard was staying at a friend's, had told her that in the morning. But still she had expected something, some form of life. She had slipped up the stairs, pushing open the door to her parents' room, thinking that she would check on her mother, because Mum worries when Dad goes out, when he forgets to call. But finding only an empty bed, duvet still pulled taut across the mattress.

She had stood there for a moment, trying to remember. They must be out together. Her mother must have told her and she had forgotten, that was all. Still that strange feeling in her stomach, of the world being a little off its balance. She had gone to bed then. They were grown-ups, would return when they were ready. But still she had lain awake, waiting even though she hadn't meant to.

Her mother had returned about an hour later. Freya had known it was her from the clip-clop of her heels on the tiled kitchen floor. She had listened, waiting for the sounds of her father's heavier step. Had heard nothing.

They hadn't talked about it, when they woke up the next morning. She hadn't asked her mother, because in truth that just wasn't what they did. They didn't poke, or pry, they let things be. Her father hadn't come down for breakfast. Still hadn't surfaced by the time she left for the university.

Her mother had been quiet, replying in one-word answers.

What was going on with your father?

Freya crouched down, pulling at the laces, knotting them tight. Then pushed herself up, darting down the stairs, light steps.

She had hoped that the family would be asleep, that she could pull on her coat and grab her bag, letting herself out of the house and into the car without ever having to answer a question. Because this is how they do things here, this is how their family normally works.

But she was never going to be that lucky today. There were voices coming from the kitchen. Her grandmother, trilling, incessant. Her grandfather, low, rare. Freya hesitated, hung in the hallway. Didn't seem to be breathing. She'd just grab her keys. Go.

'Freya. Is that you?'

Freya stopped. Sighed. *Bugger.* She could still

119

go. Before they could ask her where. She sighed again and turned, heading to the kitchen.

Her grandmother was crouched on the floor, corduroy trousers hiked up revealing freckled legs, Minnie Mouse socks. Bottles of bleach, counter sprays, bin bags, coffee filters, arrayed on the floor before her, the cupboard beneath the sink hanging open. Her grandmother's arm swallowed whole by it, her shoulder moving back, forth, in wide sweeping movements, as if she's trying to fight off a monster that's eating her a bit at a time. Her grandfather sat at the kitchen table, *Daily Telegraph* spread out before him. A glance up, a quick nod, toast crumbs scattering across black and white pages. 'My God, how many bottles of bleach does one house need? Look at this, two, three.' Her grandmother scrabbled furiously, shoulders vibrating beneath her peach blouse, stopping briefly to scratch at a stain on the cupboard floor with a fingernail.

'Grandma? What are you doing?'

Her grandmother glanced over her shoulder. 'I was getting a new bin bag. Have you seen the state of this cupboard? Shocking.' She paused, a frown flitting across her face. 'You're going out?'

Freya hesitated, glancing at her grandfather. He was looking at her too with a slight frown.

'I . . .' She tugged her coat on, trying not to look at her grandmother, her face dark, overhung with warning clouds. 'Yes. I . . . I'm going to the crash site.'

The kitchen stilled.

'What?' Her grandmother's voice was trimmed with ice.

Her grandfather was watching her. 'That's ridiculous, Freya. Why would you want to do . . . Nonsense. You don't need to see that. George. Tell her.'

'Tell her what?'

'Tell her that she shouldn't go.'

'I'm not telling her that.'

'George! Would you speak to her?'

'What do you want me to say to her, Bets?'

Her grandmother sighed in exasperation. 'Anything. Good God!'

'All right, fine. Freya. I think that's a very brave decision and I'm proud of you.'

'George!'

They hung there for a moment, stalemate. Then her grandmother tsked, a small noise, a minor nudge to break the spell. Her grandfather flapped the pages of his paper, brushing toast crumbs on to the floor, her grandmother muttering, returning to the cupboard, arm swiping furiously at the stains. Freya looked down, buttoning her coat. 'Grandad?'

'Yes, love?'

'Don't tell Mum. Okay?'

CHAPTER 19

Tom: Saturday 17 March, 11.01 a.m.

'Jim,' said Tom, 'you know I need to ask?'

Jim was leaning over the kitchen table, gaze fixed off in some middle distance. Ethan sat beside him, his chair pushed back, arms folded tight across his chest. Tom cradled his coffee. The kitchen clock ticking extraordinarily loudly.

'I know.' Jim had pushed himself up, squared off his shoulders. Preparing himself for what was to come.

'I could . . .'

'No, it's okay, Tom. Go on.' His fingers were tapping the tabletop, a fast beat, as though that way he could hurry the investigation forward.

Tom flicked open his notepad. 'When did you see Libby last?'

'Tuesday. She came to dinner. Essie, she likes to cook. Worries Libby doesn't eat enough . . .' Jim's voice stumbled over the words, and he looked down at his hands. A breath, another, a moment to grieve for his wife's grief.

'So,' Tom said. 'Tuesday evening?'

'She was here, six till, I don't know, ten maybe?' Jim looked at Ethan. A slow nod, not meeting his father's eye. 'Ten. We were all here.'

'And how did she seem to you?'

'I don't know.' Jim shrugged. 'Better, I suppose.'

'Better?'

'Yeah, she'd been, I guess, off, recently. You know, not herself.'

'In what way?' Tom asked.

'I don't know, withdrawn. Quiet.' Jim rubbed at his face with thick hands. 'She just, she wasn't herself.'

'Did you ask her about it?'

He nodded, a pause, swallowed. 'Yeah, she . . . she just, she laughed it off. Said she was tired.' Shook his head. 'I didn't push her. Thought she would tell me if she wanted . . . if she needed to talk.' He looked down at his hands. 'I should have asked. Pushed a bit harder. You think there's always time.'

Tom nodded, a fleeting scribble. He hadn't seen Cecilia this morning, had been gone before she got up. Had briefly considered stopping, a quick knock on her bedroom door, but had decided against it. Could get away with that, considering himself a good husband because he let her sleep.

Tom couldn't remember when it was she had migrated from their king-size bed into the occasional double, how long ago. Some flimsy excuse: *I'll be home late, don't want to disturb you.* He had known in his gut that it was one of those moments, the ones when you set out your stall. But he had nodded, like it meant nothing. Then the next night, when she had gone to bed early because she was tired, hoping that it wasn't his bed that she had gone to. And the relief when he went to bed two hours later, finding it empty.

'Sorry.' Jim shook his head.

Tom looked back up again, a smile. 'Not a problem. Do you want a minute?'

'No. Let's just, let's do it.'

'How long had Libby seemed withdrawn?' asked Tom

'Um, a while, I guess. A couple of months.'

'And you have no idea why?'

Jim shook his head. Ethan shifted in his chair, glanced up at Tom, then back down, looking to his fingers.

Tom watched Ethan for a moment. Kept his face flat. 'So, Jim. How did Libby get home on Tuesday night?'

'Ethan.' Jim nodded towards his son. 'He drove her home.'

'I see. What time was that, Ethan?'

'Huh?' Ethan looked up. 'Oh, um, I guess about ten, maybe ten thirty.'

'Right. So what did you guys talk about?' Tom was watching Ethan, felt Jim move, sensed the frisson of tension spiking the room. A flash of something crossed Ethan's face. Tom wondered if it was guilt. Looked at his hands, unwrapped from his chest now, splayed on his knees, large, thick-fingered.

'Nothing.'

'Nothing? It's, what, a twenty-minute drive?'

'Well, I mean, not nothing. Just nothing important. Just stuff, you know?'

A silence settled heavily on the room.

'There was something going on with her, though.' Ethan's words seemed to tumble faster. 'I don't know what, but it was, I guess, like she was afraid.'

'Afraid?' Tom repeated.

'I don't know. Maybe not afraid. Nervous.' Ethan knotted his thick fingers together.

'What makes you say that?'

'I . . . You'd have to know Libby. You . . . Did you know her?'

Tom shook his head. 'I met her, just the once, when she first joined.'

'It's like she's never afraid of anything. Is she, Dad?'

Jim smiled then, shoulders untensing. His eyes had filled with tears.

'But the past couple of weeks.' Ethan shook his head. 'She's been . . . I don't know . . . Jumpy, I suppose. I mean, she came to ours for dinner the other night . . .'

'When was this?'

'Last week. Monday. We – me, Libby and my wife, Isabelle – were in the kitchen, around eight o'clock, you know, so dark, and we had the lights on. And . . .' He looked up again. 'It's just that she wasn't happy. About the light. You know, that you could see in from outside. She kept, like, looking over her shoulder. Twitchy.'

Tom frowned. 'Did she say why?'

'She thought, said she thought she saw something. Someone. She laughed. Said she was imagining things.' His voice had shrunk, he wasn't looking at Tom now, but down at the table.

'You didn't tell me this.' Jim was staring at him, voice hard as rocks.

'I know. I . . . It wasn't . . . At the time, it wasn't a big deal.' A little boy, caught throwing stones at a greenhouse.

'You don't know that, though, do you?'

'I . . .'

'You realise that it could have been him? The one who killed her.'

'Jim.' Tom glanced from father to son. 'Let's not jump to any conclusions.'

'No, no. Let's get the facts on the table, now.' Jim smacked his hand flat against the tabletop. 'You said your sister was afraid. So obviously you went and looked? That's right, isn't it, Ethan? You went outside to make sure there was no one there?'

'Jim.'

'When your little sister was frightened, when she said that someone was outside of that window, you went to look, didn't you?'

Ethan was crying now, head bowed down low.

'Jim. Come on. Leave it now.'

Jim pushed back his chair, the wooden legs scraping against the floor.

'Okay, Ethan. Did she say anything else?'

Ethan was watching his father. He looked like Jim, a little taller, a little broader, a little less worn down by a life serving as the thin blue line. Jim stood at the window, back turned to the room, shoulders drawn in tight. Ethan shook his head.

'So she never told you why she was nervous?'

He didn't answer for a moment. Then, in an explosion of sound, 'Fuck. It's my fault. Oh my God . . .'

'Eth.' Jim had turned now, hand on his son's shoulder, eyes red, cheeks wet. 'It's . . . I'm sorry. I'm sorry. I'm just, I'm taking it out on you, and that's not fair. It's okay.' He sank into a kitchen chair, hand on his son's shoulder. 'I'm being a prick. I'm sorry, son.'

Tom watched them, father and son.

'Sorry, Tom. I'm sorry.' Jim wiped his eyes.

'It's okay, Jim. We can leave it there for now . . .'

'No. It's okay. Please. Go on.'

'Did she, was there a boyfriend?'

Jim shook his head. 'There was a boy, in school. But they broke up years ago. He left for university. Durham, I think. Libby, she said it was for the best. There's been no one since.'

'Did she date?' asked Tom.

'Not really. Focused on her job, friends.'

'Did she ever mention anyone? Anyone that she had problems with?'

Jim shook his head again.

'I need to ask . . .'

'I know,' said Jim. 'It's okay.'

'Jim, where were you on Wednesday?'

'Essie and I went to visit her parents – they live in Bath. We stayed the night and got back Thursday lunchtime, around one maybe. I can give you their number.'

'Thanks.' Tom made a note, then looked up at Ethan. His arms were crossed again. 'What about you, Ethan?'

'Why do you need to know?'

'Eth!'

'No, Dad. I'm asking. What, am I a suspect or something?'

'Eth, they've just got to eliminate us. It's procedure.'

Ethan sighed heavily. 'Look, I went to work. I work for the council – you can check with them if you feel the need. Then I went home.'

Tom watched him. 'Okay. And your wife – Isabelle, was it? She can vouch for you?'

Ethan fixed him with a look. 'She was there when I got home, then she went to the cinema with her sister.'

'Right.' Tom nodded, slowly. 'Okay.' Tried not to look at the man's hands. 'Just one more question. Anyone, anyone at all, you can think of with any reason to wish Libby harm?'

'No one that I know of. No.' Jim shook his head

'I mean, she's . . . Libby has always been such a popular girl. Always.'

'Ethan?'

Ethan shook his head too. 'No. Everyone loved her.'

Tom nodded, not saying what he was thinking, that no one is loved by everyone.

CHAPTER 20

Freya: Saturday 17 March, 11.30 a.m.

The snow had stopped falling, the sky a vivid blue. Freya picked her way through the slush, past the silent Talgarth church, grey smothered in white, along ribbon pavements.

It was quiet, most people choosing to stay indoors, their curtains closed. Those who did come out, who had to, they walked with their heads down, their collars pulled up, chins tucked in, as if they were marching into a hurricane. They looked down, or at worst straight ahead. They didn't look at the mountain, where the tail of the plane had gouged a black gully into the snow. They didn't look at the pall of smoke that still seemed to sit in the air, marking the spot where death had been.

Freya walked along the country lane. Shivering. Telling herself that it was from the cold. She had left the car by the old mill. Had smelt the coffee, freshly baked bread. She imagined painting it, the church and the snow, thinking about colours and where she would feather the brush, how the tones would work, the light fall.

Her mobile had rung as she had driven the winding mountain roads. Luke. It wasn't the first time he had rung, or even the second. She wondered if it was the crash. If he had heard, wanted to see if she was all right. Or whether he was going to ask her out again. He had once, the night before the plane crash, had drunk too much, wrapped thick arms around her, mumbling into her hair, had said that he had always fancied her. Freya had felt her insides go cold. Had smiled politely, breathing in the sweet smell of alcohol, and unravelled his arm, thinking how much he looked like her father.

She rounded the corner into the hospital grounds. Couldn't imagine painting any more. The narrow village lane gave way to debris. Fragmented metal. Scarred earth. Red bricks tumbled across the snow, a collapsed Lego tower. Everything black and charred and broken. And in there, somewhere, her father.

She stared, feet stuck into the icy granite ground. Felt that swirl of unreality, that any moment now she would wake from this dream. Because this didn't happen, not in real life. You didn't wake up one morning, your father dead because his plane had tumbled from the sky. Life just didn't happen that way, not really. A heat rushed through her. She thought that she might be sick.

She turned her back to the wreckage, facing the line of trees still black with the heat of the fire.

She wanted a memory, something to cling to that would wash clean the image of charred white bones, crimson sinew, black ash. Him teaching her to ride a bike, reading her a bedtime story, anything would have done. But there was nothing but the ghost of him, moving through her life, barely touching it.

She stared at the trees, the way the branches hung down, spindly thin and black. She hadn't cried. Not once. When her mother wept and her brother wept and her grandmother wept, she had watched and had comforted and hadn't cried. How could she do that? How could she be human and a daughter and not want to cry?

She stared at the trees, the ring of snow melted by the fire that killed her father, and willed herself to cry.

But there was nothing. Just this low thrumming in her chest where her heart used to be.

She didn't see him. Had been too caught up in the sight of the ruined building to pay attention to the figure standing at the cordon line.

'Pretty shocking, isn't it?'

Freya turned with a start. He was late thirties maybe, tall and thin. His face was awash in five o'clock shadow, dark eyes ringed with dark circles. She didn't recognise him, not at first. Then she noticed the black leather jacket, got a wash of cigarette smoke, and remembered the cameraman who had followed her along her path, red light blinking.

He was watching her, assessing.

Freya stared at him for a moment. This was a terrible idea. She should never have come. Her feet turned, willing her to walk away.

'You're Oliver Blake's daughter? Right? I saw you at the house. Yesterday.'

She looked at him, her mouth set into a hard line. 'What do you want now?'

He studied her for a moment, then gave a half-smile. 'Why did you come here?'

'That's none of your business.'

'No,' the man allowed with a slight shrug. 'Probably not. But I am a reporter, so I tend to ask anyway.' He glanced back towards the ruined building, the yellow jackets and white hard hats swarming across it like flies on a carcass. 'Quite a sight, huh? They've been out here all night. Probably will be tonight as well.' He shivered ostentatiously. 'Wouldn't fancy that.'

'Indeed.' She should just walk away. She should never have come. Couldn't now remember what it was she'd been thinking. Just that she'd wanted something to cling to. Some final piece of her father that she could point to and say, look, he was a good guy.

'I'm Ian Slater, by the way.' He didn't offer his hand.

Freya didn't reply.

Would it have repaired itself? In time, after he

had walked her down the aisle, after she had given birth to children and he had played with them, doted, been a grandfather for them even though he could never really be a father to her. Would they have found peace eventually? Perhaps even joy in one another's company? But now he was gone, lost in the metal and the snow and the bricks, and they would never know.

'Tell you what. You look like you could use a drink. Only, ha,' he glanced at his watch, 'okay, a little early. But a cuppa. You could use a cuppa? Yeah? Come on. There's a café, just down there. I'll buy you one.'

Freya stared at him.

'What? Look, I won't question you.' Ian held up his hands. 'Promise. And I've had a chat, with some of the guys working the site. People, they talk. They say things even when they shouldn't.'

Freya started. 'You know something?'

'Well, ha, I mean, I know a lot of things.'

Irritation bubbled in her. 'Forget it.' She turned, away from the paltry remains of the plane and the tumbledown building. Should never have come.

'Wait.'

The reporter had reached out, gripped her elbow. 'Look, I'm sorry. Okay? I know this is a shit time for you. It's just, okay, I have to report on this stuff. I mean, it's my job. If my boss – the guy you met earlier, remember? If he had been here, the story would already be out. But you're here, and I'm supposed to call in, was just about to in fact. But the thing is, I know . . .' He shook his head. 'I know what it's like to lose a parent. It's rough. And . . .' He let go of her elbow, tucking his hands back into his pockets. 'I think you should know first. I think you deserve that.'

'Was it fast?' Freya asked, taken aback by the uneven quality of her voice.

'Huh?'

She bit her bottom lip. Surprised by how much she needed to know. 'My father. When he died. Did it happen fast?'

'Yes.' But it was too quick. He said it without thinking. Because she needed to hear it, not because it was true.

Freya studied him for long moments. Then, tucking her coat tighter around her, gave a half-smile. 'A cuppa would be good.'

CHAPTER 21

Freya: Saturday 17 March, 11.44 a.m.

'Look, right, the thing is, I'm a chatterer, okay. I mean, I'm a reporter, so that's kind of part of the job.' Ian grinned at her. 'So, I, like, hang around, and I talk to people and they get comfortable with me and they tell me things that they probably shouldn't. So, I popped up here last night, hung out in the bar a little, where some of these guys are staying. You know, the investigators, the guys helping out on site. And so I get talking to them.'

Freya shivered, a sudden chill in spite of the unnatural heat of the doll-sized café. Took a sip from the thick china mug. The coffee was good, bitter and sweet. The air smelled of breakfast, radio humming low in the background. The reporter spoke quietly, leaning forward, even though they were the only ones there.

'One of the guys, well, he had a bit too much to drink. Just enough to make him chatty. He tells me that they found the flight data recorder – the FDR. They found that and they found the cockpit voice recorder on the night of the crash, so pretty much straight away. Now, what my guy tells me is that they took them up to Farnborough, listened to the CVR, looked at the FDR and what they're seeing is that the flight had problems, pretty much from the get-go.'

'What kind of problems?'

'He says that the engines were straining. Says that it was like they were struggling to pick up speed. Now, he was very careful to say nothing definitive, too early to tell, blah, blah, blah. But he also said they were investigating the possibility that there was ice . . . on the, ah, whatsit, the wing chord.'

'So they're thinking it was the weather?'

Ian looked down, studied his coffee. His fingers drummed against the side of the cup. 'Look, my guy, he says that they're thinking that weather played a part. Probably. But that wasn't all of it.'

'Okay?'

'He said that the pilot – your dad – he had a chance. There was talk early on about the ice. He had time to abort take-off. His co-pilot seemed to think that he should. But your dad seemed . . . confident. That was what my guy said. He chose to press on.'

Freya took another sip of her coffee, thinking of her father. Confident. Always confident. Even when he was wrong.

'The scuttlebutt is that they also got some pretty interesting information from the flight data recorder. What my guy told me was that there was some kind of problem with the plane, that they don't think there's any question about that. But the issue they're having is in the level of difficulties.'

'How do you mean?'

'Well, the ice and shit, it had made the plane tough to fly. But not impossible. They're saying that they don't think the problems your dad had would be enough to bring down a plane.'

Freya stared at him. Couldn't seem to make sense of what he was saying. 'I don't understand.'

Ian sighed. 'Look, there were problems, right? But there were also solutions. In the first place, he could have aborted the take-off. Or he could have called for a divert, could have returned the plane to the ground. The plane was struggling, but it was flyable.'

'So what . . .'

'All right . . . now you're going to have to bear with me on this, 'cause this is a long way beyond my wheelhouse.' He pulled a notebook from his pocket.

Freya saw it, leaned back.

'No, it's not . . . Look.' He flashed a page at her, black with scribbled notes. 'I didn't understand the technical stuff, so I did some research. Like I said,' he gave her a fleeting grin, 'not my wheelhouse. Okay, from what I could find out, when you have a build-up of ice on the wing, you get a number of effects. Reduced stalling angle of attack. Reduced lift. Increase in drag and stall speed. What

138

I think that shit means is that you're at greater risk of stalling because the airflow over the wing is interrupted. Now, sometimes that can just make a plane unflyable. But in this case, from what we can see from the FDR data, that wasn't what happened. The plane became difficult, unwieldy, but not unflyable.'

'Then what happened to it?'

He was looking down at the notebook now, fingers tapping against it, wouldn't meet her eye. Freya felt a creeping sense of foreboding.

'Ian. Please?'

He gave a deep sigh. 'When they were nearing a stall, they would have known, any pilot worth his shit would have known, that the way to deal with it was to lower the nose. Help the airflow over the wing. This would have helped the plane pick up speed. Moved them away from the stall.'

'But that's not what my dad did?'

'No. From what I can make out, what they're saying is that your dad, he pulled the nose up. Now what that means is that by increasing the plane's angle of attack he was also increasing the drag. That would have lowered the speed of the plane. It would have essentially forced it to stall.' He was moving his hands, palms down, teaching. 'His co-pilot. Now he was doing something different. He was trying to lower the nose. He was doing exactly what he was trained to do in a stall situation. So essentially what you have is these two guys fighting against each other for control of the plane.' A long pause. 'Your father won.'

'He . . . So my dad . . . he made a mistake?'

'Yes . . . maybe.'

'Maybe?'

He still wasn't looking at her. 'Look, we talked about this yesterday. He had been flying for a very long time. He had been flying this type of plane – a turboprop – for a very long time. He knew that plane. He knew what it could do. He also knew what it couldn't. What my guy told me was that if this had been a new pilot, someone new to this type of plane . . . I don't know. Maybe they'd be thinking something different. But they cannot figure out why the hell he would have chosen that as an option, when he would have known, had to have known, that bringing the nose up, when the plane is already on its way into a stall, bringing the nose up was the one way of guaranteeing that a stall occurred.'

The air became thicker. Freya leaning forward. 'What are you saying?'

He shook his head. Didn't answer.

'Are you saying that you think my father committed suicide?'

CHAPTER 22

Cecilia: Saturday 17 March, 11.45 a.m.

Cecilia's legs were concrete. Her insides ached, like she was hollow.

Maisie was asleep when she left, had fallen into an uneasy drowse, chin resting awkwardly on her chest. Would shudder occasionally, too many tears just for the waking hours. Cecilia had sat a while, watching her, holding her hand like she had in the snow. She knew that she should leave. Knew that she had nowhere to go. Glancing up as the nurse leaned past, checking the IV. Wondering if she should tell her who she was.

'Poor love.'

Nodding, couldn't think what to say.

Sighed. 'I do hope they find him. If they don't . . .' Another sigh. 'It's good that you're here. She's told us so much about you.'

'She has?' Looking up, feeling something fluttering in her chest.

'Are you kidding?' The nurse had smiled, squeezing her shoulder. She was pretty, in a dumpy

141

sort of way. 'She's told everyone about her solicitor daughter.'

Cecilia walked slowly now, looking down, people billowing around her. She could go home. Sit inside the beige box. There were no friends, no one who would be worried, not any more. Could ring her mother. But her mother was holed up in a new-built flat in the outskirts of Glasgow with her new boyfriend. They had spoken, briefly, after Ben was born. Her mother had promised to visit. She had never arrived. Cecilia could have rung her father, but he had given up pretending he was just a social drinker, had taken it on as a serious occupation. He rang her every couple of weeks, long, meandering calls where he talked more than listened, about her mother, their marriage and his bitter mistreatment. The calls often ended in wrenching tears. There was nothing left now but a shadow of the handsome, charming man she had grown up with.

She turned a corner, slowly, getting in people's way. The information desk was still there. The woman was still there, drinking a bottle of sparkling water, coral lips clamped around the plastic bottle. Her fingernails were painted black, too long, looked like claws. She started when she saw Cecilia, water spilling in rivulets down on to her dove-grey blouse. 'Oh, my, oops.' Dabbing at the water spots with her hands. 'Oh, sorry. Um, all right? Did you . . . Everything okay?

'I, I was wondering . . . Maisie's husband . . .'

142

'Maisie?'

'Mrs Collins.'

'Oh.' Still dabbing at her blouse. 'Now, he was on the plane too, was he?'

Cecilia looked down at the scarred linoleum. It crackled with flames. She could smell flesh. 'Is there news?'

'Um, right, I'll . . . Oh dear, well that's just made it worse.' Sighed, turning to her papers. 'Let me just . . . Collins, Collins . . .'

'Ernie.'

'Ernie.' The wingbeat of papers as she flicked forward, forward. A pause as she reaches the end. Then backwards. Maybe his name will be there this time. 'Um.' She had reached the beginning. The black talons drummed on the Formica. Then a sigh. 'I'm sorry, my love. It's an awful thing. Awful. But you've got to focus on the good. Got to, it's all you can do at a time like this.'

Looking at her like she's speaking a foreign language. 'The good?'

That compressed smile, so that she's all puckered lips, flared nostrils. 'You made it. When it comes right down to it, that's all that matters. You're here, my love. You survived. And your husband,' nodding towards her hand, 'he must be so relieved.'

Sixty years next year we've been married. Happiest day of my life.

Her wedding ring pinched at her. The woman was staring, waiting for her to speak, but the words wouldn't come. They'd crumbled into free-flying

143

letters. Nothing in her head now but images and smells and sounds.

Cecilia turned and walked away.

The light was beginning to dip, a sepia noon. Clouds had rolled back in, low-lying and bulbous. There were more people now, bundled tight against the cold, slopping their way along the footpath, through the snow. It was visiting time. They carried flowers.

Cecilia ducked her head. It was cold, her body shook wildly. She walked quickly, even though it was slick and slippery, through the knots of people, flowing like salmon upstream. Then out, with a sweep of relief, into the car park with its mounding snow, secret puddles of ice. Quiet here, cars abandoned, owners already inside, smiling, trying to hide their fear. She reached into her handbag, fingers questing for keys, pulled them out, careful, but her fingers shook, narrow keys slipping. They landed on the iced ground with a clatter. She stood, watching them fall.

There was the crunch of footsteps, fast, nearer, nearer. The feeling of breath on the back of her neck.

Cecilia turned sharply.

He wore the same coat that he had worn in the lobby, too thin for the weather. He bent down, movements swift, enfolding her car keys in gloved hands, and she watched him as he unfurled. Tall, far taller than she. Lean, angular features.

She almost backed away, a spurt of fear shooting

through her. But there was a look about him, a scared little boy. Couldn't be more than seventeen, eighteen at the most. She smiled at him, in spite of herself, almost. He was just a boy, and she thought of Ben and how she should have gone to see him today if she was any kind of a mother.

He looked tired, like he hadn't slept for weeks. Familiar, even though she couldn't place his features. He held out his hand, the jangle of metal. She'd forgotten about her keys.

'Oh. Thank you.' She reached out, her fingers touching his as she took the keys. 'I'm so clumsy.'

He didn't respond, was still looking at her, and she thought of a sparrow watching a cat. A bitter cold wind springing from nowhere, disturbing the snow that lay on the cars, sweeping it towards them like confetti at a wedding. She shivered, and the boy tugged at the collar of his coat, chin tucking in.

'You . . .' His voice came out quiet, was pulled away from her by the wind. 'I heard you. You were talking to that lady, the one on the desk. You were on that plane?' he looked down, scuffing his feet into the snow. 'The one that crashed?' He looked up at her, a desperate look, hungry almost. He wiped snow from his forehead, his hands trembling.

Cecilia nodded, hands shaking. 'I, I was a flight attendant. I am a flight attendant. I helped. I got the passengers out.'

They stood there, in the car park, for what felt

like the longest of times. Although maybe that was just because of the snow and the bitter cold wind. The boy looked down at his feet a lot, seemed like he couldn't look at her. Embarrassed maybe. He could be Ben, fifteen years from now. She almost reached out, touched him. One shining, flickering moment when motherhood was what it was meant to be. Then she remembered: he wasn't her son. And she remembered that it didn't matter anyway. That she had built the walls so high that she had no idea how to scale them. The boy glanced up.

'I heard you say, to that woman back there. I heard you say about the crash. Sorry. I . . .' The boy glanced back towards the hospital. 'My dad. He just died.'

Cecilia's stomach sank, and without thinking she reached out. Touched his arm.

'Do you . . . This is weird.' His voice was snatched away, torn by the wind so that she could barely hear him. 'I know it's weird, but do you maybe, like, want to get a coffee?'

He looked so plaintive and hopeful and sad that how could she say no? And there was a whisper somewhere in her saying that this was a good thing to do, spend some time with this terribly sad boy when he needed someone the most, and that maybe somehow that would make the difference in the grand scheme of things.

'Sure.' She smiled. 'Coffee would be good.'

They pushed through the slush, heavy with silence. Moved through the knotted crowds of visitors. Cecilia looked down, studying the concrete, the slush, the slippery, slick linoleum. Could hear the scuffing steps of the boy beside her.

'It's half day today, mind.' The coffee shop was dimly lit, snow bringing on an early twilight. The woman behind the counter dumped down half-full mugs of orange tea. Peering at Cecilia, across to the boy.

Cecilia held out a five-pound note. Suddenly realised that her hand was shaking, probably from the cold.

The woman stared at it. Sighed. Plucked it from her with sausage-fat fingers, heavy with thick gold rings that grew from inside the folds of fat, muttering about her shortage of change.

They sat down amongst a forest of chair legs, upturned on tables, cast in shadow. The boy sat across from Cecilia, visible only in the periphery of her vision, shoulders hunched forward. There was a rattle, a cart on a gravel-rough road, as the woman pulled at the metal shutters, half covering the wide-open mouth of the doorway. The snow was falling again, heavy now, thick flakes tumbling past the long windows. Scuffed counters wiped and wiped again, woody pine, gleaming under low lights. The woman watched them with folded arms and narrowed eyes.

'So . . .' Cecilia watched him, trying to look like she wasn't. 'I'm sorry about your dad.'

The boy didn't look up. Murmured, 'Thanks.'

'Do you . . . have family?'

'Yes.'

'Your mum, how is she doing?'

He shrugged. 'Bad, I guess. In bed. I can't talk to her.'

Cecilia nodded, tried to suppress the rush of emotion, the feeling that this child had chosen her, sought her out when he needed a mother. Didn't really stop to question the why of it all. A boy approaching a stranger because he heard that her plane had crashed. She'd think about that later. For now it was enough to feel a little like a mother, even if it couldn't be to her own child.

The boy looked up at her then. 'The plane. The crash. What was it like?'

Cecilia froze, words stoppered up by a barrage of flitting images of fire and wind and a giant hand pinning her to her seat. 'I . . . I don't know. I . . .'

'Please?'

She stared at him for a moment. She didn't want to talk about it. Couldn't talk about it, because if she did, the flames would come back and that stomach-empty sense of tumbling. But he was watching her, eyes fluttering from her eyes to her lips, waiting, like her words and her words alone could save him. 'It was . . . I didn't realise what was happening. Not at first. When I did . . .' Wanted to stop, because if she stopped, maybe the heat and the smell of burning would dissipate, vanishing back into the linoleum floor. But the words tumbled from her, unbidden. 'I keep remembering that feeling, like I'm falling. Like in one of those dreams, you know? But it's like that all the time. I can't close my eyes. Every time I do, it starts again.'

He was watching her now, and she could feel it, that sensation of falling.

'I'm so tired. I just want to sleep. But then I have those dreams. People screaming at me, begging me to save them, the ones falling out of the plane when it pulls apart. They're screaming things, like they're angry at me.'

Her fingers shook, slopping stewed tea in a wave over the rim of the thick white mug, her arm throbbing.

'I keep seeing things. I mean, all the time. Even when I'm awake. Fire. Bodies. And faces, all these faces. Jesus. It's all I can think of. I mean, even when I'm talking to someone, like I'm talking to you. I can still see them. You know? And hear things. Like that noise when the plane broke up. All the time.'

Her hands would not stop shaking, and she hoped that he hadn't noticed.

'Have you ever had that? You know? That thing where you just keep seeing the same thing over and over again?'

Her fingers had crept forward, crawling across the tabletop, begging this stranger, this kid, to pull her back over the cliff edge. He wasn't looking at her, but his hands seemed to tremble, mug clattering against greasy Formica. Then a quick nod, and in a soft voice, 'Yes.'

'I feel like everywhere I go there's these ghosts following me.'

He glanced up at her, eyes darting, then down, and for a fleeting moment it occurred to Cecilia to wonder who he was.

The scree of metal chair legs on linoleum. A loud sigh. Enough to distract her. The woman was staring at them, shaking her head.

'I shouldn't be here. I should be dead.' Cecilia watched the woman, not seeing her, seeing instead flames and pitch-black night sky. 'I wasn't supposed to be in the back. My seat, the seat I was assigned, it was up front. I should have died. But they were talking . . . Vicki and Sarah. Vicki was getting married. In April. God, it was all she talked about. She was so excited.' Her voice dwindling away. 'She was telling Sarah about . . . I don't know . . . something with the band, some problem, and I just thought, "Jesus, not again." I didn't want to listen. I mean, it was all the time, just on and on about this wedding, and I didn't want to listen to it, not that day. I'd . . . It had been a bad day. I wanted to be by myself. So I said I'd go to the back. I made it sound like I was doing them a favour. That it was so they could carry on talking. But it wasn't. It was me. I didn't want to hear about it.'

The voice that came out didn't seem to be hers, not under her control any more. 'It should have been Vicki. She was the one who was meant to be at the back. She was the one who should have survived. But I took her place, because I didn't want to listen to how happy she was. What kind of a bitch does that make me? She had everything . . .' Tears were building, her voice shuddering under the strain. She shifted her gaze out to the falling snow. 'Her fiancé, Jason, nice guy. Really nice. Nothing to look at, but . . . he really loved her.' A tear had fallen. She didn't bother to wipe it away. It was as if she had forgotten he was there, the words spilling out of her, the flushing of dirt from a wound. 'I don't get it. I really don't. Why me? Why did I . . . I mean, all these people. They had lives. They had futures. They had so much to live for. But I'm the one who survives. I don't understand. Vicki, Sarah. They had people who loved them so much, who wanted them to come home. And they're the ones to die. And Oliver, the captain. Married with two kids.'

There was a clatter. She didn't see what happened. She was looking at the snow, waiting for it to drown out the faces. But when she looked back, the tea was puddled across the tabletop, the mug rolling on its side. A scraping as the boy she didn't know pushed his chair back, the tepid liquid cascading towards the floor. The woman was bustling forward, heavy sigh, throwing a cloth on the table, sweeping it from left to right, face a storm.

'We're closing. It's one o'clock on Saturdays.'

'Yes. I'm sorry. We'll go.' Cecilia moved to push

her chair back, gaze dropping away from the heavy scowl.

'Did you see it?' The low voice seemed to come from nowhere.

Cecilia started, dropping back into the seat. 'I . . . What? Did I see what?'

'The plane. The rest of it.'

The woman spun on her heels, a *tsk* jabbing at the air, stalking away.

'No, I, the tail, where I was, we broke away. I, no, I didn't.'

'Why did it crash?'

She was staring at him, not understanding now. 'I . . .'

'The plane. What happened to the plane? Why did it crash?'

'I, I don't know.'

'Look, we're closed. You need to leave.' She was standing beside them, had come from nowhere, foot tapping loud against the floor.

'Okay, um, sorry.' Cecilia stood. It seemed like her brain wasn't working. The boy stood too. He was watching her. 'I . . .' Then something occurred to her. A dawning realisation. 'Your father. You said he died. He was on the plane, wasn't he?'

The boy stood there for long moments. Then a tear spilled down his cheek. 'Yes.'

'Oh God.' Cecilia's fingers flew to her mouth. 'I'm so sorry. I didn't think. And I was just prattling on and on, and, oh God, I'm sorry. I just didn't think.'

'It's okay.' He gave her a half-smile, wiping at the tears with the back of his hand. 'I asked you to tell me. It's just . . . it's nice. No one will talk to me. No one will tell me. I needed . . . I needed to hear what it was like for him. At the end.'

Cecilia reached out. Gripped the boy's hand. Smiled. 'I just realised, I don't even know your name.'

He seemed to hesitate for a moment. 'It's Richard.'

CHAPTER 23

The grating of metal rings on a metal pole, thick velvet curtains billowing outwards. A large window. Libby lay beyond the glass, Snow White in a crystal coffin. Her eyes were closed, and Tom found himself wondering who had closed them, grateful that they had. She could be sleeping now; if you ignored the greyness of her pallor, the blood that crusted her scalp.

'I have to see her.' Jim had been waiting for him when he arrived at the house that morning. Arms folded across his chest, ready for a battle.

Jim's fingers rested on the glass, shoulders slumping like the bones had been stripped from him. Policeman posture slipping away on to the dark-carpeted floor. There was a noise coming from him, something low that Tom would be willing to bet he didn't know he was making. A quiet keening. Tom remembered his father talking about Jim – the big J. *You should have seen this guy in the St Paul's riots, facing down the fury.* Had said

154

that they had stood shoulder to shoulder. But then the crowd had surged, Tom's father slipping on a ground slick with gasoline and anger. Feeling hands tugging at him, boots digging into his soft flesh. *Then,* he had said to Tom, *these hands reaching in, picking me up.* That was Jim.

Jim was trembling now, a full-body quiver like a newborn left outside in the snow. The mortuary attendant watching him, an exercise in inconspicuous sympathy, hands folded at his waist, head bowed.

'You know you don't need to?' Tom had said. 'The DI, he's already done the identification. It's okay.'

'I know. I want to.'

'Look, why don't you take a little time? Don't make this decision now. Have a chat with Esther. Maybe . . . perhaps it would be best to remember her as she was.'

The scent of disinfectant grazed Tom's throat. Beyond that, something else, darker. The smell of decay.

'I have to see her, Tom. Have to.'

Libby's hair pooled, dark puddles on purple cloth. They had covered her, pulling a sheet up until it grazed her chin, as if she could still feel the cold.

Jim let out a soft moan.

Tom looked down, not wanting to see any more. There was an uncomfortable feeling in his stomach, nausea. Tried to tell himself that it was because he hadn't eaten, because hadn't he done this too many times for it to be anything else? Trying not to think about it, a father mourning his child, that sensation in your gut like your insides have been pulled out and now you have to go on living, even though you've been emptied out and there's nothing left but a hollow shell. Don't think about it. It's a body. That's all it is. Done this a thousand times before. Just part of the job. Narrow hospital hallways. Doors swinging open. Knowing that if you look left or right there will be bodies, inside out. The shriek of a saw on bone. And you laugh, because what else do you do? Just part of the job.

Tom clasped his fingers together, thumb running across soft skin, trying to find it again, that place where he is just a detective and not a person, where all of this can be tinged with an air of unreality, because you can't look at it like everyone else does, because there are things that you have to see that they can be allowed to miss as they wallow in the tragedy.

But it doesn't seem to be there today. Today he wants to cry.

'I just . . . I want you to be sure this is what you want. You don't have to do this. Not if you don't want to.'

Jim hadn't answered. He was already putting on his coat. Ethan watching him. He didn't want to go. But Jim's jaw was set, and his shoulders squared and he looked like a bulldog. Tom felt a thrill of something, like when you're at the top of a roller-coaster and you know that things are going to get worse before they get better. Watching this man, who has been stripped of everything, ploughing on regardless, because he understands that you have to fall before you can begin to climb again.

Tom realised that the thrill felt an awful lot like envy.

Jim hadn't spoken in the car, had stared straight ahead, jaw clenched so tight that the veins pulsed. Hadn't sat frozen to the seat when they pulled up outside, or hung back as they trudged through slush towards the mortuary door.

Tom had held the door open for him. Had watched him walk through, his head held high. Had wanted to grab for him, say: *Don't do this. You don't have to see everything, sometimes it's okay to pretend. That way you can be a better man than your father and you can keep your family together even if it's a family in name only. But at least you are staying and you are there, and so what if you're lying, to yourself, to everyone else. Your son gets a mother and a father. And that's what matters.*

But he hadn't said a word, of course he hadn't, had stepped aside, allowing Jim to pass, had sat in silence with him in the claustrophobic waiting room and hadn't commented when the man's hands shook so badly he could barely sign the forms.

Once you know, you can't go back.

Tom had found it by accident, a week or two ago. He had been looking for shoe polish. She had to have some somewhere. She had ten thousand pairs of shoes. He hadn't opened it right away, had sat there for longer than he would have thought possible, envelope resting on his lap. Then he had pulled at the edges.

A dark image, black, a ghostly grey outline. A baby scan. The whisper of a child.

'Can I go in?' Jim hadn't turned, still looking straight ahead at his daughter. His voice still the policeman's voice.

The mortuary attendant's head raised, expression a struggle between alarm and condolence.

But then Jim shook his head, a heavy sigh. 'I'm sorry. The PM. I know.' His voice dropping to a whisper, a different voice now, softer, the father. 'My little girl.'

At first Tom had thought that the scan was Ben. He had been surprised, hadn't thought that she would have kept it. Then he had looked at the date: a year before they met.

Once you know, you can't go back.

'Cecilia?'

She had been getting ready to go to work, had been slicking her lips with deep crimson lipstick. Hadn't turned to look at him when he came into the bathroom. 'Yeah?'

He stood, frozen to the tiled bathroom floor. 'I found something.'

'Okay.' She was blotting her lips, still not looking at him. A quiet sigh of impatience.

'Cecilia? What is this?'

She had turned then, looked at him, face set, like she was irritated with him. Then her gaze dropped towards the picture. Froze.

'Where did you get that?'

It seemed like he could hear her heart thrumming, although surely that was memory rewriting what was.

'I found it. I was looking for shoe polish in your wardrobe. It was in a shoe box. What is this?'

She reached out with manicured nails, snatching it from his fingers. 'You shouldn't be in my stuff.'

'It's not Ben. The date is wrong.'

She had turned away from him, back towards the mirror, but he could see her hands, shaking.

'No. It's not.'

'So . . .?' Annoyance built in him. 'Who the hell is it?'

Cecilia was looking down. Holding on to the edge of the vanity unit. Her voice quiet. 'That was my baby, okay? My first baby.'

Tom had hung there, after a body blow. Had felt it crumbling, then, right there. Because it was, after all, a pretence. This marriage, this life. This family that he had sacrificed so much to preserve. Watched his wife, saw her pushing herself up tall, pulling her long dark hair into a ponytail. Her hands were shaking, even though she was pretending that they weren't, her lips set into that thin line, the one that says that her contribution is over, that you've gone as far as you're going to go with her and beyond this is nothing, just a no-man's-land of silence.

'What happened?'

She didn't answer him. Tugged at her hair so that the strands yanked at her scalp, a fleeting facelift.

'The baby, Cecilia. Did you give it up? Did you have it adopted? Or . . .'

'For fuck's sake . . .' She spun, letting her hair spill down over her shoulders. 'It's gone. Okay? I had an abortion. Are you happy now? I didn't want it. I didn't want to be a mother.'

The words sparkled, casting long shadows.

And they had stood there, like they were frozen.

You should know what to do, at times like this. When it is your wife, and the mother of your child. You should know what it is you're supposed to do. But Tom hadn't, had just stood there, staring at her, thoughts chasing one another, fighting to clamber their way from his mouth.

She had been shaking properly then, thin tracked tears snaking their way down her cheeks, burning channels through her bronzer. Didn't look at him, and it had struck him suddenly how rarely she did. And he had stood there, and she had stood there, and the knowledge had settled on to him like a stone. He didn't know this woman at all.

Tears had begun to spill down Jim's cheeks, but he made no move to wipe them away. Just stood there staring at his dead daughter stretched out on a mortuary slab. Tom wanted to turn away, even though it wasn't his tragedy. Because it was all too stark, too raw, and he couldn't stop thinking of burning planes and how close he had come to being the one standing beside glass, staring at a dead wife. And how his grief would have been a dull mockery of this man's.

Tom hadn't wanted Cecilia back. They had dated. They had stopped. She had gone. And that had been fine with him. He hadn't loved her. At times he had found himself wondering if what he felt could even be described as liking. They had amused each other, a little, for a short time. Then they had gone their separate ways. Just like they were supposed to. Life had moved on, and there had been Maddie. His stomach clenched, thinking about her.

And then had come the call, and the knowledge that he was going to be a father, and suddenly all the decisions had already been made. He was a father. He would be there for his child. So he would marry his child's mother. They would be a family. And he would pretend. For the rest of his life.

It seemed like hours, although in truth it could

have been little more than minutes, before Jim's hand dropped, and he stepped back from the glass. The mortuary attendant half turned, watching, and then pulled gently on the curtains.

Jim stood as his daughter disappeared behind thick velvet.

CHAPTER 24

Freya: Monday 19 March, 10.30 a.m.

'You okay, Rich?' Freya smiled at her brother, his hair all standing on end, fresh from his bed. Tried to keep her voice light. She was still in her pyjamas, hadn't slept. Seemed now like she couldn't remember when she had last slept. The landing carpet was warm under her bare feet, caught in a patch of sunlight.

'Yeah.' Richard rubbed his eyes with the palm of his hand. 'Didn't sleep too well.'

'I know. Me neither.'

Richard leaned against the frame of his bedroom door, caught in slanting sunlight working its way in through the hallway window. 'You see the news last night?'

Freya felt her heart stop in her chest. 'Rich.'

He wasn't looking at her, staring down at the floor, his eyes full. 'You heard what they're saying? About Dad? They're saying he did it on purpose.'

She hadn't told him. When she had returned from the crash site; hadn't told anyone. Because how did you even begin to say that? *Our father might have killed himself. Might have killed everyone else.* Felt like there was barely room in her head for it, let alone anything else. Her stomach rolled. 'I know, honey.'

He looked up at her then. 'Is it true, Frey? Did he?'

She wanted to lie to him. Wanted to lie so desperately. Looked at him, and the words were forming on her lips, ready, right there. 'I don't know.'

Richard nodded. A tear rolling down his face. 'Yeah.'

Freya leaned, kissing him on the cheek. 'Why don't you go get some breakfast, kiddo? Grandma's been cooking.'

The ghost of a smile flitted across his face. 'Don't you think I'm a little old for that now?'

Freya smiled. 'You'll always be my baby brother. No matter how old and ugly you get. Go on. Have some food.'

Her brother hesitated, for a moment looked like he would argue like most seventeen-year-olds do. Then his shoulders slumping, a slow nod, too tired to do anything but agree.

She waited until the kitchen door was closed, then turned.

Her parents' bedroom was empty. I can't sleep here. Please don't make me sleep here. Her mother leaning heavily on her grandfather. I can't be here without him. They had put her in the spare room.

164

Her grandparents were sleeping on the fold-out sofa in the living room.

It smelled of her father. Dolce & Gabbana. Freya leaned against the bedroom door, letting it shut tight behind her. Only then did she realise that she was shaking.

What was going on with your father?

Freya had experimented with pretending, telling herself that the reporter had it wrong, or the investigators did. That somebody did. Because surely it couldn't be possible. Her grandparents hadn't asked her about the visit to the crash site, her grandmother contenting herself with the occasional loud sigh, a forlorn shake of the head. Her mother still hadn't come out of her room. It would be so easy, here in this house, to let it slide. To slip back into the party line. Their father, just one more tragic victim. So she had showered and dressed and watched TV and pushed her food around her plate, and then undressed and gone to bed, and all the time a vision of her father standing in the snow rolling through her head.

What was going on with your father?

Freya had come home early on Wednesday, the day before the crash – wasn't supposed to be there. Had said that she would go straight to Carly's, that she would get changed there. But she had worn the wrong shoes, and it had started to snow, tumbling flakes sneaking inside the thin leather, soaking her feet. She was cold and she was uncomfortable. She would go home, take a hot shower, change her clothes. Her father wasn't expecting her. It was a rest day for him, wouldn't be flying until the next evening.

At first she had thought the house was empty. Had slipped off her boots in the hallway, leaving behind puddles of melting snow, padded her way into the kitchen, thinking that she would make a quick cuppa, something to warm her from the cold. She had started when she saw her father. He was standing in the back garden, shoulders rolled up tight. One hand was jammed into the pocket of his jeans, the other held his mobile phone to his ear.

Freya had known, with that sinking feeling that children have when they have catch their parent in yet another lie.

Had considered turning, walking out. After all, this wasn't her fight, was it? Her parents had chosen the way their marriage would play out, and if this was their choice then surely that had little to do with her?

Back in the present, she pushed herself away from the door, padding softly on the thick carpet. Gripped the bronzed handles of the wardrobe door. Her father's wardrobe.

Her father's shirts hung neatly, lined, pressed, a regimental army in whites and blues and greys. Then jackets. Then trousers. And he would walk in, at any moment, and reach past her, plucking a shirt from the rail, and then he would be gone

166

again, hidden in plain sight, as his family drowned in the secrets that he kept. She stood there for a moment, staring, and she felt that feeling that she had always had around her father. Or for as long as she could remember, at least. An unsteadiness, as if she was standing on the deck of a ship that for a moment, or for an hour or for a day, would drift on a millpond, and then, without warning, would hit a wave and buck, throwing you from your feet. Remembering fleeting moments: chasing her and her brother around the swing set in the garden, dropping to all fours so that they could ride on his back, and then the phone would ring or he would remember something and suddenly he wouldn't be fun Daddy any more. Now he was angry Daddy, and you would never know why, and even when you asked your mother, you would see that look in her eyes, a wall going up, and even though you were little, you would know not to push it any further.

Freya pulled at a cotton shirt on a wooden hanger. Lilac. She plunged her fingers into the pocket.

A white shirt. Then a blue. Then another white. She didn't know what she was looking for. Just knew that she had spent her childhood smothered in secrets, always knowing that there are questions you don't ask, places you don't go. You just had to take Daddy's word for it. You just had to let him lie to you, even if you knew it was a lie.

Earlier that week she had kept her coat on as she'd stood in the kitchen watching him, pulling the red padded material tighter around her, colder now in their home where Victorian radiators pumped out heat than she had been in the snow. Her father wore a navy cashmere sweater, white shirt collar, blue jeans. No coat. The snow littered his shoulders. Freya couldn't hear what it was he said. But then she didn't really need to. The tightness of his neck and the way his fingers clenched up into baby fists was enough.

She had felt a sinking in her insides. Plunging déjà vu.

Now she pulled at the trousers, neatly lined up like toast slices in a rack, lightly done, medium, burnt; pulled the fabric towards her, dipping her hands into pocket after pocket.

She remembered how her father's right arm had dropped, pulling the phone away from his ear, staring at it. A long pause, and then his head had sunk.

He had turned then, facing back towards the house, eyes red like he had been crying.

Hangers scraping on the rail, Freya worked faster, her head swimming.

She had wondered distantly what she would do, as he turned towards her, phone dangling helplessly in his fingers. Turn and walk away. Pretend she hadn't seen. Do what her mother would do. But her feet had planted themselves against the travertine tiles, and then, suddenly, it had been

168

too late. A lightning-fast flash of emotion flying across her father's face, footsteps frozen on the snowy ground, and then an effortful smile as he pushed open the patio door, voice far, far too loud.

'Hiya, love. I didn't know you were home.'

There was a way these things worked. They all knew it by now. You lowered your head, gave a light, ignorant smile, started on with some nonsense about the weather or the rugby or something else that no one cared about. Anything to avoid talking about what was there in front of them.

'That was work.' His words had been too fast, tumbling one after the other, gaze flitting across the kitchen counter, to the clock, to the radio, anything to avoid looking at her. 'It was . . . it was work.'

Strange, Freya had thought. *He's normally a better liar than that.*

Then there was nothing left. The hangers shoved roughly from one side to the other, wardrobe gaping, no secrets to tell. Nausea welled. Freya sat down hard on the carpeted floor. What had she been looking for? What had she hoped to find? There was nothing that could make this right, nothing that could take this away. No answers waiting for her inside the wardrobe; just the paltry remnants of her father's life. Her hands began to shake. She leaned her head back against the bed. Could feel it, the sudden upswell of grief waiting there, just beneath the surface.

Was it possible? Could they be wrong? Could it have been an accident after all? The phone call in the garden just work, like he had said? And her, so conditioned to believe her father a liar that she saw lies when there was only the truth.

Freya closed her eyes. Tried to breathe.

What was going on with your father?

CHAPTER 25

Jim: Monday 19 March, 12.12 p.m.

Jim's footsteps crunched deafeningly loud on compacted snow. There was a swish at his back, cars hurrying through slush up on the main road. But the cul-de-sac was quiet. Just him, the snow and the falling light. He kept his head down. Snowflakes falling steadily into a thick curtain, creeping their way beneath his collar, down his back. The cold jarred him. Reminded him that he was awake, that all of this was real.

'Drop me off here, Tom.' He hadn't looked at him when he said it. Had waved with a hand that felt ridiculously heavy now.

'I can take you to the door. If you want.'

He could feel Tom looking at him. Assessing. A dim memory of what it was like to be that side of the car rather than this. Wished like hell that he was.

'Could do with the walk.'

He felt rather than saw Tom nod. Understanding.

Had got out of the car slowly, an old man now. A nod to Tom. Had closed the car door carefully. Turned to face the snow.

Libby was in front of him. Although that was impossible in any practical sense, still there she was. His daughter. Lying dead on a trolley.

Jim blinked, rubbed at his eyes. The snow stung. Everyone had their lights on, even though it was early, only just noon, the snow plunging them into a pre-emptive night. Life going on beyond the windows, undented by tragedy. He paused for a moment, watching as the guy from number 9, the one he had always referred to as a bit of a prick, played with his kids. He wished like hell that he could be that prick.

He turned, looked along the road to where his house stood. He squinted through the snow. His house, the one right up on the end, double-fronted, with the large drive, the only one without the lights on.

Jim couldn't remember how many bodies he had seen. An occupational hazard, one blending very much into another over the years. By the end, you didn't really look at them. Not as bodies, anyway. Certainly not as people. They were evidence. A series of clues, the answers to the questions you had to know how to ask.

He remembered his first. Everyone did. A little old lady, living alone. Had slipped on her way to the toilet, hit her head. Had been found the following morning. He remembered how it had jarred him, standing in the room with death, how fragile it had all felt.

But you couldn't live like that, could you? Not doing what he did. So you became invincible. Pretended to yourself that this was something that happened to other people. Until the day it happened to you.

He was walking slowly. Inching towards the house, like he was afraid of breaking a hip. Glanced up. Six houses left. Far enough to wipe the vision of his dead daughter from in front of his eyes? Far enough to learn to breathe again, to compose his face, so that when his wife opened the door she wouldn't see this burning, pulsing knot of pain?

He slowed down a little more.

Funny thing was, now that he thought about it, he didn't want to stop seeing Libby lying there like that. Was that weird? He didn't know. All of the victims over the years, he'd never once thought to ask. Was it normal to want to cling to this? Your last, precious moments with your little girl. Was it normal that when they'd pulled the curtain back, even though he'd steeled himself for it, and even though it was horrific, his heart had still swelled up fit to bursting, the way it had every time he'd looked at her ever since she was the tiniest of babies with a grip like a professional arm-wrestler.

He stopped. *Breathe. Breathe.* Looked up into the falling snow.

You weren't supposed to have favourites when

it came to your kids. He didn't know much about much, but of that he was fairly sure. You were supposed to love them both equally.

Sometimes he justified it to himself, saying that he was young when Ethan had come along. That he'd been busy trying to establish a career, support a young family. Hadn't been there as much because he couldn't be, not because he hadn't wanted to. The truth of the matter was that Ethan had scared him. Ridiculous. A grown man scared of a tiny child. But it had been the truth. He hadn't known what to do with him. And as he had grown, it had become apparent, to Jim at least, that his son had inherited from him the worst of his qualities – a tendency towards laziness, an unwillingness to listen. And his temper. Ethan had definitely inherited that.

Esther said that he was too hard on him. That he was a good boy, that Jim just needed to lighten up. *There is so much good in him. Why can't you see it?* It was easier for her. Perhaps because she had so many years of experience loving the father in spite of all his flaws that loving the son came naturally.

Then Libby had come along. It was different with her. Had been from the get-go. Maybe because he had done it before, made all his mistakes with Ethan. Maybe because she had won the genetic lottery, inheriting his best instead of his worst.

And now she was dead.

Jim closed his eyes. Snow littering his face. It

was cold. Bitingly so. He could stay here, like this. Maybe he would just drift away. They would find him, tomorrow or the day after that. A real-life snowman. He allowed himself one last moment. The tear sliding down his cheek.

But Esther was waiting for him inside. Esther needed him.

Roughly brushing the tear away, Jim turned and began slowly trudging towards the house again. Ethan's Audi in the drive. He'd stayed with his mother, then. That was one thing to be grateful for, at any rate.

Jim's breathing had become more ragged now, a pit opening up in his stomach as he began rehearsing the lies. She looked peaceful. They said that it was very quick.

And then, before he was ready, his time was up, the front door swinging open. Orange light flooding the snow-bound path.

'Dad.' Ethan wasn't wearing a coat. Hurried down the drive, arms wrapped tightly around himself, and Jim felt a flush of unreasonable irritation. Just put a fucking coat on.

He shoved it down. 'Hiya, Eth.'

'How was it?'

How the hell did you answer a question like that? How the hell could you even begin to describe the feeling of staring at your dead daughter, knowing that some evil bastard had done this to her, that you had failed when you promised that you would always protect her?

'It wasn't the best, Ethan.'

'No. Well. No . . . Did they . . . Have they found anything?'

'What?' Jim could feel the irritation building, doing his best to suppress it. Failing.

'The police, I mean . . . Do they know who . . .'

Jim was about to snap. He truly was. Then he looked beyond his son to the patch of light just inside the doorway. To his wife, looking so much smaller than she ever had before.

'No.' He answered briefly. 'Nothing.'

Then he turned and prepared to lie to his wife.

CHAPTER 26

Freya: Monday 14 February 1997, 10.58 a.m.

Afterwards it was the tiniest of details that Freya would remember. The purple sky that darkened to grey. The chattering of the wipers, pushing a path through the pounding rain. The way four-year-old Richard's breathing cut through the thrum of the heaters, a gentle snoring. The shine on the red coupé blocking the drive, like it belonged there. And the smell of violets.

Freya had been ten years old. Sick. Had been sitting in class while her teacher talked about something that she couldn't remember, her head swimming. Had raised her hand to ask to see the nurse. Hadn't been fast enough. The vomit had pumped from her with volcanic force, coating the floor, the desk, her uniform in murky yellow. The other children shrieking with delight and mock disgust.

Her teacher had led her from the class, her arm tentative around her shoulder. Let's call your mum. Steering her down ghost-empty corridors tickling with the sounds of distant children's voices.

She would remember the trickle of warm tears down her cheeks, even though she was trying so hard to be a brave girl; the tang of acid in her mouth.

It's Freya. It's nothing to worry about, just a little sick, that's all. Think she wants her mummy. No. No. I tried your husband. I knew you were working. No. Yes, house and mobile. No answer. Okay. Okay, we'll see you soon.

Mummy's on her way, Frey. Have a seat. She won't be long now. We, ah, we couldn't get hold of your dad, so Mum is going to leave work.

She would remember the look, one teacher to another. The pungency of it. She would remember wondering for a moment what it meant, and then just giving up, giving way to the sickness and the way the world spun.

Her mother arrived, in a flurry of skirts and jasmine. Encasing her in her arms. *I'm sorry, I would have been here sooner but I had to get cover.* Her teacher smiling one of those tight smiles that adults give when they don't really mean it. *Don't worry about it, Adele.* Her mother, slipping Freya's arms into her coat, like she was a toddler. *I don't understand where Oliver is. He's off today. I don't know why he isn't answering.* The teacher not looking, playing with some papers that were splayed like groping fingers across the desk. *Sure it's nothing. Sure everything's fine.* Freya looking at her mother, wondering if she knew that her teacher was lying too.

Come on, love. Let's go home. Her mother had taken her hand. *We'll pick Richard up on the way.*

Freya would remember her mother's face, the tight lines, lips pressed flat. The sparking anxiety that rolled through her stomach like tumbleweed on a prairie. An old friend. Sitting up straighter in her seat, trying to catch her mother's eye, to smile, pretend she wasn't so sick so that at least her mother wouldn't have to worry about that as well.

They collected Richard from the childminder, his eyes so heavy he could barely keep them open.

They drove, so slowly that it seemed to Freya that she could walk faster.

She would remember the rain, bulbous drops smudging the Cardiff skyline. The cold of the window against her forehead. She must have dozed off, because the next thing she remembered was the jolt, her body straining against the seat belt.

She couldn't see her mother's face, but she could see her back, her shoulders, the muscles in her neck standing proud, her jaw working, chewing invisible gum. Freya sat forward, fingers clinging to her mother's seat.

The cherry-red car sat at the end of their drive. She didn't know what car it was. A sporty one, with the kind of top that you could roll down. But she knew that it didn't belong there, where it sat, blocking her father's car. Her mother was staring at it.

Freya wanted to ask. There was something here, something not right. But she was ten and she didn't know what. She opened her mouth, but then she saw the light glistening, catching on the single tear that rolled down her mother's cheek.

'Mummy. I'm sleepy.' Richard had woken, startled awake by the hard braking, and now he was fidgeting, tugging at his seat belt. 'I want to go home.'

Their mother didn't answer, just sat there staring at the car that shouldn't be there, fingers clinging to the steering wheel as if she thought that it was going to drift away.

'Mummy!'

'Shh, Richard. It's okay.' Freya stroked his arm, stroked his forehead, the way their mother did to them when they were sick, still not looking at him though, watching their mother with her tight lips and pale face.

'No. I want to go in.'

'Okay, it's okay. We're going.' Their mother's voice sounded drum tight.

Then they were out in the rain, her mother carrying Richard even though he was too big for that now. Freya trailing behind, heart thudding, even though she didn't know why.

'Here we are.' Her mother's hand shook, key scritching against the lock. 'Home.' Voice too high.

There was a black leather handbag, lying on the hallway floor. A grey coat slouched over the banister. And the smell of violets.

Her mother knelt, placing Richard on the ground. Staring at the bag, the coat.

There were sounds, distant, the kind that you hear at eleven o'clock at night when you wake and your parents think you are asleep. The sound of someone jumping on the bed.

Freya seemed to be frozen, feet welded to the tiled hallway floor. It was wrong. It was all wrong. The smell of violets and vomit, the tightness in her mother's face, her eyes flashing like Freya had never seen before. Freya wanted to turn and run away, dragging her mother and her brother with her.

'Wait here.' Her mother's voice sounded strange, scarily so.

Freya looked up at her, wanted to catch her, stop her, but before she can she's gone, taking the steps quickly, with light, silent footsteps. There is laughter, somewhere in the house. Freya watched her mother crossing the landing, face set so that she is barely recognisable as soft Mummy, kind Mummy. Now some new kind of Mummy. Then the bedroom door bangs, laughter turning to screams. Her mother's voice, roaring like thunder. Somewhere in the melee, their father's voice, pleading.

Freya reached down, pulling Richard in tight to her.

'Where's Daddy?' His face was tilted up towards her.

'Shhh, Rich.' She should pull him away, take him

to the kitchen, give him some milk, some biscuits. Wait for the storm to blow itself out. But she was too slow, because before she could move there was a creak of floorboards, a figure emerging, skinny, with long dishevelled hair the colour of sunsets. Pulling a lilac blouse over a fuchsia bra, eyes downturned, scuttling past. No sign of the cream suede jacket she had worn this morning at the school gates as she kissed Kayla goodbye. Kayla was in Freya's class. Sat three seats over. Was skinny and pretty with a laugh that was too loud.

The woman brushed past Freya, didn't look at her. Then she was gone in a wash of perfume.

Freya didn't know how long it was that they stood there. Remembered hoisting her little brother up on to her hip, even though he was much too heavy and it felt like her back would break. Remembered him softly sobbing, his tears hot against her flushed cheek. Remembered her mother's screaming, the sound of a slap.

They stood there until her parents re-emerged. Her mother marching down the stairs, barely looking at them, shaking. 'Come on, you two. Into the kitchen.'

Knowing that they had to obey, because Mummy was really mad, but doing it slowly, because there is the creak of floorboards and footsteps and now her father is emerging, coming down the stairs. Not looking at Freya, or at Richard, but at their mother. A livid red mark with five bright fingers splayed across his cheek. 'Adele.'

Richard was crying. Her mother didn't answer and Freya wondered if she had heard.

'Love. Please.'

Freya was looking at her, at her father, back to her mother, expecting something, but not knowing what.

'Oliver, go fuck yourself.' Her mother's head snapped up, words flaming, and Freya jumped, tears building in her eyes.

Her father stood frozen, shocked. Richard, wailing, rearing back, because he doesn't recognise this mother and now she's scared him.

'I'm sorry. I'm sorry.' Pulling Richard up into her arms. 'It's all right. Let's go into the kitchen, okay? Let's get some hot chocolate.'

But still they all stand there, dolls in a doll's house.

Then her father. 'I . . . I'll go and get dressed.'

Her mother looks up at him, a brittle smile that she doesn't really mean. 'Yes. Perhaps you should.'

CHAPTER 27

Tom: Monday 19 March, 5.47 p.m.

Tom leaned back in the office chair, closing his eyes. He could still see the drifting snow, white flecks on black. Could still see Libby. Jim's hands folded at his waist, somehow staying upright even though he's swaying, corn bending in the breeze. Never taking his eyes off her as the thick velvet curtains sweep shut, even though that's his little girl lying there dead, and his shoulders are shaking, feet turned like they want to run away, are prepared to run without him, tears pouring down his face. His jaw is bulldog set, chin tilted upwards, and you can see that he's enduring, that's all he's doing, because he has to and he has a wife and a family and for them he will stand, even though all he wants to do is fall. That he will not allow himself the luxury of blindness.

Tom knew that there was a phone on the desk in front of him, less than six inches away. He knew that he should pick up the receiver and call his wife. But instead he keeps his eyes closed,

184

listening to the low throb of conversation, the click-clack-clack of keyboard keys, and tries not to think about everything that he should be that he isn't.

He had dropped Jim off on the corner of his street. *Tomorrow, okay? I'll be by tomorrow. Have to talk to Esther.* Had thought that Jim would protest, would say that she had been through enough. But he had just nodded slowly, sadly. *I'll see to it that she's ready.*

Tom rubbed his eyes, trying to break up the image of Libby dead on the mortuary table. Would have to ring his mother, check on Ben. Should ring Cecilia. A feeling rising up in him, the panic that you get when you've swallowed the wrong way and it seems that you'll never catch your breath.

'Hey.'

He opened his eyes. Madeleine nodded towards the mug that she carried, her other hand resting on the gentle slope of her belly. 'Thought you could use this.'

Madeleine was beautiful, even though he hadn't seen it for a long time. Not beautiful like Cecilia, where there's that sense like she should be on the cover of a magazine and that you shouldn't even stand next to her lest you mar the perfection. More ordinary, easier to miss. But there are dancing eyes, lips that curve into a perpetual smile like she's thinking of some joke and if you can just get close enough then she'll share it with you. She'd filled out a little, wasn't as stick-thin as she used to be, cheeks fuller, hips a little wider. It suited her. Her dark blonde hair was pulled up into a high ponytail, clothes loose to allow room for her expanding stomach. Diamond wedding ring that caught the light.

Tom pushed himself up in the chair. 'Whisky?'

'Tequila. I took the worm out.' Madeleine gave a brief smile, setting the coffee on the desk. 'This is shit, isn't it?'

'You're not wrong.'

'She was such a nice girl. She'd applied to be a police officer. Did you know? They started the application process a couple of weeks ago. We had lunch. Chatted about the interviews.' Maddie's eyes had filled, a tear sliding down her cheek. She wiped it away with a hand. 'This job sucks sometimes. I mean, you prepare yourself for it, when you're wearing the uniform. You know, the trouble, getting hurt. But at home . . . she should have been safe there.'

'I know.' Tom wanted to reach out, take her by the hand. Kept his fingers knotted tight together.

It had been an indecently short period of time – a week, maybe, after Cecilia had stopped taking his calls. He'd softened it, saying that he'd known Maddie for ages, years, that they'd been friends for so long that it was almost as if this had been building, bubbling under the surface. It was love. He knew that. Had known

it the following morning when he'd woken, arm
dead with the weight of her head resting on it,
watching her, nose furrowing with dreams. He
hadn't said it. Wasn't the done thing, was it?
But it had felt like finding a pair of shoes that
fit you perfectly, so there's no need to break
them in, treading carefully in case the unfamiliar
presence grates. They had just fitted.

'How was it?'

He shrugged, trying not to look at her belly. 'You
know. Shit.'

'Yeah.' Sipped her own coffee, looking at him
over the top of the mug. 'You okay?'

He looked away from her, couldn't look directly
at her because then she would see everything. She
always did.

'I'm fine.'

'You're lying.'

Tom grinned, now looking back at her, and
there's that bubble of emotion. 'Yeah. I am.'

It had been six weeks, of him feeling like the
luckiest man alive, knowing that for the first time
in his life everything was exactly as it should be.
Then his phone had rung, Cecilia's voice flooding
the line, and his world had changed. She was
pregnant. He was the father. Maddie had taken
it in the way he knew she would. Had held his
hand, had nodded patiently, had turned her head,
pretending that she was looking for something so
that he wouldn't see that she was about to cry.
Then she had stood, had kissed him on the cheek

187

and told him that he was a good man, and she had left. She hadn't gone very far. They still worked in the same office. So he still saw her every day as he rushed into a marriage and bought things for a baby and settled into the realisation that the shoes that he had ended up with rubbed terribly. They would pass the time of day every now and again. Brief, nothing personal. But she told him when she met someone, about a year later, she told him when they got engaged, even invited Tom and Cecilia to the wedding. Of course they couldn't go.

Madeleine leaned against the desk, shifting a little to get comfortable, and glanced over her shoulder at the falling snow. A deep breath as she refocuses. Becoming the detective once more. 'Snowing again. You hear that initial forensics are back on the house?'

'And?'

'They didn't get too much. Someone's bleached all the surfaces down, but they got some blood remnants in the kitchen. Counter top, the floor, some down the side of the cupboard.'

'What about prints?'

'Not much there either. They found a partial underneath the seat of the kitchen chair. No sign of forced entry either. Doors and windows were definitely locked.'

Tom bit his lip, thinking about Libby stretched out dead on the mortuary table. 'So she did let them in?'

'It looks like it.'

Someone she knew, someone she trusted. Should she have seen it? Opened her eyes to danger coming? Or was it that she didn't want to see it, because it was easier not to?

Tom sighed, rubbed his eyes. 'Family said they don't think she had a boyfriend. But there were the condoms, the wrapper in the bin. So she's had . . .'

'Action?'

'Yeah. She's been sleeping with someone. Recently.' Tom shook his head. 'I'm going to see her mother. Tomorrow. Maybe she'll know more. I guess it's not really the kind of thing you discuss with your dad.'

'Yeah. I talked to the other PCSOs, the people on her shift. As far as they knew, she was single. But the condom . . .' Maddie sighed. 'Put it this way, if she was seeing someone . . .'

'She kept it pretty quiet.'

'Yeah.'

'So the next question is, why?' Tom leaned back, stretched his arms above his head. 'What about the glove? They get anything?'

Maddie wrinkled her nose. 'It was immersed in water, overnight presumably. They said that what was there has been diluted so much it's pretty useless. They've managed to type the blood, matched it to Libby, so we know that there's a connection there, but as for any DNA from inside the glove . . .'

'Nada?'

'Nada thing.' Maddie shrugged. 'It's not a surprise, but still . . .'

'Disappointing.'

'Yeah.' She was watching him. 'How's Cecilia?'

Tom shrugged. 'Okay. Broken arm. Other than that, she's all right.'

'I'm so pleased. I really am happy for you, Tom.'

He didn't look at her, because if he did, he would see that she meant it. She had married a paramedic, a good man who looked at her with something very much like adoration. She had moved on.

'I'd better get back to it.' Madeleine pushed herself to her feet. 'Oh, I nearly forgot. The DI asked if you'd ring the pathologist. He's been called into a meeting.'

'No problem.'

A brief smile flitted across her face, lighting up her eyes, and then she was gone.

Tom stared at the snow. It was getting heavier. He should go home. He pulled the desk phone towards him, punching numbers, trying not to notice the lingering scent of Maddie's perfume. 'This is Cecilia. I'm not free right now. Leave me a message.' He closed his eyes, hanging up before the beep, trying to pretend that he wasn't relieved.

Tom had been driving carefully, slipping out of the hospital car park into slow-moving traffic. Jim's voice had startled him, cutting across the swish of the tyres through slush, the whip of the windscreen wipers.

'You see your dad much?'

'I, uh, no.' Tom had glanced across at him. 'No. Not since I was fourteen.'

Jim hadn't replied, and for a moment Tom wasn't sure that he'd heard him.

'I'm surprised.' When he did speak, his voice came out low, loaded with gravel and grief. 'Didn't think he was like that.'

Tom had concentrated on the traffic, the car light on the slick surface. Hadn't intended to speak at all. 'It was me.'

'Sorry?'

'He tried. After he left. He kept trying to call, wrote to me. I didn't want to know.'

'Oh.'

Idling at traffic lights that stayed obstinately red even though there were no other cars on the road. His father had remarried, less than a year after he left. Making an honest woman of the slut, his mother had said. Tom hadn't gone to the wedding. He'd never met his half-brother.

'It's tough, I guess. That kind of situation.'

'Yeah.'

'At least he tried.'

There was a burst of laughter from the other side of the office, startling in the quiet. Then a lull as they realised where they were. Now a deeper silence, the office tight with contrition. Tom dialled again. 'Mr Henderson? DC Allison from South Wales Police.'

'Ah, Detective Constable. I was expecting your inspector.'

'He sends his apologies.'

'You want the report, I assume? On Elizabeth Hanover?'

'If you could.'

'Of course. Of course. Now, I have completed the PM. It's been rather a busy day. You were extremely lucky I could fit her in.'

Lucky. Tom closed his eyes. *Lucky*. If she had kept her door locked, if she hadn't been home that night . . . How the fuck did you get further from lucky than this? 'Thank you, Mr Henderson. We appreciate it.'

'Indeed. Now, let me have a quick look . . . Yes, cause of death, a simple linear fracture to the skull leading to a subdural bleed. The result of blunt force trauma to the back of the head.'

Did she see it coming? Did she know that she was in trouble, heart pounding, skin spiking with fear? Did she know that she was going to die?

'Can you identify the weapon?'

'Shape of the fracture . . . I'd say that in all likelihood, the most likely candidate is something hard-edged, a brick, say, or a square paperweight. We have defensive wounds on her arms, contusions and whatnot, indicative of some kind of struggle.'

Thinking she was safe. Perhaps turning away,

192

maybe to make a cup of tea, maybe chatting. Then turning back, and now the situation has changed and suddenly, from nowhere, she's in danger, and raising her hands, trying to save herself, but it's already too late.

'Under the young woman's nails I found skin cells, traces of blood. Not her own. It has gone for DNA analysis, but it will take some time. You know how these things are. Trace evidence . . . I have, ah, some hairs, not the victim's. Follicular tissue was still attached, so perhaps pulled out in a struggle. That could come in handy. DNA and such.'

Fighting – scratching and tearing, desperate. Feeling it slip away, but not giving up, not for an instant, because then she's dead and she doesn't want to die, so she fights and fights.

'Do you have a time of death?'

'Ah, now, I'm going to have to say between eight p.m. and midnight on Wednesday, based on degree of rigidity, temperature and such. Now, our victim—'

'Libby.'

'I beg your pardon?'

'Her name. It's Libby.'

'I see. Yes. Well. Anyway, when I examined the victim, I found evidence of faint lividity along the back. However, one can see true fixed lividity along the front, so I would say that the body was supine for the first few hours following death – I'd say perhaps three to four hours – and then moved

to the river location and placed into a prone position, where it remained until it was found.'
'She.'
'Sorry?'
'She. Her name was Libby.'

CHAPTER 28

Cecilia: Monday 19 March, 8.03 p.m.

Cecilia had lit a single lamp. The Tiffany one in the corner. The living room was thick with shadow, bone-chillingly cold. No one had put the heating on, and for no reason that she could understand, Cecilia was angry. She knelt, the cold from the hard wood floor seeping its way through her jeans. The damn fire wouldn't light. She jammed her thumb down hard on the ignition. Click, click, click, click. Fuck.

What kind of a fucking husband was he? Not to be home on a night like this.

The boy – Richard – had walked her to her car, their feet slopping through the snow, an unsteady rhythm. She could feel him, gaze ahead, but every now and again dropping to her when he thought she wasn't looking. He hadn't said much, and she had struggled to keep pace with his long stride. He had opened the car door for her, had watched her as she slid inside. The slip of paper clutched in his hand. She had written her number, handwriting awkward and spiky, a strip from today's newspaper. Wasn't sure why. She already had one child, surely didn't need another. But he seemed comforted somehow, being in her presence, even though she had no idea why it was that he needed comforting. And she felt . . . what? A tiny whisper nestled in the back of her brain. Like a mother. And even though she had spewed her sad, sad story out to this poor boy, she had somehow felt . . . okay. Had felt like she did in that field, with the plane on fire and the snow falling and all the death. That perhaps she was helping someone in some small way. That perhaps she wasn't entirely useless after all.

The fire sparked to life, heat rolling out. Cecilia stared into it, flames small at first, then climbing, climbing. Her hand grasped the dial, turning it, so that the flames stretch higher, until they reach the treetops.

There was the low squeal of brakes, a flood of light illuminating the snow outside of the wide open curtains. The thud of a car door. A moment, two, then another thud.

Cecilia pushed herself to her feet. Her heart beating faster.

'Come on, kiddo. Let's get you in.'

The front door thunked into its frame. Then the slop of footsteps on the mat.

Cecilia was frozen, standing in the shadows, and for a fleeting moment it felt that she was invisible.

But then they are in the doorway, her husband starting. He sees her.

'Hi.'

'Hi.'

She wasn't looking at him. She was staring at her son, carried high on his father's shoulder. Tiny frame buried within a thick winter coat. His head hung, heavy with sleep, nose pressed to his father's neck. The bruise is still there, flowering purple. There was a soft sound. He was snoring.

'He's tired.'

'I didn't know . . . I thought you would . . . I thought he would stay at your mother's.'

Tom was cradling her son, arm wrapped protectively around him. 'I thought . . . maybe you'd like to see him.'

She knew that she should move, step forward, take him into her arms. But she was scared, frozen, feet planted right into the walnut floor.

She had woken up early on Wednesday morning, the air thick with the promise of snow. Hard to believe that was only four days ago, seemed a lifetime. But then, it was a lifetime. Thirty-six hours before the flight. Thirty-six hours before falling back to earth. *My mother, she's sick, some kind of stomach bug.* Looking at Tom, wondering why he was telling her this, why she would possibly care. She never looked after Ben. Still not piecing it together, and then finally the slow realisation dawning that he was asking, or trying to without framing the words. Looking from him

197

to her son, a mounting fear because she knows that she's not up to it, and he should know too. Hadn't they agreed that it was best if his mother did the childcare? Hadn't they discussed this already? What would she do with him? How would she cope?

Then hearing herself saying the words. *All right. I'll do it.* Wondering what the hell she was saying. Seeing her husband's face, relief and concern vying for supremacy. Looking out of the window, realising that the snow that has been threatening for days is finally falling, and that they won't be able to go anywhere, will have to stay here, just the two of them in this too small house. A growing sense of claustrophobia, panic.

But it's too late and Tom has to go, is pulling on his coat, glancing from her to their son, still chewing his lip as if he'll think of an alternative. Any minute now. Then time's up and he hasn't, and he has to leave, kissing Ben, that awkward moment when he tries to figure out what's expected and then gives up, a stranger's *have a good day*, and he's gone.

Looking at her son. Wondering what the hell she's done.

But the snow falls and falls, and Ben claps his hands with excitement and for a while it's as if he's forgotten that he's been left with the second-string parent. And she has a brainwave, a rare moment of motherhood, wrapping him in his winter coat, fitting the bobble hat with the overlarge bobble

198

over his dark tumbledown curls. Let's play in the snow. The whoop of excitement, and she's breathing him in, like a luxury perfume. Watching as he runs through the snow, crouching, scooping flakes into a ball with clumsy little-boy hands. Feeling a flush of something that she doesn't recognise, but that's warm and safe and complete. Wondering if maybe she can do this after all.

Then when the excitement begins to wane, and his face glows a brilliant red with the cold, calling him in, feeling like a proper mother. *I'll run you a bath.* A stroke of genius – *then we'll have hot chocolate with marshmallows. How would that be?* Her little boy clapping his hands, laughing, and she had done that.

Turning the taps, boiling hot water cascading into the claw-foot bathtub. Congratulating herself. Thinking that he's behind her. Then a sickening series of thuds, a childish scream. The sudden tearing awareness that she hasn't closed the child gate.

He was curled in a ball at the bottom of the stairs, arm crossed protectively over his curls.

Running down the stairs so fast that it seems inevitable that she will fall too. Pulling him up into her arms, and he's screaming, so loudly that it grates at the inside of her. Fear gripping her so tight that she can't think, running down the drive in slippered feet, putting him into the front seat, even though the child seat is right there and she knows he should be in it. Wheels spinning on snow.

Then waiting as the doctors examine him, as they look at her, and she can see it in their eyes that they are thinking the same thing as she is. Bad mother. Then Tom is running in, and her son's eyes spring alive and he's crying again and now she's angry that he's laying it on, reaching for his father. Cradled tight together, the perfect pair. Opening her mouth to try and explain, but Tom won't look at her, and when he does finally look at her when the doctors have gone and there's no one left but this fracture of a family, his lips are compressed, so tight that they seem to have vanished. *It's my own fault. I shouldn't have expected you to watch him.*

The words stabbing at her like a knife and knowing, finally, that she had been right all along. And now what's the point of her staying? They will be better off without her.

'Come on then, let's take this off, little man.' Tom still holding him, pulling on his sleeve with one hand. Ben shifted, rubbing his eyes with a soft moan. Her hand, her good one, twitched. Wanting to reach out, but what if she dropped him? What if he cried?

Tom was struggling. It was awkward, Ben not helping. He was too tired. He just wanted to go to bed. Finally Tom pulled the coat free, lifting the wool bobble hat from his head, dark curls flopping. Ben started to cry softly.

'He's exhausted.'

Tom was looking at her, like he was expecting something from her. But still she couldn't move.

How could she, when her son was clutching at his father with fingers that seemed to be embedded in his skin. His bandy legs clinging to his waist.

Cecilia took a step backwards.

Ben stirring, hands scrubbing at his face. Gazing blearily around the room.

Tom smiled, a bright, brittle smile. 'Mummy's home. Look, Ben. It's Mummy.'

He wasn't looking, rubbing his head into his father's coat, whining softly.

'He's shattered.' Apologetic.

'Perhaps . . . he needs to go to bed. You should put him to bed.'

'Well . . . do you want to . . .'

Then her son sat up, twisting in his father's arms. Tom's face suddenly relieved. 'Look, Ben. Mummy's home. Why don't you go and see her? Go on, then.'

He came closer, looming large over her, thrusting her son towards her, desperate seemingly.

Against her better judgement, she reached out her good arm, carefully stroking the Tigger pyjamas. He was watching her. Big brown eyes. Her eyes. Wary.

'Hi.'

But his face suddenly fell, lip trembling, spinning back towards his father.

'He's exhausted.' Tom repeated. 'Just exhausted.

Look, I'll put him to bed. Why don't you get a cup of tea? Did you eat? I'll put him to bed and then I'll make dinner. You have a sit-down.'

Ben was crying softly now, face averted from his mother.

Cecilia turned and left the room.

CHAPTER 29

Freya: Monday 19 March, 9.13 p.m.

Freya's mother had stalked into the kitchen, that day a lifetime ago, had left her father standing staring after her. Freya had watched him, his mouth moving in a silent defence, had heard the engine of his girlfriend's car growling to life. Had watched, waited for him to say something. Anything. But he never had, had finally turned, tail of his shirt hanging down between his legs, climbing the stairs, head sunk low. Freya had held tight on to her brother's hand. No one had ever mentioned it again.

Sometimes, as Freya got older, she had wondered if it had been discussed, if they had chewed it over in late-night arguments, packed with guilt and recriminations. Deep down, though, she had known that wasn't the case. Instead it hung over the house, an invisible cloud of radiation that seared their skin. She had watched her parents dancing around it, playing a grown-up game of dress-up, and she had wanted to scream.

She had almost asked about it, once, twice, more

times than she could remember. When the conversation would inadvertently circle towards it. She could feel the words, tingling at the tip of her tongue. *How could you forgive him, how could you forget?* And, perhaps most importantly, *You do know that he has never stopped?* But then she would see her mother's face, eyes wary, like she knew what was bubbling there beneath the surface, and she would stop and they would drift back to somewhere safer and they would all go on. Pretending.

She didn't know if Richard remembered it. He was so small. But sometimes she thought he did, in the way that he watched their father, the way that he positioned himself beside him, clinging to him almost, like his grip could keep him from drifting off from their family into the wide open sea.

For Freya it had been different. She hadn't clung. She had watched him too, but the way you watch a dog that is nuzzling at your leg and has already bitten you once. And her father had watched her in the same way. It was like each was afraid of the other, both knowing that they had the means to destroy the family if they should so choose. A case of mutually assured destruction. In the end it was just easier to keep her distance. Keep an eye on her mother, her brother, make sure they were okay. As to her father, keep him at arm's length. Just in case.

There was the distant sound of voices, her grandmother's shrill chirrup and, every now and again, the rolling bass of her grandfather. Freya hurried back up the stairs. The house still smelled of grease, the fish and chips her grandfather had picked up from the local chipshop. They had sat around the table, pushing pallid chips around their plates, her grandmother filling the air with a steady stream of one-way conversation. Her mother hadn't joined them, still shut away in the spare room. She should go check on her, make sure that there was nothing she needed. Freya hung on the landing, before her parents' closed-up bedroom door. She really should go check on her. Glancing left to right, she gripped the handle, slipping inside. The wardrobe doors were still hanging open. Freya stared at it. Distressed wood. Such an odd term, as if wood could feel pain. But then maybe it could. She should close it. Walk away. Let her father's secrets rest.

A shrill buzzing sparked from her pocket. Freya looked down, easing her mobile phone free. Luke. He had called her twice today already. Her finger hovered over the answer button, possible futures shuffling through her head. He was a good-looking guy, a nice guy, had a desk next to hers in the PhD office. A framed picture of his nieces tucked beside his computer. But it wouldn't work. She couldn't shake it, that whiff about him, in the way he carried himself, the way he laughed, just a little too carelessly, couldn't look at him and not see her father. And if he was her father and she answered the phone, then sooner or later she would become her mother, pretending that the world is what she wants it to be so that she can survive. Freya turned the ringer to silent. It was better this way, safer to guard yourself upfront, rather than to throw yourself away, taking a chance on someone you didn't really know. She sat for a moment, thinking about Luke, and then, with a sigh, folded the image up and tucked it away into the back part of her mind. She was okay on her own. After all, she always had been.

She heard the creak of floorboards on the landing, felt her heart thumping a little faster, the sudden flush of guilt that comes with being somewhere you really aren't supposed to be.

'Frey?' Her mother seemed to have aged a hundred years in the space of the last four days. Her eyes were crimson from crying, her face slack. She was hunched over, the posture of an old woman suddenly appearing overnight. 'What are you doing in here?'

She stood on the threshold, as if she was afraid to step inside her own bedroom. Looking from Freya to the wardrobe doors.

'I . . . I was just . . .'

Her mother wasn't looking at her, was staring at the wardrobe. Took one step, two into the room, and with arthritic-slow movements reached out with her long, narrow fingers. Pianist's fingers, her grandmother had always said. She breathed in, a deep, shaking breath. Ran her fingers across the hangers, the fabrics, down the sleeve of a cashmere sweater. Navy blue.

Freya watched her, thinking of the last time she had seen her father in it. Standing in the snow.

'I bought this for your father. Last Christmas.'

'I know. I remember.'

'He likes navy.'

'Yes.'

Her mother lifted the sleeve, holding it to her cheek, soft, a newborn kitten, cashmere stroking her skin. Breathing it in, and Freya knew that she was trying to find her father in it. But instead she must have smelled something else, because her eyes opened wider and she pulled the jumper from her face, staring at it.

Freya didn't move. Didn't speak. Waiting.

Then her mother shook her head, a small movement, one that she probably wasn't even aware of making.

'You shouldn't be in here, Frey.' Her voice came out cold, didn't seem to belong to her at all. She reached up, pushing the jumper on to the top shelf, the one that ran above eye level. Shoving it so that it was hidden in the shadows and you couldn't see it any more.

'Mum . . .'

Her mother stood at the open wardrobe door, holding on to it like she would fall down without it. Staring at the remains of her father's life. 'He was such a good man.'

Freya looked down. A pulse of something flooded

through her. It felt a little like anger. For the briefest of moments she wanted to scream. *Why is that I'm the only one who can see this?* But then she heard her mother, her breath juddering the way it does when you've been crying too long. And she pushed the feeling down.

Her mother pushed at the wardrobe doors, closing them hard on all of her father's secrets. Stood there for long moments, her palms pressed against it. 'You shouldn't be in here, Freya.' Then a heavy, wintry sigh. 'I . . . I'm going to go back to bed, I think. You shouldn't be in here.'

'Okay, Mum. It's okay. I'm going. You go to bed.' Freya's gaze fought its way back to the wardrobe doors.

'Okay. If you're okay . . .'

Freya nodded, gave a smile for her mother's benefit that struggled to stay. Watched as her mother shuffled towards the door. As she paused, looking back over her shoulder. Her gaze resting on her father's bedside cabinet. Hanging there. Her lips tightening, the way they do when she's angry. Then a sigh, and she turns.

Freya's heart thrummed.

She should leave it. That was what her mother wanted. And what Freya wanted was to make her mother happy. But it now seemed that her entire life had been lived in the shadow of her father's secrets and that she couldn't breathe for them any more.

She should leave it.

She should leave it.

Freya pushed herself up, pulled open the wardrobe doors.

The shelf was high, almost higher than she could reach. But she stretched, fingers brushing the soft cashmere. She pulled it forward, holding it close, wondering what it was that her mother had found and she had missed. Then she smelled it, a waft of perfume. Vanilla.

Freya closed her eyes. Her mother's. Must be her mother's. But it wasn't, and she knew that it wasn't. Her mother smelled of jasmine.

Her father, standing in the snow. Talking on the phone. Crying.

Freya turned, swift steps towards the bedside cabinet. Pulling at the drawer. There were papers, a dog-eared novel, a half-empty pack of Nytol. And then, behind that, something cold, hard. Freya reached in, pulling the metal box towards her.

It was a lockbox. Small, about the size of an A4 pad, hardly big enough to contain any real secrets. She glanced over her shoulder, checking that the door was closed. Something bubbling up in her stomach like that time when she was seven and she stole two penny sweets from the shop on a horrible, hideous whim, and then came home and threw up. The padlock was small, thin, had begun to rust. A lifetime of secrets. Picking up a photo frame that sat on top of the cabinet, silver-plated, heavy. Her father in his pilot's uniform. She hefted it, brought it down hard on the lock.

There was a crack, metal on metal.

There were papers inside. Stubs, tickets for concerts, receipts for hotels. And beneath, a picture. They stood before the Eiffel Tower, a lit-up Paris skyline. A woman, about Freya's age, pretty and flushed, her head on Freya's father's shoulder, smile wide, chestnut hair caught in the wind.

CHAPTER 30

Cecilia: Tuesday 20 March, 9.26 a.m.

'Good morning. This is the Flight 2940 information line. Can I help you?'

'Hi. I need . . . um . . . I . . .'

'Are you looking for someone?'

'Yes.'

'Okay. Do you have a name?'

'It's Ernie. Collins.'

'All right. Just a second.' There was a long pause. Cecilia closed her eyes, leaning her forehead against the cool of the refrigerator. 'I'm sorry. I don't have anything. But we have information coming in all the time. You should call back, maybe later today? Perhaps we'll have something for you then.'

'Okay.' She could picture him, even though she hadn't met him, or at least couldn't remember meeting him, lying in the snow, body rigid with death. Or vanished, burned to nothing. She hung up without saying goodbye.

Don't think about it.

She hadn't seen Ben this morning. She hadn't

kissed him goodbye. She had woken in the early hours, a little after five, and had lain awake, thoughts cascading. Had almost got out of bed, not sure where she would go, but not wanting to stay. A feeling all too familiar. Watched as the clock clicked past six, seven, listening because soon she knew she would hear it. Then later than she had expected, almost half past, had come the light footsteps, rain on a tin roof. Pattering towards the spare-room door. Holding her breath for a moment. Then stomach sinking as they moved further and further away. The yawning of a door. A little boy. 'Daddy.' She had turned, burying her face in the pillow.

She leaned back from the refrigerator, balancing her weight on bare feet. Couldn't seem to sit. It was as if she was waiting for something, hairs on the back of her neck on end. She hovered, halfway between the fridge and the kitchen counter. Trapped in no-man's-land. She was sweating, beads trickling between her breasts, along her brow line. The heating turned up too high to compensate for the snow. It seemed that she couldn't breathe, the air thick, crawling over her. She pulled at her dressing gown, letting it slide to the floor in a puddle, now wearing nothing but a spaghetti-strap vest, boxer-short panties. Her bare toes curled against hard, cold tiles, sparking a chill through her, like they were buried in snow.

Don't think about it.

It had been a little after 8 a.m. when she had woken again, light streaming through the thin curtains. There was movement, a rustling like pine trees. 'Let's be really quiet now.' Tom's whisper exaggerated, carrying on the still air. 'Mummy's asleep.' Holding her breath again. Waiting. 'Daddy?' Thinking that somehow it would be different, that somehow the crash would have scrubbed clean her past. 'What is it, buddy?' Stuck between two worlds, and in one she wants to be left alone, an island in the middle of an ocean, where she is safe and where no one can touch her. And in the other her fingers creep closer to the door, craving the feel of her son's hand. 'We build a snowman today?' Exhaling, drowning in disappointment, because nothing has changed. Had listened to the groan of the front door, the footsteps as they walked away from her, wondering what kind of a mother fails twice.

She stared out of the kitchen window at the falling snow. She could eat something. There were eggs in the china basket. Bread in the bread bin. She should eat something. But her stomach was full of lead; far too full for food. She could take a shower. But her arm throbbed, and the bathroom was so far away.

She wondered if there was anything left, out of the wreckage of the plane. After they had found the bodies and the fingers and the toes, what then? Would there be suitcases and tray tables and a flimsy picture, dark and unformed? Was it there, lying in the snow, just waiting for someone to find it, bring it home to its mummy?

In that first pregnancy she had gone to the appointment alone. After all, who would she take with her? The father? Had sat in a greasy plastic chair, leafed through a magazine, eyes flickering over the story of a woman who had slept with her stepfather, trying to ignore the couples, leaning in towards each other, books on a bookshelf that had overbalanced, toppling towards one another, the women cradling their bellies. Almost walked out, once, twice, ten thousand times. No idea why she was there. *I mean, what is the point?* But couldn't seem to move, welded to the seat, watching them waddling their way past her like overweight ducks, eyes bright with anticipation. Had splayed her hand across her own belly, an experiment. Still perfectly flat. You would never know it was there. Growing. Mutating. Woman after woman, coming out smiling, clutching dark photographs of an alien life form.

Had moved, about to leave. Pointless.

'Cecilia Williams?'

Hadn't looked up for a moment, apparently engrossed in the woman who gave birth to her own grandson.

'Cecilia Williams?'

If she didn't look up then it would all be a mistake, and none of this would be happening to her, and she would be back where she belonged in her apartment in Bethnal Green. Smelling of sandalwood and musk and home.

214

'Cecilia?'

But she had to look up, because the woman with the stocky build and the lesbian haircut was hovering over her, leaning too close, and suddenly she was back in the greasy waiting room.

She shivered, suddenly cold standing in the kitchen in just her underwear, but the dressing gown seemed so far away now and her arm pulsed with pain. There were tablets, there on the kitchen counter. They'd given them to her at the hospital, said not to be afraid to take them. That they would make her drowsy, take away the pain. But she couldn't seem to move, couldn't seem to make her body do anything but stare at the small white packet.

'You're Cecilia?' The ultrasound technician's voice had been too little for that big body, reedy and high.

Cecilia had nodded because she couldn't speak.

'Come on then, love. I've been calling you.'

Sticky fingers letting the magazine drop on to the table beside her, knees shaking as she stood, following unwillingly, a dinghy pulled behind a barge. And before she knew it she was flat on her back, oversized sweater tucked up beneath her bra, jeans shuffled down to her knicker line, stinging cold gel squirted on to her belly. The overwhelming sensation of panic, that she had to leave, didn't want to see it. But the woman was leaning over her, pressing so hard into her abdomen that she had wondered if she was going to kill the tiny life,

215

and thinking in the deep dark hell of her thoughts that at least that would be easier. At least she wouldn't have to do it then.

She was still clutching the phone. Looked down at the dark plastic. Maybe she should call someone. Maybe she should talk. But it was all pointless, she knew that. There was no one to call.

'Do you have a partner with you today then, love?'

A moment as Cecilia's mouth bobbed open like a fish. Not knowing how to answer, just a quick shake of her head, because she couldn't find the words.

'All right. Here we are.'

The silver clouds on the screen coalescing as she presses into Cecilia's stomach and suddenly there is a light, pulsing.

'There's the heart.'

Wondering if she's going to black out or be sick, but instead she's staring as the image pulses and moves.

'My, this one's a little wriggler. There's the spine. That's the head.'

The ultrasound technician had offered her a photo. *We got a nice profile shot*, she had said. *Think it's going to have your nose.* Cecilia hadn't answered, silence taken for agreement, and the woman had bustled, feeding paper into the printer, muttering about her busy day.

'I wanted to ask . . .'

She had glanced over her shoulder at Cecilia,

then back at the printer, pulling free a small square piece of paper. Handing it to her. Image dark, ghostly. Her child.

'Yes?'

Cecilia had looked at the picture, staring at it for what felt like a lifetime. Then, feeling like she was floating, back at the woman with the little voice and the lesbian hair. 'I wanted to ask how I go about getting an abortion.'

CHAPTER 31

Jim: Tuesday 20 March, 9.26 a.m.

Jim hadn't slept. Of course he hadn't. How could he, when even the briefest fluttering of his eyelids brought with it the image of his dead daughter? He had let himself into the house after Tom dropped him off, hadn't spoken to Ethan, even though Ethan hovered, a question half formed on his lips. Instead he had pushed past him, up the stairs, into the bathroom, locking the door behind him. He had vomited, once, twice. Had sunk down on to the tiled bathroom floor and sobbed.

Wasn't sure how long he had stayed in there. Had wanted to curl himself up like a foetus, bury his head in his hands, never get up. But he couldn't stay there for ever.

It was full dark by the time he came back out again, trudging slowly down the stairs. Someone had put the lamps on in the living room, had lit the fire. Jim had sunk on to the sofa, head dropping to his hands. Then he had heard slow, heartbroken footsteps, and he had wiped his eyes

218

and tried his best to straighten his back; had smiled, even. Esther had hung in the doorway, scrutinising his face, then had started to cry again, because even without him saying it she saw it there. Had crossed the room to him, shoulders shaking with suppressed sobs, lifting his chin with her hands, and lowered her face to his.

'Thank you.' A cross between a whisper and a moan.

Then she had kissed him. He could still taste the salt. Wasn't sure whose tears it was from.

Jim didn't know how long they had stayed there, his head buried at her waist, how long it was before she sank to the sofa next to him, folding herself into his arms. How long it was before she fell asleep, breathing thick.

He knew that it was about nine when Ethan had looked in. Knew because he remembered looking at the clock.

'You should go home, boy. Isabelle will be waiting for you.'

His son hanging in the doorway, like there was something he wanted to say, just like he had a week ago, when he had come to break the news to his father. Could it really have only been a week? Just a week ago that it seemed the worst thing that could possibly happen was the curvature of the spine, slight enough that none of them had ever noticed it, pronounced enough that the police force medical officer had. *They said I'll never be a police officer, Dad.* Ethan had cried that day too, weighted down with the crush of disappointment.

But now, a week later, he had simply stood in the doorway, watching his parents drowning in their grief. Had given a quick nod.

'You . . . you'll call me? If you hear . . .?'

'I'll call you.' Neither Jim nor his son putting it into words.

They hadn't gone to bed. Had stayed like that all night, with the lamps lit, and the dancing flames in the fireplace that seemed just too happy, as if they didn't understand what had gone on here.

It was a little after 9 a.m. that the doorbell rung. It had taken him a minute, brain running slower than it should, to realise what that meant. Esther pushing herself up, looking around, confused for a moment as to where they are, why they are sitting on the sofa with the fire down to an ember. Then another look taking over, realisation, and the colour draining from her face. Jim had kissed her, and she had clung to him, just for a moment.

'Tom. Come on in.' The wind was whipping around the detective, through the open front door, clawing at Jim's legs. His mouth was stuffed with cotton, the stale taste reminding him that he hadn't brushed his teeth.

'Hey, Jim.' He didn't ask how he was. Jim appreciated that.

Esther was still sitting on the sofa when they returned, legs pulled up under her. She didn't see them, or at least it seemed that she didn't. She was staring out through the patio doors at the garden, trees drooping under the weight of snow. Watching as a bird launches itself into flight, branches bending, springing back, a flurry of snow falling to the winding path. There were fresh tears on her cheeks. The renewed pain of recollection.

'Essie?' Jim sank on to the couch beside her, one hand on her knee.

Esther turned, the image broken down into stop-motion frames. She smiled, even though the movement looked awkward.

'Essie? Tom needs to speak to you.' There was a flash across her eyes, a quick spasm of fear, settling down into something else – resignation. *What is there to be afraid of now when the worst has already happened?*

She nodded slowly. 'I understand.'

'Can you tell me when you saw Libby last?' Tom had perched on the edge of the leather recliner, notebook in his hand.

Esther started, like the name had stung her. 'It was . . . Tuesday?' A question, a quick glance at her husband because she couldn't trust herself, not now. A nod in reply. 'Tuesday. She . . . We were all . . . dinner . . .' She shook her head, trying to shake the words free.

'How did she seem to you?'

She was watching his lips move, a foreign tongue, lost in translation.

'I . . . Okay. She was fine. Seemed fine.'

'Your husband . . .' Tom nodded at Jim. 'He said she seemed happier.'

Esther wasn't looking at them, was staring into space, a faint flutter rippling across her lips, the suggestion of a smile. 'Yes.' The smile wilting as she remembered.

'Why was that?'

She stared at him for a long moment, then a brief glance at her husband. Jim squeezed her hand.

'Esther?'

'She was seeing someone.' Her voice so quiet it seemed like it would vanish when it touched the air. Talking to Jim now, not to Tom. 'I wanted to tell you, but she asked . . . She was shy about it.'

A quick spasm of pain, another loss inflicted. Jim smiled. 'It's okay.' Because this was the way it was. This was why you had a mother and a father. A father to teach you to ride a bike, drive your first car. To help you when you apply for the police force so that you can be just like your daddy. And a mother to kiss the knees that have got scraped because you still aren't that steady on your bike, to whisper secrets to about some man who would never deserve you. Another quick flash, this time Ethan, crying on his mother's shoulder even though he hadn't told Jim he was coming over and had told him he was okay with never being a police officer, that he could move on. This was why they worked. He had his job, Esther had hers.

'Who was she seeing, Esther?' Tom asked. And Jim can hear it in his tone, the sound of a new line of inquiry opening up.

'I don't know.' Esther shook her head. 'She wouldn't say.'

'Had they been together long?'

'I don't know. A while, I think.'

'Okay.' Tom was scritching in his pad, frowning heavily. 'So you think this was why she was happy?'

Another rough shake of the head. 'No . . . I'm . . . I'm sorry. She broke up with him. That's what she told me.'

'When was this?'

Esther rubbed her forehead, like the act of thinking was painful. 'Last week . . . sometime. She didn't go into details. Just said that it was over.'

'And it was her decision?'

'Yes. She said that the relationship had been a huge mistake.'

'Did she tell you anything else about him?' Tom asked.

'She told me that he was older.'

A pause for a moment, the detective's mind working. Jim closed his eyes briefly. Knows what he's thinking. Would have thought it too.

'Is there anyone who might know more?' Tom asked. 'Anyone Libby might have talked to about this relationship? A friend? A colleague?'

'Hannah. She's . . . You could talk to her. Libby . . . They were close. Maybe she'd . . .'

'Hannah is a friend of Libby's?'

'She lives near her. Couple of doors down.' Jim's voice came out sounding strained. 'I can give you her address.'

'Thanks, Jim.' Tom paused, so long that Jim wondered if that was it, if he was done. Then, 'Esther, was Libby afraid of this man?'

A heavy silence.

'She . . . He kept calling her. After she ended it. He called her all the time. She said . . . she said that he was never going to let her go.'

CHAPTER 32

Cecilia: Tuesday 20 March, 10.15 a.m.

C ecilia carried flowers, orange carnations wrapped in silver cellophane. She had almost bought roses, but with roses there were thorns, and she thought that perhaps life had thrown enough thorns their way for the time being. She had bought chocolates too, an overlarge box of Quality Street. As if that could make up for the answers she hadn't been able to bring. She walked quickly, but was aware of the nurses watching her, the approving smiles, and she felt her head lift itself a little higher.

Maisie looked smaller if anything, hunched into a mound of pillows. She seemed to be watching television, some property show, but her fingers were plucking at the rough hospital blankets, small rapid movements, her lips moving in silent prayer. Didn't see Cecilia until she was right alongside her, the crinkling cellophane announcing her arrival. She looked up. She smiled.

Cecilia felt her eyes pooling, a rush of warmth. Felt better than she had felt in days.

'Hello. Wasn't expecting to see you.' Maisie tried to push herself up, but there were too many pillows and it was like watching someone push against clouds. 'And you . . . Are those for me?'

Cecilia smiled. Was surprised to realise that she meant it. 'Of course. Thought this place could do with brightening up.'

'Well. Isn't that just lovely? And chocolates. Well. Gosh, aren't I spoiled. Sit down, my love. Go on, sit.'

Cecilia set the flowers down. She'd have to ask for a vase, make sure they had plenty of water.

'Well . . .' Maisie folded her hands across her lap. 'This is just lovely. You shouldn't have come. You're a busy girl, with your family and everything.'

Cecilia played with the cellophane, trying to get it to lie flat. A spurt of guilt. 'Oh well.' Tried to laugh, although it came out false. 'I'd rather be hanging out with you anyway.'

Maisie was watching her, eyes squinting. 'You okay, love?'

Cecilia tried a smile. 'Sure.' Couldn't stop the tears, though; they sprang up whether she wanted them or not.

The abortion had come about a week after the scan. She had floated aimlessly about London. Hadn't gone to work, hadn't been near the place. Not since Eddie. They had called, once, twice, must have been a dozen times in the end. Red light blinking messages demanding to know where she was. She had deleted them. Had never called back. Her notice of dismissal had come in the post finally. She had read it, had crumpled it up, throwing it in amongst the skeletal remains of week-old takeaway cartons. She hadn't told anyone about the pregnancy. Had spent her days drifting, unnoticed, through crowded Hammersmith streets, stopping to stare at women with prams, the baby clothes shops that seemed to occupy every corner. Changed her mind a thousand times.

Maisie reached out, folded Cecilia's small hand into hers. Cecilia stared at it, veins blue and proud. 'You can tell me, you know. It's okay.'

Cecilia looked away, out of the window. The sky was blue today. 'I keep remembering. All the time. Everything.'

'You mean the plane?'

Cecilia shook her head. 'No. I mean everything.'

She could keep it. After all, wasn't it hers as much as his? She would occasionally slip, allowing herself to spin out this little fantasy where she kept it, raised it on her own, a young single mother. People did it, didn't they? Youngsters with belly rings, cigarettes hanging from their thin lips, grubby babies resting on narrow hips. If they could do it then she could do it. She could be a yummy mummy, a career woman with a roll-on bag in one hand, a car seat in the other. Then she would remember the letter from the airline, balled up on the floor. Her dismissal. Would remember that even if she still had the job, she would never be here, because wasn't that her life, wasn't that what she had loved about it? The chance to escape. And how could you raise a baby when you were always running away from it?

And then, tumbling after, would come the other fantasies. The ones she tried to push down, that only broke through at night when she was drifting into an uneasy sleep. Of Eddie, his hands tugging at her, a pain that crumbled her. And this baby, a mirror image of his father. She would dream of giving birth and looking down and expecting this rush of love, but instead recoiling in horror because she had given birth to a monster.

Then the day of the appointment had come, tumbling fast on the heels of a turbulent night full of evil dreams: babies that clawed their way out of her womb, dead eyes looking at her with loathing and triumph. And she woke wanting to climb out of her skin, just so she could get away from this thing that was inside her.

So she went.

Another sterile room, a hard-faced nurse, a sharp pain. And then blood as the little life leeched out of her. She had gone to bed, a hot-water bottle pressed against her abdomen. Had pushed her face into the pillow and cried and cried and cried. Because now all she could see was the perfect little baby and the family that she had flushed out of her. Had clutched the scan photo in her fingers, letting the image scald itself into her memory. That way she would never forget what she had done.

'You're having nightmares, love?'

228

Cecilia felt a tear spill. 'Yes. But it's not just that. It's like I have no filter now. All of the things that I try not to think about.' Looked down. 'The bad things. It's like they're coming back for me. It's like they're all I can think about. The crash and . . . other things. They're all around me. All the time.' She was crying properly now. 'I just . . . I just want to lie down. To stop thinking.'

Cecilia had never forgotten. Couldn't even if she wanted to. Because every time she saw her son, she also saw the child she'd killed. And in her darkest moments, she found herself wondering if it would have been easier with that one, if she would have been a better mother, if she could have given that one more.

'I know, love.' Maisie stroked her hand. 'It's okay. We've been through it. We've all been through it. And you . . . you were so *brave*, love. So brave. We just . . . we have to ride it out, you know. God never gives us more than we can handle.' She squeezed her fingers, tighter than Cecilia would have thought she could. 'You're going to be all right, my love. You just have to hang in there. Keep trying.'

They sat there, long minutes. Then Cecilia lifted her head, brushing her tears away. Picked up the box of Quality Street, sitting it on the bed.

'So where's your little boy today?' Maisie reached for the chocolates, arthritic fingers picking at the cardboard flap.

Cecilia didn't look at her, but reached over and

229

slid a nail under the flap, releasing a waft of sweet chocolate. Her breath shuddered in her chest. 'He's with his grandmother.'

Maisie sighed, squinting into the brightly coloured wrappers. 'It would have been nice if Caroline could have come. My daughter, you know. But then . . .' She shook her head and leaned closer to Cecilia, voice dropping to a hoarse whisper. 'We're not close. Now don't get me wrong. I mean, I love her. But . . . Ernie, he says we're too alike. Says that's why we rub each other up the wrong way.' She shook her head again, looking back into the chocolate box. 'Are you close with your mum?' She selected a purple-wrapped chocolate, offered the box to Cecilia.

Cecilia studied the chocolates. Felt thick, stuffy, the way you do after tears. 'We were. When I was younger. You know, she used to take me to ballet, do my hair, girlie stuff. And she was thrilled when I got a job as a flight attendant. It was what she always wanted to do. You know, before she got married and had me.' She selected a strawberry cream and handed the box back to Maisie. The normality of the moment suddenly leaving her breathless. How long had it been since she had felt that? Normal. 'She used to come up and visit me in London – this was when I worked there. Said I was living her dream life.' She wasn't looking at Maisie, was picking at the silver foil. 'After that . . . things changed. We, ah, we grew apart.'

Cecilia had called her mother after she had

walked in on her ex, Kyle, screwing a blonde in their bed. She had been crying, expecting sympathy. Instead the phone had thrummed with a long, sharp silence.

Then, 'So?' Her mother's voice had razor blades in it.

'What do you mean, "so"?'

'Men cheat, Cece. Jesus. Grow up.' A heavy sigh of disappointment. 'Where are you?'

'I moved out. I got my own flat . . .'

'You moved out?' her mother had shrieked. 'What the hell is wrong with you?'

'Mum. I caught him. Shagging in my bed. Two years we've been living together. Two years and I've done everything for that sodding man. And he does this!'

She hadn't answered right away, and for the most fleeting of moments Cecilia had hoped that she was reconsidering, that there was still room to repair what had already been said.

'Cecilia. Come on. You think it's just you? You think you're the only one this has ever happened to? Now, I'm telling you this because I'm your mother and I love you. You've got a good thing going there. A nice house. A good-looking man who makes plenty of money. He's a pilot, for God's sake. These things happen. Put it behind you. Go home.'

Cecilia had been angry, had hung up the phone in a temper. That was why she changed her mind, why she decided to go out, even though she had planned to stay in, watch a movie. Instead she had got dressed up, had done her hair, and gone to the club, where the music was pulsing so loud that it washed her thoughts clean. That was why she had bumped into Eddie. And that was when everything had changed.

She hadn't known Eddie well. Just well enough to know that he was trouble. You could see it in his eyes sometimes, a hunter tracking game. They stayed away from him at work, when he was called in to make repairs, with his smell of grease and his proprietorial stare. But that night she hadn't cared. She had gone out to get drunk. To forget. Had been feeling bruised and reckless. That was why she had let Eddie buy her a drink, even though she knew better. That was why she had let him walk her home.

She would wonder afterwards if she had screamed. Couldn't remember. She had tried to scream, she was sure of that. But the sound was drowned out in music and laughter. It was the laughter that she would remember.

They had walked past pubs, nightclubs. Then he had suggested a little turn, a detour. Quicker this way, he had said. And Cecilia, dizzy from vodka and Coke, had giggled. Eddie had slipped an arm around her, all cosy and nice, and Cecilia had known that she should pull away, but she was cold and lonely and so she had left it there. He had steered her into the dark alley. Then his hand had snaked down to her backside.

Cecilia had started then, pulled back. But by then, of course, it was already too late. His hand had whipped out, impossibly fast, had wrapped itself around her throat. His palm pressing down, choking. She tried to grab for breath. Could feel darkness closing in. Then he was on her, other hand diving into the front of her blouse, grabbing at her breast, pulling at her skirt. Pushing her against the wall, rough bricks tearing at her skin.

She was going to die. Remembered thinking that she was going to die. Had looked up, staring at the shattered remains of a broken street light. Felt a sharp, searing pain that cut into her. Watched the street light. Never once took her eyes off it.

He had left her lying in amongst the five-day-old bins, weeping, her skin alive, crawling. She had found out later that he had bragged at work about fucking her, *that snooty stewardess bitch.*

She had barely left the house. Had showered and showered and showered but still, no matter what she did, couldn't get rid of the smell of him, the feel of his fingers. She had never called the police. Had never really occurred to her. After all, wasn't it her own fault, with her short skirt and her vodka and Coke, and hadn't she known, deep down, that he was dangerous and gone with him anyway? She took to wedging a kitchen chair under the handle of her front door. Just in case.

It was nearly a month later that she had found out she was pregnant.

'I like this programme.' Maisie's voice was

muffled by the chocolate she was eating, disguised by the crinkle of the wrapper she rolled through her fingers. 'People starting out in life, making themselves lovely homes. It's nice. Do you like this programme?'

Cecilia reached across, smiling briefly, and took the wrapper from Maisie, slipping it into the bin that sat beside her chair. 'Yes. It's a good programme.'

CHAPTER 33

Tom: Tuesday 20 March, 7.36 p.m.

Circling the cloth, around and around. Tom looked out of his kitchen window, saw his own reflection looking back at him. Could dimly make out the fence in the back garden. It would need revarnishing this year. The water scalded his fingers.

Esther had fallen back against the cushions, energy spent, face slack with grief. She hadn't looked at him; by the end, Tom wasn't even sure she knew he was there. Eyes dark with the death of her little girl. Clinging on to Jim's hand, and him clinging on to hers as well, his head low, eyes studded with the loss of his daughter and of the relationship that he'd thought they had.

'Will she be okay?' Tom had stood on the doorstep, watching the cold wind send cyclones of snow swirling around the silver Audi on the drive. Not asking if *he* was okay. Giving him that much. He jammed his hands into his pockets. Glancing back up at Jim as he shook his head.

'If there's anything I can do . . .'

'Just be straight with us. That's all I ask.'

Lifting the plate up high, lowering it to the draining board and laying it to rest. The radio burbled. There was a dishwasher, less than three feet away. Tom never used it. Preferred to use his hands.

He glanced up at Cecilia, hovering in the kitchen doorway. 'Why don't you take a bath? Read a book?'

Cecilia looked down, hands shaking a little.

The book was on the plane. Like everything else was on the plane. Tom shook his head, cursing himself for reminding her of it, no matter how unlikely it was that she had forgotten, even for a moment. Seemed to be always this way, with his wife. That he would always know how to say just the wrong thing. 'I'm sorry. I didn't think.'

Cecilia glanced up at him, gave a small shrug. 'It's okay.'

Then they stood, hung in stasis in their own kitchen. Tom plunging plates, one after another, through the bubbles, water bitingly hot, turning his fingers red. Trying to think what the hell else there was to say. Cecilia bit her nail.

'So,' he scrubbed at a patch of dried-on food, 'what did you do today?'

'I went to the hospital.'

'The hospital? Are you okay?' Tom turned, looked at her.

'Yeah, no, it's not me. Maisie. One of the . . . the survivors. I went to see her.'

'Oh?' Another swish with the cloth; Tom pulled the plate from the bubbles.

'Yeah.' Cecilia wasn't looking at him, still picking at her nail. 'She's nice.'

'That's good.'

'Yeah.'

There was a silence. Tom wondered if she had gone.

'I think . . . Maybe I will take a bath. Okay?'

'Sure. Yeah. That'll be good. You go. Ben's already asleep, so you won't disturb him.' He didn't watch her go, heard the sound of her footsteps on the tiled floor, the creak on the stairs. Wanted to sink into the floor. How was it possible this could be his life? His wife a complete stranger. The barest of conversation seemingly beyond them. How the fuck had it come to this?

He dumped the plate hard on the draining board. Couldn't stop thinking about Jim, Esther. The way he looked at her, so many years and so completely in love. And Tom was jealous. He was jealous of a guy who had just learned that his daughter was dead. How sick was that?

Pipes creaked, groaning with water weight, the aching of floorboards above his head. He plunged the plate back through the bubbles. One final swipe. Then music, his phone sparking to life, vibrating hard against the counter top. A quick wipe of his hands.

'Tom Allison.'

'Hey. It's me.'

'All right, Dan. How was house-to-house?'

'Fucking freezing. My arse still hasn't warmed up.'

'You still in?'

'Just about to head home. The DI said you'd asked to be updated . . .'

'Yeah. Please.'

'You sure now? I mean, you're at home with the family and everything . . .'

Tom glanced around the empty kitchen, living room dark beyond.

'Ben's in bed. What you got?'

'Not much. Neighbours on one side are away. Don't know where or when they'll be back. The other side, the guy is like ninety. Almost completely deaf.'

'What?'

'Ha ha. Didn't hear a thing.'

'Well, he wouldn't.'

'You're a funny guy. I always say that about you whenever anyone asks; I say, funny guy that one. Twat. Yeah, well this guy may as well have been blind as well, 'cause he didn't see anything. He did say that his dog, this annoying fucking yappy thing, went nuts at about nine. By the fence adjoining Libby's.'

'Was there someone there?'

'I don't know. He didn't know. He did say that there was a lovely car parked outside Libby's all night the night of the murder. He's a car buff apparently. We had a *fascinating* conversation about his Skoda.'

'What car?'

'Mercedes S-class. Black. Blue maybe.'

'Plate?'

'Nah. Lovely car, though.'

'Awesome. Did you speak to a Hannah Thomas?'

'Um . . .' A short pause. 'Number forty-three?'

'Yeah, I think.'

'No answer. I'll try again tomorrow. How are Libby's family doing?'

Tom pulled out a kitchen chair, sinking into it. Gaze caught by his reflection in the window. Beyond, just darkness.

'Not good. You know.' He sighed, running his fingers through his hair. 'Turns out Libby had a boyfriend.'

'Who was he?'

'I don't know. The family as a whole had no idea. She only confided in her mother.'

'Why the secrecy?'

'I don't know. They'd been together for a while. Mother wasn't sure how long exactly. She knew that he was older, but not much else.'

'Married?'

'I was thinking the same.'

'Did the mother know?'

'Said she didn't want to pry.'

'Fuck, wish she was my mother. Do you know, last week I told my mother I had a date. You know what she did? Bought me a box of condoms. Ribbed.'

'Nice.'

'Yeah. DI said we're releasing the house, Libby's. Forensics have got everything they're going to get. And I got the phone records.'

'Anything?'

'Lot of family calls. Friends. The usual. Couple of odd ones, though. Unregistered numbers so we can't track them. Pay-as-you-go. The first one came into use almost a year ago, early February. Initially the calls were sporadic, once a week maybe, then every couple of days, increasing in frequency over a couple of weeks. After that it was every day, pretty much. Long calls, an hour, sometimes two.'

'The boyfriend.'

'I'd say. And with an unregistered SIM? This guy's married.'

'When did they stop?'

'Huh?'

'The calls. When did he stop calling her?'

'The frequency increased in the days before her death. Ten, fifteen calls a day. Most of them she didn't answer.'

'That tallies with her mother's theory that he was pursuing her.'

'Last call came in the day she was murdered. Probably a couple of hours before.'

'Nothing after that?'

'Nothing.'

'Shit.' Tom closed his eyes. 'We need to find the boyfriend.'

'Yeah. I'll be back on house-to-house tomorrow. Someone'll know something.'

'So how was it?'

'What?'

'The date. How was it?'

'Yeah, not bad. Good-looking. Smart. Breath like a toxic fucking dump.'

'Nice. Use the condoms?'

'Not so much.'

'What about the other number?'

'Yeah . . . that one started later, around July. On average a couple of times a day. The interesting thing is that every call was short.'

'How short?'

'A second, two.'

'Hang-ups?'

'Looks like. Every single one of them.'

'When was the last call?'

'The day she died.'

'Shit. Okay.' Tom pushed himself up, leaning heavily on the kitchen table. Staring at his reflection in the window. He looked old. 'Look, let me track down this Hannah one. I'll try and see her tomorrow.'

'You sure?'

'Yeah. If you get anything else . . .'

'Yeah, I'll call you.' A long pause, and Tom can tell he's thinking about something, wondering how to phrase it. 'Everything all right? With Cecilia?'

'It's fine. No worries.' Tom rubbed his hand across his eyes, sighing heavily. 'You know how it is.'

'Yeah . . . look, I know we're blokes, but if you need to talk . . .'

'You'll laugh your arse off at me?'

'Damn right, you skinny fucker. No, I'm serious. And if you, you know, ever needed a place to stay . . .'

Black bags lined up against the front door that swings in the breeze as his father loads the plastic remnants of their family into the boot of his Nissan. Eight-year-old Tom watching him, face pressed against the bedroom window. Air creaking with the sound of his mother's sobs. Then his father stops, rubbing his hands over his face, and if it were anyone else, Tom would have thought that he was crying, but this was his father, and he doesn't cry. Looking up. Tom pulling back from the glass, so fast that he jars his neck, pain racing up into the back of his skull.

'Thanks, mate. But I'm okay.'

'You sure?'

Tom glanced around the kitchen that he fitted and the toys that he bought, knowing that he will never leave, no matter what it costs him, because he cannot be his father and he cannot breathe without his son. So he'll stay, and he'll absorb the cost like a blow to the body, because then his son will never have to press his nose to a pane of glass, watch his father walk away.

'Yeah. Thanks, though.'

'Well, look, offer's there.'

'Yeah, whatever. You love me, I know.'

'Ah, bite me.'

'You wish.'

'Speak to you tomorrow, mate.'

'All right, cheers, Dan.'

Tom let the phone slip from his ear. The reflected him looked at him and shrugged. *You look like shit, mate.* Then there was something. A dart of movement, caught out of the corner of his eye.

His heart suddenly racing.

He crossed his kitchen in three quick steps, pulling at the back door. Unlocked. Out into the snow, into the empty garden. Nothing. A bat wheeling overhead. Thick silence. Shuffling through the snow in his slippers, crossing the patio towards the kitchen window. No rustling. No voices. Just paranoia taking hold now after all that they had been through. He was about to turn, go back into the house, when he saw the two perfect footprints that lay beneath his kitchen window.

CHAPTER 34

Freya: Friday 23 March, 11.03 a.m.

The minister leaned on the podium, sausage-fat fingers curling around the red wood. Freya watched a solitary bead of sweat work its way beneath his bristle-stiff hair, down his forehead, along the grooves that ran by the side of his nose, past his lip, watched it dangle there for a moment before it let go, landing on the lectern in front of him. She imagined that she could hear the splash.

'. . . the souls of the righteous are in the hands of God . . .'

'I don't want to go, Frey. I can't do it.' Her mother had leaned against her. Sunlight bright in the spare bedroom.

'It's okay, Mum. We can do this.' Freya had helped her from her bed, slipping listless arms into a black silk blouse, the dark trousers that she wore for work.

'I just, I miss him so much, Frey.'

'I know, Mum.'

'He loved me, Freya.' Her mother had sat back on her bed, legs folding beneath her. Had allowed Freya to slip on her shoes. Hadn't looked at her, gazing off into middle distance.

'I know, Mum.'

'No . . . I know . . . I know what you think about your father. But he loved me. He told me. And everything was going to be okay. It was all . . . It was all going to be okay, now.'

There were colours, a kaleidoscope scattered across the tiled floor, purples and reds and a dark bitter orange, sunlight through stained glass. It smelled of polish, damp clothes, the creeping sweetness of roses. Her mother's eyes were closed. She was crying, softly, quietly. There was an empty space beside her where Richard should have been. Freya wondered if it was deliberate, if her grandmother had sat a little way off, thinking that he would change his mind. Or if it was just the way of families when one member was missing. You leave a space. She wondered about her father, whether a space would remain for him, how long it would take those of them remaining to grow into the vacuum.

'. . . no torment will ever touch them . . .'

They had been standing in the hallway, sunlight filtering through the swirling stained glass of the front door. Dressed in their funeral black. Looked like they were all dead too, a collection of ghosts,

245

waiting. That was when she had realised that Richard was missing.

'I'll go get him.' She had turned, running quickly up the stairs. 'Rich? Kiddo?' Three quick taps on his bedroom door. Silence. 'Richard? We're ready to go.' Fingers dropping to the handle, twisting it. Then the door swinging open, and he's standing there, a loose-fitting T-shirt, jeans that have scuffed at the bottom. Letting her eyes fall to his bare feet. Then looking up, trying not to be impatient, because what right does she have, honestly? 'Rich, it's time for the memorial. We need to leave. You want to get dressed? I can iron a shirt for you really quickly . . .'

'I'm not going.' He hadn't looked at her, had studied the tips of his toes. His voice was so small, like it was his first day at school.

'Rich.' She wanted to hug him, wrap him in her arms, tell him it was okay, but how could she tell him that when she knew damn well that it wouldn't be. 'Honey, I'll be with you. We can do this together.'

But that was the wrong thing to say, and now not only was he not looking at her, but he had turned away, and there were tears spilling over his cheeks. Shaking his head, whispering almost. 'I'm sorry, Frey.'

'In the eyes of the foolish they seem to have died, and their departure was thought to be a disaster.'

There was a sound, towards the front of the

church, not crying, keening. An animal caught in a trap. A woman leaning forward, folded in two with grief. A man beside her, his arm around her shoulders, face pulled into a silent scream.

'. . . and their going from us to be their destruction; but they are at peace . . .'

Freya didn't know how long she had sat on the floor of her parents' room, cradling the photo. Wondering who the hell this woman was. Then she had heard floorboards creak, had felt a flush of panic, stuffing the lockbox back into the drawer of her father's bedside cabinet. The picture she kept. Had slipped it into her handbag. Didn't know how many times she had looked at it. Enough to memorise the wave in her hair, her father's bright smile. One she had never seen on him before.

But then that shouldn't be a surprise, should it? Seemed like she had known almost nothing about her father, and what he was or wasn't capable of.

'For though in the sight of others they were punished, their hope is full of immortality.'

The minister bowed his head, his lips still moving. Then a deep bellow of sound and he glanced back at the organist, dropped his head again, a slow shuffle along the aisle towards the flung-open doors. He passed, arthritic and painful, a waft of cinnamon. The crowd turned, trudging, and Freya followed, arm wrapped tight around her mother. Passing airline officials in their black suits and their stiff upper lips. A hand on her shoulder, her grandfather's face tight. Her grandmother beside him, tears staining her cheeks.

The dark aisle gave way to a bright sky. Patches of crisp snow, broken by hopeful grass shoots. Gravestones testifying to the long-forgotten dead. Flowers had been left against the outer wall of the church, reds and greens and orange and yellow vivid against grey stone, white snow. The cellophane caught the low winter sunlight, blinding them.

'Freya?' Her grandfather's voice was quiet, almost lost in the crunch of footsteps on gravel.

She glanced back over her shoulder.

'I thought he wasn't coming?'

'Who?'

Her grandfather nodded towards the graveyard, beneath the widespread arms of the draping yew, to where Richard stood. He wore jeans, the same ones he'd worn earlier, had thrown on a jacket that was far too thin for the wind that had sprung up. Wasn't looking at them. Freya tracked his gaze, towards the wrought-iron gate, and for a second her breath caught in her throat. Chestnut hair falling to her shoulders, tousled into a rough curl. Her arm held awkward in a sling. And for one perfect moment it was crystal clear. The woman her father was sleeping with was an air hostess. She was with him on the plane. She survived. It felt almost like a breath of relief. The throng of questions queuing up, waiting to be asked. But then Freya looked again. The woman was taller, older. It wasn't her. A quick breath out, a moment to steady her heartbeat. Then looking back at Richard, still staring at the woman with the chestnut hair, oblivious to his gaze.

CHAPTER 35

Cecilia: Friday 23 March, 11.15 a.m.

'. . . t he souls of the righteous are in the hands of God . . .'

Cecilia stared down at her hands, the nails chipped, bitten like when she was twelve. Hadn't wanted to come. Hadn't answered when Tom had knocked on the spare-room door, first at seven, then again at eight. Had closed her eyes, squeezing them shut. Didn't want to go. Didn't want to see. The mountains and the snow and the people with their grief-ravaged faces. Better to stay here, with her eyes closed. Better to pretend that it had never happened.

She couldn't breathe. People stuffed together, a sea of black. Could feel the gazes, grazing her face, her arm, back up to her face, knowing that they knew. Couldn't decide if it was sympathy or judgement that she saw. Wanting to say, *I saved people, I got people off the plane*, as if that alone would pardon her from the iniquitous crime of surviving. Scanning the faces. Waiting for that tickle of familiarity, someone to look at her with recognition and relief. To say to others, *Look, that's her, that's that stewardess, the one who saved us.* But there was just grief and horror.

'. . . no torment will ever touch them . . .'

It had been a little after 8.30 when the door opened. She hadn't moved. Had kept her back towards the door.

'Cecilia.' Tom had spoken, voice low. 'The memorial.'

She hadn't reacted. Hadn't murmured.

'I think we should go. It's important.'

Why couldn't he just shut up? She squeezed her eyes closed, pressing her lips together.

'Cecilia? If we leave soon, we'll make it.' A waiting silence. 'I know you'd rather not. But . . . I think that maybe it would do you good. I don't think . . . We can't just pretend it didn't happen.'

Flames and falling and a tearing pain that penetrates deep into her. A grey figure on black. The look on the ultrasound technician's face, lip curling into disgust. She had pushed herself up from the bed, not because she wanted to. She had moved because there were too many things now, and all of a sudden she couldn't remember how to forget.

'In the eyes of the foolish they seem to have died, and their departure was thought to be a disaster . . .'

They had arrived late. They were already singing. She had wanted to cry with the absurdity of it all. Had wedged themselves in, standing with backs pressed against the door. Studied her shoes. Black

Armani boots with a narrow heel. Scuffed, stained with mud and slush. Didn't want to look up and see speckles of the familiar in a sea of unfamiliarity. Vicki's fiancé Jason, his hair wild, tie crooked, because Vicki wasn't there to straighten it. Looking like he could barely stand, leaning heavily on a woman she took to be his mother. Two rows in front, a middle-aged woman, familiar for some reason that Cecilia couldn't put her finger on. Then it occured to her: Oliver's wife. She had seen her once, picking him up from a late flight when his car was in the garage. She had been attractive, could be more so if she made an effort. But now she looked like death. She was leaning on a young woman. Their daughter. She dimly remembered Oliver making some fleeting mention of a daughter, a psychology student or something like that. There was a son, too, younger. Cecilia watched the family, looked for a boy who would fit. But then perhaps he was younger than she remembered him being, too young to come to something like this. She looked anyway, anything so she didn't have to listen to the minister and his droning tone and the low, keening grief. But there was just an elderly couple, their gazes darting sideways to the mother and daughter, the main players in the tragedy.

'. . . and their going from us to be their destruction; but they are at peace . . .'

Cecilia had dressed in the spare room, her room as she now thought of it, running a brush through her hair, knew it needed washing, rolling itself into the curls that she had spent so long trying to fight. Had pulled on black trousers, a black blouse. Studying herself in the mirror, thinking that she looked sick, like a cancer patient. Swiping foundation and bronzer and mascara, still little but the ghost of herself. Hadn't noticed that Ben wasn't there. Hadn't even occurred to her to ask. Too swamped in the memory of the tablet she had taken to get rid of the foetus, the pain gripping her stomach, the blood as she flushed the life out of her, and then, from somewhere older, the memory of hands, smelling of grease, wrapping themselves around her neck.

'For though in the sight of others they were punished, their hope is full of immortality.'

It was getting warmer in the church, seemed like all of the air had been sucked out. Looking up at her husband, because she doesn't know where else to look. He is watching the minister, his face is the policeman face, the one that he uses when he doesn't want to give anything away. The one he uses with her. He glanced back at her, a brief smile, eyes wary. As though he was considering something. Then he reached an arm out, wrapping it around her waist. She froze. Now she can't breathe, wants to get out, has to get out where there is air and space. There was a movement behind them, wind rushing in like a gasp of relief, and she turned, shaking off her husband's grasp, not waiting to see if he would follow.

Feeling the cold wind slapping at her cheeks,

feet slipping on slush. Walking past the bank of flowers set into the snow, looking straight ahead, because she's done her bit now, and all she wants to do is go home, and swallow those painkillers, the ones they gave her at the hospital. *They'll make you drowsy, mind.* Sinking into bed, gripped by that heaviness that pulls dreams away, until you're just left floating in a sea of silence. Could hear voices behind her, footsteps on the path. Didn't turn.

Cecilia reached for the gate, pulling at it. Heavy and old, it stuck, grating against the stone wall. Could feel eyes on her. Someone watching. She kept going as fast as she could go in the slush.

CHAPTER 36

Tom: Sunday 25 March, 6.01 p.m.

'You're the policeman? Libby's dad said you'd be calling me. He said you needed to talk to me?'

Tom nodded, handing her his warrant card. She wore sweat pants, long blonde hair pulled into a loose plait. Rimless glasses sat low. It looked like she had been crying. She studied the warrant card, glancing up at Tom, back down at the photograph.

'Would you mind if I asked you a couple of questions?'

'Of course. You want to come in?'

'If that's okay.'

'Jim said. He said you'd want to talk to me. Because me and Libby . . .' She turned abruptly, Tom followed. The living room was spartan, wooden flooring, stark white walls, the chimney breast smothered in dark crimson paper. 'I'm sorry. I'm so sorry I wasn't here. I've been working away. I didn't . . .' She choked down a sob. 'I didn't know. Not until I came home last night.'

255

Hannah shook her head, brushing at the tears with her fingers. 'Her dad, Jim, he'd left me a message. Asking me to call.'

'You and Libby were friends?'

She had sunk on to the black leather sofa, long stick-thin arms stretching between narrow knees. 'The best. We moved in on the same day. Stinking weather. I saw this removal van a couple of doors down, and we're both running back and forth and getting drenched. The next thing you know there's this knock on the door, and Libby was standing there with a bottle of wine.'

'You guys hit it off?'

'Like you wouldn't believe. Saw each other like every day.'

'So you knew Libby as well as anybody?'

'Yeah. I did . . .' She still wasn't looking at him, voice drifting off into nothing.

'When did you see her last, Hannah?'

'Uh, Monday. We were going to go get lunch, but I had to cancel. I had an appointment with a new client – I'm an accountant – so we got together for breakfast instead. I'd been away. Bournemouth, on my sister's hen weekend. I wanted to see Libby, wanted to tell her, I mean, my sister, she's marrying a prick. A real prick. And Libby and I, we'd been talking about this. She was going to come over.'

'How did she seem to you?'

'She was good. We laughed . . .'

'Did she tell you anything about having just gone through a break-up?'

She looked up at him, gaze wary.

'Did she?' Tom could feel a well of frustration rising.

She looked like she was considering it, almost like she wasn't going to answer. Then she sighed. 'She was seeing someone. For the past year. Met him on a night out. She was with a bunch of school friends in Swansea, and he came on to her, wanting to buy her drinks, you know the drill. She said she wasn't interested at first. She thought he was too old for her. And . . . there was other stuff.'

'Was he married?' His tone was harder than he had meant it to be.

She didn't answer at first, just folded her hands into themselves. They were thin hands, long fingers. Like Cecilia's. Knotted tight together. Just like Cecilia's. She hadn't spoken to him after the memorial. In truth they had barely spoken since. Two ghosts drifting past one another, just inhabiting the same space. Cecilia had left the church, got into the car, shoulder rested against the passenger-side window as if she was afraid that Tom would try and touch her again. She needn't have worried. He had driven a little faster on the way home, a little less careful than perhaps he should have been. He had wanted to get home. Had wanted to drop her off, leave. Had work to do. After all, they were in the middle of a murder investigation. Had thought about the case, about Libby, only sparing a fleeting moment to wonder about the boy standing amongst the gravestones

257

watching his wife, whilst she stared, oblivious, into the cold bright sky. It occurred to him that he should have been curious, perhaps even jealous. Something. He had tried, effortfully mustering his energies, but there was nothing there.

Hannah shook her head, tears beginning to flood down her cheeks. 'I told her he was bad news. Fucking jerk. He told her that he was unhappy, wanted to leave his wife. He was persistent. And, I don't know, she just gave in. But the thing is, he didn't make her happy. She seemed to be miserable all the time. He was letting her down, left, right and centre. He'd keep her hanging on, saying he was going to leave, then coming up with all these excuses why he couldn't. She finally had enough.'

'When was this?'

'Last week. He was supposed to be coming to see her, they were going to do like a pretend Christmas, exchanging gifts and stuff, but he just never showed up. She really lost it. Told him it was over.'

'How did he take it?'

'Not good. Not good at all. He was crying on the phone to her, kept calling, leaving messages, showing up outside her house. She was getting all these calls, all hours of the day and night. Then she'd answer. No one there. It was getting really weird. She came around one night, all freaked out, said that someone had been in her garden. There were footprints, a broken plant pot. In the end, she answered one of his calls. That was when she was here on Wednesday. Said she'd had it. She was really calm, just said to him, look, you don't make me happy, I can't rely on you. He said he'd change, he'd leave, you know. But she said no, I don't want you to. I don't want you.'

'And what did he say?'

'Nothing. She hung up on him then. When she left, she said that she was changing her number, was going to do it later that day, but . . .'

'And you didn't see her after that?'

'No.'

'Do you know his name?'

Hannah shook her head. 'Oliver. I don't know his surname. I think she was trying to protect him. In spite of everything.'

'Oliver. What about his work? Where he lived?'

'I don't know. I know he used to travel, would go away with work. I know he wasn't based in Swansea. I think maybe Cardiff way, but I'm really not sure.'

'Was she afraid of him?'

She chewed her nail. 'I don't think she was afraid. Libby wasn't afraid of anything. But she didn't like the calls. She said she kept feeling like she was being watched. It weirded her out.' Hannah looked up at him. 'I was afraid for her.'

'Why?'

'He seemed so manipulative, so determined. I didn't think he would let her go.'

Tom nodded. Watching her. 'Did he have a key to Libby's house?'

'Yes.'

His mobile phone sparked to life, making them both jump.

'I'm sorry, let me just . . .' Glancing down at the display, heart tightening a little. 'I'm sorry. I just need to get this. Hi. Everything okay?'

'I'm sorry, love.' His mother sounded strained, awkward. 'I know you're working.'

'That's okay. What's wrong?'

'Well, nothing. I mean, I'm sure it's nothing. It's just, well, you said that Cecilia was going to pick Ben up. That was right, wasn't it?'

It had been his suggestion, on the way to the memorial that morning, as the snow-bound scenery hurried by and he'd looked for something to say. *Why don't you go and get him? I'm sure he'd love to see you. It'd be nice. For the two of you to spend some time.* She'd nodded, he was sure she'd nodded, made some sound, something that he'd taken to be acquiescence.

'She hasn't been?'

'No. And it's not that it matters. I mean, I can hang on to him. That's fine. It's just, you said she'd be here, and to be honest, I was worried.'

'Okay. I'll give her a call. She said she'd be at home this afternoon.'

'There's no answer at the house. Or on her mobile. That was why I was ringing. I can't seem to find her anywhere.'

'Okay, don't worry. I'll give her a call when I'm done here. I'll let you know.' He was watching

260

Hannah, biting the edge of her thumbnail, her fingers shaking. Hung up. 'Hannah?'

'Look, I . . . I don't know if this is relevant, and, I mean, I feel awful even saying anything, you know, they're going through so much . . .'

'What is it, Hannah? Anything could be of help to us.'

She sighed deeply. 'Well, you know about the row, don't you?'

Tom frowned. 'What row?'

'The night before she . . . you know. Libby was at her parents' house. Her brother gave her a lift home.'

'Okay.'

'Well, I mean, I'm sure it meant nothing, but they had a row.'

'Ethan and Libby?'

'Yeah, I mean, she was gutted. They've always been really close. But he just lost it with her.'

Tom felt a tingling along his spine. 'Why?'

'I think it was because of the news he'd just had – you know he applied for the police force, don't you? I mean, he's been trying for years and years, but he's had problems with the fitness test. And there was this weird thing between them when Libby got in and he didn't. But he had applied again this year, really sorted out his fitness, so he passed that bit. But then last week he had the medical and they told him he had curvature of the spine. They said he'd never be able to be a police officer. I think that was what triggered it

261

off. Libby said he just lost it with her. Started laying into her about how it wasn't fair, her getting to do it when he couldn't. That it was all bull . . . you know. She was really upset about it.'

He was aware that his heart was beating faster.

Then Hannah stood up, frowning, moved to the front window, peering out into the street, now bathed in plunging darkness. Glanced back at him. 'Do you smell smoke?'

CHAPTER 37

Freya: Sunday 25 March, 6.03 p.m.

Freya slipped through the puddle of light spilling from the living room window. The darkness was creeping in, oppressive, bringing with it a harsh cold. She shivered. Should have put a coat on. Stuffed her hands into the pockets of her sweater, brought her shoulders up tight. She stepped through the snow. It had begun to melt, a green and white patchwork quilt. Her feet crunched on ice, and she glanced up. It was cold enough to snow again. But the air was clear, stars shining brightly.

Freya had tried to get to her brother after the memorial, as he stood there under the snow-laden tree. But there were bodies everywhere, pressing into her, and by the time she had pushed through them, he was gone. She had waited, with her mother, her grandparents, hanging in the narrow village street with its thick banked-up snow, the smell of wood burning. Had waited until the bells had stopped ringing, until all that remained was the whispers of the yew trees. Searching face after

263

face. But none of them were him. Finally they had given up. He was already home when they returned, had beaten them back. She had tried to talk to him, but he had locked himself in his room, turning his music up until she could barely hear her own voice above the thrum of the bass.

Freya pressed the key fob, opening the passenger door. She climbed into the Mercedes, tugged at the glove compartment, pulling it open with a force that would have made her father angry. He loved this car. His pride and joy. She pushed her hair back from her eyes, and the snow dripped on to the black carpet, staining it grey.

There were CDs, neatly stacked. She pulled them out, watching them as they tumbled into the footwell. The Beatles. Status Quo. Dire Straits. She leaned forward, picking up a CD, tucked neat into its case. Remembered him playing it, all those nights when he was too stressed from work, too tired to talk to his children, when his voice would bellow out across the room shouting at them to *be quiet, for God's sake*. Her little brother, his lip trembling, eyes sparkling with tears. She snapped it in two. Behind the CDs there was the log book, the manual. She pulled them free, leafing through the pages, even though she wasn't sure what it was she was looking for. Then she dropped them on to the floor, pages spreading open in supplication. A glint of light, buried in the gloom of the glove compartment. A silver lighter and a packet of Benson & Hedges, so light in her hand it seemed that it would fly away.

Freya stared at the cigarettes, and she almost laughed. It would be funny if it wasn't so damned sad. The extent of the facade.

She pushed open the passenger-side door, climbing back out into the snow. She had watched the woman, moving through the snow-bound churchyard. Beautiful and tired, wounded. Not the woman in the picture that her father had guarded so closely. That sinking feeling, as the answers moved further away. The back seat was empty, crisp, clean, the mats on the floor still wrapped in plastic. She wasn't surprised.

She wondered who the woman was. She wondered why her brother was staring at her.

A feeling clung to her, cigarette smoke on her skin: the sense of waiting, that there was another shoe just about to drop.

Freya's footsteps crunched on snow, and she pulled at the car boot. Ice-cold metal on her bare hands. The lock sticking, fighting to keep its secrets to itself. He had stood in the snow that day, with his shoulders drooping, his head sunk low. He had got on to a plane, filled it with people who trusted him to protect them, and then had allowed it to tumble from the sky.

Why?

It raced around and around in her head, tugging at her, pinching.

She gripped the lever harder, yanking.

The light was fainter in the boot, sickly and pale. And there was something else, a smell. It clambered its way out, striking her square in the face. Her stomach lurched. She pulled back, leaning over the snow, gasping in the bitter cold air. It smelled like gone-off food, maggots and rot. She scanned the boot: almost empty. There was an old jacket, one he never wore. She picked it up, shaking it so that the zips rattled, knotting the material tight in her fingers. Trying not to breathe. Plunged her hands into the pockets. A packet of gum. Wadded-up receipts. And cigarettes.

The woman, the one in the picture. Freya knew that it was her he was talking to on the phone, in the snowy garden, the day before he died. It was her that he had spoken to the day before he drove his plane into the ground.

She leaned further in, gagging. The cream interior scarred with dark stains that she couldn't make out properly, not in this light. And there at the back, wedged right up against the seats, was a sports bag. She tugged it free, pulling it towards her.

Papers. Papers and papers and papers. Credit card bills with her father's name, a stranger's life. Freya scanned them, knowing what she was going to find and knowing what it would mean. Hotels. Jewellery stores. Florists. Then there were the phone bills. One after the other after the other. She pulled one free, a recent one, a month ago, maybe a little more. Holding it closer to the insipid light so she could see.

One number. Again. And again. And again.

Freya sank on to the boot edge, metal cold through her jeans, holding the sheet of paper in her hands. Jesus. Hung there, for long moments, wondering what the hell you did next. She glanced back over her shoulder, back into the bag, her eyes wandering as her brain worked to calculate her next move. There was a patch of darkness, a ball of material that she hadn't seen before, tucked into one of the side pockets. She reached in, pulling it free. A glove, the solitary one of a pair of dark grey Thinsulates, large, so as to encompass her mother's long fingers. Her mother had laughed that she could never wear dainty women's gloves. She held it up to the light, her stomach flipping. She recognised them. Had seen them last as a pair. When she gave them to her mother for Christmas.

She sat there, in the cold, holding the phone bill, the glove. Her mother's glove. If it was there . . . what the hell did that mean? That she'd been in the Mercedes, in this bag, had seen the phone bills, the receipts, the clumped-together evidence of her father's infidelity?

Freya didn't think about what she did next. If she had, perhaps she wouldn't have done it. Punched the numbers into her mobile phone, fingers trembling. She told herself that it was from the cold. Then suddenly it was ringing, and she knew what she was going to say. *That man, the one you've been fucking? Well, he's a liar. And he's dead.*

Then the ringing stopped, the phone answered, and she held her breath. But it wasn't the soft woman's voice she was expecting, full of hope, fear.

'Hello?' A man. Tired. Heavy.

Heart thundering, Freya hung up the phone.

CHAPTER 38

Cecilia: Sunday 25 March, 6.25 p.m.

Cecilia walked, even though her head floated, ground shifting beneath her. She was dimly aware of a hollow sound, a clack, clack, clack. Her heart beating a little faster, looking for that sound in amongst the cacophony of a ruined plane. But it was just her shoes, heels against scuffed hospital linoleum. There were people, so many of them.

It was the first time she had left the house, the first time she had left her bed, since the memorial. Hadn't spoken to Tom on the drive home, had stared out of the window at the plunging mountains and the patchwork snow. She had opened the car door almost before it had stopped, engine thrumming in their half-empty street. Everyone at work or shopping or just living. And there she was, a ghost cutting through the middle of them. She had been out of the car, stepping too quickly, inappropriate shoes on slick tarmac. But then it felt like she was always falling now. She hadn't said goodbye to her husband, hadn't looked at him.

269

Her head was still too full of the people waiting for the ones never coming back.

She had wanted a shower. Needed one. The grief clung to her skin like cigarette smoke. Skin crawling. Seemed like she couldn't breathe. If she could just take a shower. But the key shook in her hand, the lock moving so that she couldn't catch it. The revving of an engine, loud, then growing softer and softer, until Tom was gone and she was alone, standing in the snow.

She shouldn't be here. Shouldn't be anywhere. Shouldn't have been one of the thirteen survivors. The lucky thirteen, the media were calling them. Lucky.

She had finally managed to open the front door. Had stumbled up the stairs, across the landing, into the room that was now her bedroom. Had swallowed two of the tablets, the ones they gave her at the hospital. Looked longingly at the rest. Then the world was swimming, fuzzy at the edges.

She had slept, on and off, through the intervening days. Waking just to use the bathroom, take another couple of tablets and wait for them to sink her into unconsciousness again. Had a dim recollection of Tom coming into the room, leaving behind a plate of toast, butter pooling on its surface, tea, curls of steam dancing from it.

Then, this morning, she had awoken with a start. Maisie. She had forgotten Maisie. She had said that she would visit, was supposed to have gone yesterday, or was it the day before? And she hadn't, hadn't even rung. She had felt a splurge of guilt, that unsettling feeling of yet another failure settling in her stomach.

She was in the car and driving before she realised what she was doing. Hadn't really paid attention to the journey, the car steering itself into the hospital car park. Back to the place where she could be a better version of herself. Where there was some hope, a chance that she could do something, be someone worthy of the title. *Lucky thirteen.*

She didn't wait for the lift. Turned into the stairwell. Quiet here, footsteps echoing. She could have rung the helpline, should have rung the helpline. Found out the latest information, a gift for Maisie in lieu of flowers. Instead she was going emptyhanded, a sick feeling in the pit of her stomach, wondering if her presence alone could possibly be enough.

Through the double doors. Nurses with brittle, bright faces. Visitors smiling, because you have to make an effort after all, even here. They glance at her, curious, at her arm and the bruising, a sickening yellow now above her eye. Quiet mutters. It's another one. One of the lucky thirteen. They look at her, judging, and they can see that something has gone wrong, that a mistake has been made. Shouldn't be her. Should have been the stewardess with the fiancé who's crumbling from grief without her. Or the mother and her little girl. Or Ernie.

She turned into the ward.

The curtain was closed around Maisie's bed. Visitors huddled across the room, quiet conversations punctured by the sobs that tore from behind the curtain. They were trying not to look up, not wanting to intrude. But their gazes struggled, straining to wander back to the sound of crying.

Cecilia's feet had sunk, drowning in linoleum. Wanting to move, because people were looking at her now, and the whispers have chased her in here as well, only now they seem to be louder, so loud that they almost drown out the sobbing. Watching as the curtain twitched, a narrow nurse stepping out. Her lips were pursed, but then she realised that she was being watched, pulling them into a tight smile.

'You're here to see Maisie?'

Cecilia wondered why the woman didn't wear make-up. Foundation to cover the splaying fingers of rosacea. Lipstick to fill out famine-thin lips. Then she wondered what would be the point. She nodded, couldn't seem to speak.

'That's good. That's good.' She lowered her voice, leaning closer to Cecilia, so that all she could smell was breath mints and grandmother perfume. 'Just had some bad news. She'll be glad to see you. Needs her friends.'

The sobbing had blurred now, becoming a low moaning.

Cecilia stared at her, and it seemed that her brain

272

wasn't working, that she couldn't seem to piece things together. 'What?'

The nurse looked at her, hard, as if struggling to believe that anyone could be so stupid. Then glancing down at the arm and up at the bruise, and realising. Face softening, taking her companionably by the arm, the good one, pulling her further away from the bed.

'It's her husband. Ernie? They found him. Poor love. We guessed that this was coming. I mean, you try to prepare them, but what can you say? She really thought that he would make it.'

Looking at Cecilia, expectant. As if she thinks that she can do something. As if anything she could ever do could make a difference.

Cecilia stepped back, pulling her arm free.

'Are you all right?'

She stared at her, almost laughed. *Am I all right?* Lucky thirteen. An entire life swamped in the guilt of a dead baby, the recollection of Eddie's rough hands violently pulling at her, breath sweet with alcohol, so close to her that she would wake up, night after night after night, and want to scream, but she can't scream because there's another man asleep next to her, and another child, one who lived, asleep down the corridor. And she's awoken in a life she barely recognises, with someone else calling her Mummy, and what the hell is she supposed to do with that? Then, when it all finally gets too much, when there's no sleep at all any more and food chokes her and touch makes her want to die, she runs away, only to tumble from the sky like a wounded bird, falling straight back into the life she has tried so hard to escape.

'No. I'm not.'

She turned away from the nurse, walking quickly towards the sound of Maisie's sobs.

CHAPTER 39

Tom: Sunday 25 March, 6.26 p.m.

There were flames climbing their way up the red wooden door, tongues of fire licking, tasting. The snow lit up crimson, scarred an acrid black. The heat rolled, barrelling outwards so that the knot of people gathered in the street recoiled, turning their heads towards the cold night. A sound like champagne corks popping, the tinkle of glass, and clouds of dense smoke billowing from the now-shattered windows. The police tape had been taken down this morning.

'Shit.' Tom pulled his radio free from his jacket pocket, toggling it to send. 'DC Allison, I've got a fire at the residence of Libby Hanover. We just released it as a crime scene. I'm going to need the fire service, quick as they can.'

The crinkle of static. 'Received. Casualties?'

'Negative. House was empty.' But there was something, a nudge at the edge of his consciousness that made him hesitate. Scanning the street. What had he seen? Then a break in the crowd, a tiny movement, and he saw the car. A silver Audi,

275

an A5, paintwork bubbling under the force of the heat. 'Shit.'

'Repeat last, please?'

'There's, shit, there's someone inside.'

'Oh my God!' He had forgotten that Hannah was there, standing in the snow, hand clasped to her mouth. 'That's Jim's car. He's not . . .'

'Is there a back way?'

Seemed to take her a lifetime to answer, the nod, and she turned, hurrying through her own house, the living room, kitchen, footsteps clacking on tiles, pushing open the back door, down into the garden, still ankle-deep in snow. Quieter, just the distant crackle of flames. She tugged on the back garden gate, frozen shut, one final tug and it fell open, dislodging a flurry of snow, spitting them into a private car park, small, lined with garden gates made from cheap wood, warping with the weather.

'That one, on the left.'

Tom pushed past her, slushing through thick snow. Tried the gate handle, twisting, then pressing his shoulder against the wood, bracing, a shove and it tumbled inwards. The garden was quiet, quilted heavy with white. There was a light on in the kitchen, the blinds open, pooling the patio with an orange glow. Tom's stomach lurched, and he strained, trying to see signs of life through fingers of smoke. There was the spike of a chair back, folds of fabric hanging down until they scraped the ground. A glint of light, metal reflecting. Car keys left on the table.

Tom's stomach knotted, fingers grasping the handle of the patio doors, pressing down as hard as he could, but there was nothing, no give. 'Shit.' He banged hard on the glass with balled-up fists. 'Hey. Jim? Jim.'

The concrete slabs of the patio were buried in white. Snowdrifts clambering over twisted iron furniture. Tom turned, pushing his way through the snow. There must be something. Fingers questing in the dark.

The chimenea was heavy, ice-cold wrought iron. Tom grabbed for it, fingers burning from the touch of the cold metal. Hefted it and swung, bringing it down hard on the glass of the doors. Hitting with a *whump*, a line of fracture creeping across the glass. Swinging it back again so that his shoulders screamed in their sockets, back around, *whump*. The glass gave, shattering, clouds of grey barrelling outwards, smothering Tom in acrid smoke. He heaved, fingernails clawing at the inside of his throat. Turning, swinging the chimenea again, widening the hole. Dark smoke flooded out, the dam breaking. Tom pulled at his jacket, yanking it up over his mouth, trying not to breathe. Ducked in through the opening.

There was no light. No air. Just black smoke. A searing heat that burned him on the inside. He tried to call out, but when he opened his mouth the smoke poured in, an avalanche of poison.

Grabbing on to anything he could, fingers wrapping themselves around the back of a chair, running across walls, questing, an opening, a doorway. Hotter here, unbearably hot. Dropping, whether because he chooses it or because he simply cannot remain upright he doesn't know, on to his hands and knees, crawling on linoleum that burns when he touches it, carpet.

So hot, the house itself seemed to be shoving him backwards, driving him out. Tom ducked lower to the ground, pushing onwards.

Can't breathe. Seemed like he couldn't think. And now he's gripped with fear that he's made a terrible error, that there's no one here at all, that he will die needlessly, that he will leave Ben alone.

Then he saw it, a movement so small that he shouldn't have been able to see it at all. Pulled himself forward towards it. Fingers crawling across carpet, feeling the tread of the staircase, then something soft, yielding. A hand that closed around his.

Tom gripped the hand, lifting himself up, even though it's hotter, and now there's a pillow over his face, pressing down on him. Moving his fingers forward until he feels arms, the hard line of a chin. Gripping the arms, wrapping his fingers so tight that they scream with pain, and then pulling, pulling.

Seems like nothing's happening, that there's no movement, and he feels a moment of despair, that he's too late. Then Jim's body gives, so suddenly that Tom almost tumbles backwards.

Tom's chest was trapped in a vice. Couldn't see,

didn't bother trying, just inching backwards the way he had come, away from the worst of the heat, back to where there was air. Arms, shoulders, back, all screaming that he can't do this, *he's too heavy, you can't breathe, just drop, just give up, get out.* He gripped Jim's arms tighter, pulled harder. Inching backwards, carpet giving way to tile, and then, finally, the smoke becoming lighter, grey not black.

Tiles grainy under his feet, crunching on shards of glass, then a searing pain across his arm, and he stumbled against the door frame. Almost falling, catching himself.

He gave a final tug, yanking Jim's lifeless body through the remains of the shattered door.

Blissfully cold snow, air rushing into his lungs, and he turned, vomiting. Hands wrapping themselves around his shoulders. A voice that comes from a long way away.

'It's okay. You're going to be okay.'

CHAPTER 40

Freya: Sunday 25 March, 11.03 p.m.

Freya stared at the leaping flames. A blue-checked blanket was pulled across her legs. She still cradled the phone. Had dialled the number five times, six. She would be breaking a man's heart, she knew that. And he would hate her for it. But it would be better, in the end. Not questioning for whom. Had punched the numbers in, wondering just how many times her father had done the same thing, calling this man's wife. The phone had rung and rung.

She should probably go to bed. Her grandparents had gone up hours ago, her mother earlier still. But still she sat there, the television flashing a cacophony of colours in the darkened room, volume low. Some eighties comedy, a late-night special.

She had come in from the car, could hear her grandparents' voices in the kitchen. Richard was out, had left earlier that afternoon, said that he was going to get together with some friends, and Freya had been relieved, hoping that her brother's

280

friends could help him with his grief where she could not. She had paused in the dimly lit hallway, listening to her grandparents argue about something and nothing. Then, slowly, she had taken the stairs.

The light was off in the spare room. Freya had hung on the landing, almost turning around. But then she knew that was never really an option. Slowly, she had twisted the handle, hearing it scree loudly in the darkness.

'Mum?'

'What is it, Freya?'

The curtains were open. Her mother was lying in the bed, head tilted on stacked-up pillows, staring out of the window at the stars.

'Are you okay?' Freya asked.

Her mother didn't answer for the longest time, then sighed heavily. 'I guess.'

'Mum?'

'Yes?'

'I . . . I need to ask you something.'

'Okay.'

'Dad . . . was he . . .' How the hell did you say it, how did you even form the words?

'Was he what, Freya?' Her mother's voice had taken on a glassy edge.

Freya hovered in the doorway. It wasn't too late. She could say, *Nothing*, turn and leave. Her mother wouldn't bring it up again, because that was just the way they were. 'Mum, I found the bag. In the car.'

'What bag?'

'I . . . The bag. With the . . . I found the picture, too. The one in his bedside cabinet.'

Her mother didn't answer, just let the room fill with a soupy silence. 'I asked you not to go in there.'

'I know,' she said. 'Mum? You knew, didn't you?'

A heavy sigh. 'Freya . . .'

The word hung there for so long that Freya didn't think she would say any more.

'Freya, please just let it go.'

Freya stood, absorbed the implication. 'You knew?'

'It's done. It's over. It's been . . . it's over. Your father . . . he loved me, Freya. Me. Just let it go now.' Her mother had turned then, had pulled the quilt up over her head.

Freya had wanted to cry.

The fire in the grate crackled and bounced. Freya shivered. Seemed like she just couldn't get rid of the chill. Looked down at the phone, pressing the numbers again. She knew them by heart now. Couldn't shake the feeling that the answers were right there, at the end of the line. What would make her father do something so horrific? What had happened to him, on that last day? She couldn't let it go. Couldn't shake this fear that had begun to build in her. It had burrowed under her skin like an addiction, nerve endings craving the truth. Nothing, still hopeless ringing.

Then there was a sound, the creaking of floorboards. Didn't know how she knew it was Richard, but she knew it anyway. Just a little boy driven from sleep by the death of his father. There was a feeling in her stomach when she thought of him, something that felt suspiciously like guilt. She should have taken better care of him.

'Hey, Frey.'

Richard's hands were tucked into his pockets, eyes brighter than she had expected.

'Hi.' Freya smiled. Seeing him hidden in the shadow of the trees. The woman with the chestnut hair, cradling her injured arm. Recognising that look; had spent her life seeing it in him every time their father was near. A poisonous mixture of adoration and fear. 'You okay?'

'Yeah,' he said. 'Thanks.' He sank to the couch. 'What are you watching?'

'Nothing much. Just waiting for the news. So, you're okay?'

'Yeah. It's cold out there.'

Freya watched her brother. His hands folded in his lap, leaning forward, all awkward angles, and for the most fleeting of moments she wanted to ask him why he has done what he has done. Then the light changed and she remembered, the son rather than the father. She looked back at the television.

'It was cold at the memorial.' Her voice came out light, airy almost.

'Mmmm.' He rubbed his eyes, his smile fleeting. 'It's stopped snowing, anyway.'

Freya nodded. 'Rich?'

'Yeah?'

'Why didn't you come with us?'

He wasn't looking at her, had sunk back into the sofa, staring at the television. 'I don't know. Just . . .' A shrug. 'Couldn't face it, I guess.'

'But you came on your own.'

'Changed my mind.'

'Oh.'

They sat there, for long moments. Richard not looking at her, staring at the TV. Something had filled the room, the sense of words waiting to be said. Freya watched her brother. Waiting.

'Frey?'

'Yeah?'

'I miss him.' That was it, the bursting of the dam. He looked back at her, eyes swimming, looking so much younger now, and she wanted to cry herself with pain, frustration.

'I know, honey.' She pulled him to her, his words dissolving into little-boy sobs, his tears trickling warm along her collarbone.

'Why . . . why did it have to happen?'

Freya bit her lip, could feel heat stinging the back of her eyes. 'I don't know, Rich. I really don't know.'

'I didn't . . . I . . . Dad . . . He . . .' Then there

were no more words, or none that she could make out at least. Just wrenching, tearing sobs.

Freya cradled her brother. Wanted to tell him it was all going to be all right. But now she was thinking about that family holiday they took in Florida, the one where they got stuck in the hotel because of a looming hurricane, trying to entertain themselves with jigsaw puzzles and reruns of kids' shows that they didn't really get. And her father. Telling them it was an adventure. Saying it would be a great story to tell when they got home. Making them cry laughing with his efforts at charades, and, when the wind picked up and the sky darkened and they had become scared, pulling them all under the duvet on the king-size bed – Freya, Richard, her mother and him – telling them stories by torchlight. Being the father that she had always wanted.

Tears built up behind her eyes, rolled down her cheeks, and she kissed the top of her brother's head. 'I miss him too, kiddo.' And it didn't feel like a lie.

It took long minutes for the sobs to subside. Finally, Richard pushed himself up, scrubbing at his eyes with the balled-up sleeve of his jumper.

Freya watched him. Didn't bother to wipe away her own tears. Felt good to have them there. 'Rich. You can't keep all this stuff to yourself. You keep locking yourself in your room. You need to be able to talk to someone.'

He didn't answer, then glanced sideways at her. 'I am talking to someone. There's a lady. She's been nice to me. She . . .' He looked down. 'She was on Dad's plane.'

Then Freya remembered the churchyard and the yew tree. 'You're talking about the woman at the memorial?'

He was looking at her now, startled. 'How did you . . .?'

'I saw you. Saw you looking at her.'

He nodded. 'Do you think it's weird? I . . . I can't talk to Mum, because, well . . . you know. But this woman, I can tell her stuff and she gets it because she was there.'

Another spasm of guilt, because that should have been her role, the big sister. But she'd been distracted, hadn't she? Had been chasing ghosts while her brother struggled. 'Of course it's not weird.' She could ask him now; the lid was so tentatively closed that all it would take would be a little nudge, a gentle poke, and it would spill out of him. And that was her job. She was his sister. But on the television beyond him, the credits were rolling. Any second now the news would start. She didn't want him to see it. Didn't want him to get hurt once more.

'Rich, you're shattered.' She kissed his forehead again. 'Why don't you pop off to bed?'

He sat there for a moment, then pushed himself up. 'Yeah. I think I will go to bed. You going too?'

286

'In a few minutes. You go on. I'll see you in the morning. And Rich?'

'Yeah?'

'You can always talk to me, too.'

He stood for a moment, considering. 'I know. Who do you talk to, Frey?'

Freya shrugged, aiming for nonchalance, feeling like she missed it. 'I'm tough. I can handle myself.'

Richard smiled. 'You need a boyfriend, sis.' Then he leaned over, kissed her cheek and trudged slowly up the stairs.

Freya stared into space for a moment. Thinking about her brother's words. But then a flash from the TV caught her and she was trapped in a moment of dislocation. Seeing herself, with her arm around her mother, in their dark suits, their tight faces, standing in the snow like a bleak Christmas card. The camera zooming in on her mother, looking like death. She reached for the remote control, turning up the volume.

'. . . families mourning the victims of downed Flight 2940. Investigations into the cause of the crash are still ongoing.'

Then the image changed, and now there is a house ablaze – one of those box houses, starter homes, on a cardboard cut-out estate. Another everyday disaster.

'. . . former police superintendent Jim Hanover is in a serious condition in Morriston hospital after being trapped in a fire at his daughter's home.

Officers are still investigating the murder of Mr Hanover's daughter, Police Community Support Officer Libby Hanover.'

Freya looked back at the television. There was a photograph on the screen. A young woman with a wide smile, chestnut hair. The woman in the picture.

CHAPTER 41

Tom: Monday 26 March, 1.38 p.m.

Tom's footsteps echoed, rebounding from pastel hospital walls. A gentle skip, skip step, in harmony with his own. Ben's head swivelling, left to right, running along walls, across chairs, a lean to glance out of the window into the courtyard below. Clinging to his father's hand.

'You okay, bud?'

'Yes. Daddy?'

'Yeah, mate?'

'Is your friend sick?'

Turning the corner into the ward, doors flung wide open, the low beeping of machines, forgotten flowers.

'He is. He'll be okay, though.'

'Oh.' Ben skipped a little, dancing across zigzag cracks in the linoleum. 'Does he have a cough like you?'

Tom's throat throbbed, chest pulling at itself. It had been late when he had picked Ben up, a little after ten, even though the doctors had wanted to keep him in, because *You can't be too careful, your body has been through a lot, just to be on the safe side.* Had smiled and nodded and then said, *No. I'm going home to my son.* Had picked up Ben's sleeping form, breathing him in, even though his insides felt scrubbed raw, his shoulder screaming where they had stitched it.

Cecilia had been asleep when they returned. He hadn't bothered to wake her.

'You've got to be extra quiet, okay, bud?'

Ben's shoes squealed across the floor. ''Kay. Daddy?'

'Yeah?'

'I love my Mickey.'

'I'm glad.'

It was Ben's birthday. Today. The little boy had awoken fizzing with an excitement that he was too young to identify. Had wandered around the pile of presents, looking up at his father, back down at the brightly wrapped gifts, bemused. Tom had bought Ben's birthday presents weeks ago, seemed like the only lone father in the store. The assistant had offered him a sympathetic smile as he paid for the dancing Mickey Mouse, assuming that he was divorced, a weekend dad. He'd returned it tepidly.

The ward was quiet, nearly empty. Esther looked like she hadn't slept. She balanced on the hard plastic chair, tilted forward so that her elbows pressed into the hospital bed, fingers steepled in supplication. Her forehead rested on her fingertips. Jim's eyes were closed, breathing strained.

'Esther?'

She started, nerves frayed by too much pressure, spinning quickly in her chair. Looking at Tom, eyes fearful, wondering what fresh hell he was bringing her. Then her gaze dropped to his son, her expression softening. 'Hi. Hi, Tom.'

'How is he?' Tom nodded towards Jim's sleeping form.

'He's . . . okay. He'll be in for a little while. Smoke inhalation.' Esther's voice piano-wire taut, trying not to cry. 'And who is this handsome man?' A smile that she is trying very hard to mean.

'This is Ben. Ben, this is Esther.'

'Hi.' Ben was watching her, a glance up to his father, to the man sleeping in the bed.

'Buddy, could you do me a favour? Just pop yourself in that chair right over there for two minutes, okay? Right there by the TV. I just need a quick chat with Esther.'

''Kay.' His son nodded blithely, walked away in that meandering manner that toddlers have.

They didn't speak for a moment, watched him pull himself up into the chair. Crossing his arms across his chest like he was seventy years old.

'He's lovely,' Esther said.

'Thank you. Esther,' Tom pulled a chair forward, sitting down next to her, 'there's something I

291

need to ask you about the night Libby was murdered.'

Saw her recoil, bitten by the words.

'Okay.'

'Do you know where your son was?'

She stared at him for a moment, then sighed heavily. 'You know about the argument.'

Tom watched her, feeling a pulse of something akin to anger. 'I do. What I want to know is why I didn't hear about it from you.'

Esther shook her head. 'I should have told you. I know. But I knew what you would think. I know what he would have thought.' Nodding towards Jim, breathing still even. 'You know, if he was in your position.' She looked down at her fingers. 'You need to understand. Ethan's been going through a really rough time. This job, it's all he ever wanted. He's been telling me that since he was five. He tried to be happy for Libby, when she got what he wanted, but you could tell that it really stung. Then when he realised he was never going to get it . . . I'll be honest, he fell apart a bit. I know that he had a go at Libby. He told me. But I also know that he didn't kill her.' Her voice cracked on the word.

'Esther . . .'

'No. He was at home. He told me.'

'Okay. But his wife wasn't there. So he has no one to vouch for that?'

Esther gave a small smile, eyes bright with tears. 'You'll learn, Tom. When that little boy is old enough to give you headaches. I know my son. Ethan loved Libby. He would never, *never* have hurt her.'

Tom nodded, looking down at his hands. 'Okay, Esther. You understand . . .'

'I understand. You're doing your job.'

'Daddy.' Ben had turned around, was half hanging off the chair.

'Yeah, Ben?'

'There's no 'toons on.' He bit his lip, watching Esther. 'It's my birfday. I got a Mickey.'

'You did? Well isn't that wonderful.'

Ben looked around the room, doubtful. 'Did you get presents?'

Tom smiled. 'He's having a little trouble with the whole birthday concept.'

'Well, I mean, who wouldn't? It's not my birthday, sweetheart.' Then Esther smiled, miniature fractures at the edges. 'I did get a present, though. He's right here. Your daddy gave him to me.' A quick glance at Tom, eyes filling.

'Hope you kept the receipt.' Jim's voice was thick, rough. Eyes bloodshot-red; he struggled to open them. 'How you doing, Tom?'

'I'm okay. You?'

'Yeah. I'll live. Thanks to you.'

Esther pushed herself up from the chair. 'Why don't we go get a milkshake, Ben? What do you say? Your daddy can talk to my husband and you can tell me all about what you got for your birthday.'

Ben watched Esther, considering. 'Can I have chocolate?'

She smiled. 'You are the birthday boy.'

''Kay.'

Tom watched as they walked away, Ben slipping his hand into Esther's. Cecilia had got up, had come down a little after nine, when they had already been up for hours. *Keep some of your presents, buddy. Wait until Mummy gets here.* Cecilia had poured herself coffee, buried herself in the corner of the sofa, her legs pulled up, staring into space. Ben had opened his presents. Tom doubted that Cecilia would have been able to name one of them.

'You saved my life.' Jim wasn't looking at him, watching the retreating form of his wife.

Tom shrugged, like it was nothing at all. 'Right time, right place.'

'Whatever it was, thanks.'

'Don't mention it.'

'Someone did it on purpose.' The way Jim said it, it sounded like a question. Even though it wasn't.

Tom nodded, leaning forward, his chest and his throat and his shoulder hurting. 'Fire investigator says yes. There was an accelerant, poured through the letter box. Probably petrol.'

Jim nodded, grimacing with the movement. 'I was upstairs. It was stupid. I shouldn't have been there. But Nat, he said they were releasing the scene and, I don't know, I just wanted to be

294

near her, you know? I told Esther I was popping out for milk. I lay down on her bed . . .' His voice trailed off. Tom looked away, not wanting him to say the rest: that he lay down to weep, resting his head where his daughter last rested hers. 'I guess I must have fallen asleep. I can't have been out long. Fifteen minutes, twenty maybe. The house phone woke me, but when I got to it there was no one there. I was, you know, disoriented, you know the way you are when something wakes you. But I remember hearing footsteps, someone running. That was when I smelled the smoke.'

'Did you see anything? Anything at all?'

Jim shook his head. 'No.' Scrubbed his hands across his face, turning to Tom, pleading almost. 'Who the hell would want to do this? Burn down her house? Hasn't she been through enough? Haven't *we* been through enough? Shit, when I think about it, if you hadn't been there, Jesus. Esther. I mean, what she's been through, and if I had gone too . . . doesn't bear thinking about.'

Tom nodded, like he understood. But the truth was, he had no idea. No notion what it was to have to wake up every morning, because your wife needed you. And you can push it back and push it back and pretend that you're doing the right thing, but you know and she knows that this isn't right and that it never has been, but you have become so used to pretending that you

295

forget it isn't real. That it wasn't supposed to be like this.

He didn't look at Jim, afraid that if he did then he would see. 'You're a good man, Jim.'

Jim laughed, a ravaged, throaty laugh. 'Yeah. Fucking saint, me.'

Tom's mobile rang, loud in the quiet room.

'Shit. Sorry.'

'Ah, answer. The Nazi nurses are doing handover.'

Tom grinned, hitting answer. 'DC Allison.'

'Hiya, Tom. It's Donna in the control room.'

'Hey, Don. How are you?'

'I'm good. I'm good. Look, Tom, I've got something on the Libby Hanover case. You're on call, right?'

He wasn't. He was supposed to be spending the day with his son like any normal man on his son's birthday. But Jim was watching him, expectation hanging in the air like storm clouds, and he can see it in his face, the longing that this is the call, that they will have answers for him, because that's the best that he can hope for now. His daughter is dead, and all he has left to hope for is the truth.

'Yeah. I am. Go ahead, Don.'

'We've had a call. A woman saying that she thinks her father was sleeping with Libby.'

'All right. Is this, ah, you know . . .'

'A crazy? I don't know. I don't think so.'

'Who is she?'

296

'Name's Freya Blake. She said her father's name was Oliver.'

Tom's stomach lurched, hairs on his arms standing on end. Watching Jim watching him. Not wanting to give too much away too soon, not until he knows and he is sure. 'You said was?'

'Yeah, was. She said that he was the pilot. The one who crashed the plane.'

CHAPTER 42

Cecilia: Monday 26 March, 5.55 p.m.

Cecilia shivered. The snow had stopped falling at last, leaving behind a black sky, pinpoint stars. She tucked her hands into the pockets of her coat, pulling the front door behind her. A careful tread on the path. The light pooled from the living room window. All looked so welcoming. Homely. She bowed her head, fighting back the drowning irony. More comfortable out here in the snow and the cold.

Richard stood at the end of the drive, folded in on himself.

She had stayed at the hospital until late. Holding Maisie's hand as she wept and wept. Cecilia didn't speak. What was there to say? So instead she sat. A fleeting thought: this must be what other mothers felt like. Holding their children while they cried, making the tears easier just by being there. Running her fingers along the veined ridges of the old woman's hands. Wondering why it was that she could do this here, be this here, and yet not at home, with her son. With her husband. But then, when you came right down to it, when you thought about it (although she generally tried very hard not to do that), wasn't her husband just one more man keeping her somewhere she didn't want to be? Would it have been different had Eddie never happened? If she had met Tom when she was a different person, less damaged and scarred. The wall wouldn't have been there, that gust of ice that swept the room whenever her husband came near her, touched her. That fear. Would it have been different then?

But she was what she was. And Eddie had happened and the baby had happened. And no matter how hard she tried, she was irretrievably scarred and damaged and scared.

The other visitors had left, faux-cheerful voices, flurries of goodbyes. The curtains moved, once, twice, nurses ducking their heads in, tight-lipped gazes falling on Maisie, Cecilia. Cecilia had ignored them. She didn't know how long it was before the tears dwindled, sobs beginning to ease.

Finally, when the ward was quiet, Maisie shifted. Seemed so small, a child buried in a mountain of pillows.

'I'll have to tell Caroline.' Her voice sounded raw, little more than a whisper. 'I'll have to ring her.'

'I can do that for you.' Cecilia felt a thrill of fear at her own words. 'I can ring her. If you want.'

Maisie had sunk back into the pillows, was watching Cecilia from what seemed to be a very long distance. 'Thank you, love. But it should be me.' A shuddering sigh. 'I don't know how I'm going to tell her. They were always so close.' She shook her head. 'Ernie always said I should try harder. Let my guard down a bit with her. I'm going to have to do better now.' Her voice strengthened at the end.

Cecilia started.

'What, love?'

'Nothing. I just . . .'

But Maisie shook her head, a brief smile. Saw it without Cecilia saying it. 'You thought I was going to lay down and die?'

'No, no . . .'

'Love, I don't get to give up. For whatever reason, God saw it as right that he take my Ernie. Now don't get me wrong, I don't agree with that, and believe you me, I'll be having a few words with the big man when I get up there myself. But that's where we are. So I've got to get on with it. And Ernie, he wouldn't like me giving up. Wouldn't like that at all.' She sighed deeply. 'No. You can't just give up. No matter how much you want to. You have to keep on trying. It's not over until you're dead.'

They had rung Maisie's daughter. A little after ten. Cecilia dialling the numbers with quick fingers, Maisie holding the receiver, shaking so badly it seemed inevitable that she would drop it. Cecilia listening as Maisie choked over the words, and then, when the chokes turned into fresh tears, taking the phone. The daughter's words barely audible through her own sobs. *I'll get the first flight I can. I'll be there in the morning.* A new urgency, now that it's too late.

She had left the hospital late. Wondering why it was that the world suddenly seemed to have a pulse, wondering where it had been hiding all these years. A feeling of recognition, suddenly realising that what she was seeing was a glimpse of the Cecilia she had been, too many years before. But then she had pulled up outside the house, and it was dark, empty, and the wrongness of it all had flooded back in. She had wanted to cry then. Had climbed into bed, in the room that she now thought of as hers, pulling the duvet over her head.

The sun had been high when she woke. Sky crystal blue. She had gone downstairs, thick-headed and thirsty. Ben was sitting, a bird on a nest of wrapping paper; he didn't look up at her, clumsy fingers rotating a plastic tool set. Toys littered the floor, new, shiny, and she felt sick. She should have got up, should have been here when he opened his birthday presents.

'Morning.' Tom's voice had sounded rough, a cough like he'd been smoking thirty a day for the last twenty years. 'I'll get you a coffee.' He glanced around. 'He kept some presents to open with you.'

Cecilia had looked at him, a thrill of some emotion that she couldn't identify. 'Thank you.' Watched Tom pushing himself up, movements awkward, pained. 'Are you okay?'

Tom had glanced at her, seemed surprised that she would ask. But then, she allowed, that was probably fair.

'I . . . yeah. There was an . . . incident, last night.'

'What kind of incident?'

He looked down. 'A fire.'

Then she's falling again, can smell the flames, feel the heat. A sickness rises through her. 'Oh.'

'It was in Libby's house. You know? The PCSO that was killed?'

She looked at him, a long look. Trying to make sense of the words. A PCSO? What did that have to do with the plane?

'You know, the murder I've been on?'

Was it her, or was there some impatience woven through the words? 'Oh. This fire. You were there?'

'Yes.' He paused, seemed like he was considering saying something else. 'I had to go in. There was . . . Her dad, he was inside.'

'So . . . you got him out?'

'Yeah. I guess.'

'Oh.' She looked down at her fingers. Another feeling swamping her. Her husband was a good man. Was, in fact, a hero. And here he was, stuck with her.

'I'll make that coffee. Ben, show Mummy what you got.'

She stared at her son in his Elmo pyjamas, hoisting wrapped boxes over his head, toddling towards her. Felt her stomach clench. Just stay here. Just for now. Don't think about anyone else.

Don't think about the other child. Just this one. Just for now. But it was creeping in, pulling at her. The hands, the pain, the smell of bins. And the baby she had killed.

She sank on to the sofa, pulling her knees up under, wrapping her arms tight around them.

She watched as he pulled the paper off a dancing Mickey Mouse, a train set, a jigsaw puzzle with oversized pieces. Wondered distantly what she had bought him. Then realised that it was probably all of it. That Tom had done it all. Felt the sinking sense of failure again.

'I . . . I was going to take him out later. If that's okay with you. I wanted to go visit Jim, the PCSO's dad. They kept him in hospital. Thought I'd take Ben to see him.' Tom had handed her coffee. 'If you don't mind.'

She had looked up at him, smiled. Had tried to hide her relief.

It was a little while after they had left when she stood, thinking that perhaps she would take a shower. Wash free the remains of this morning and perhaps find that feeling again, the one that she had found on the mountainside surrounded by the ruins of the burning plane, that had flickered as she held Maisie's hand. The memory of who she used to be. She had stopped, looking out of the window, sun just beginning to dip lower in the sky, light pooling orange on the standing snow. That was when she had seen Richard, standing across the road, part hidden behind number 72's four-by-four, like he was unsure that he wanted to be seen.

Cecilia had felt that feeling swell in her again, had pulled on boots and a coat. Had pushed open the front door, a blast of cold wind wrapping itself around her. Felt herself standing a little taller. Suddenly feeling like she mattered.

She waved to Richard. A fleeting look of panic crossed his face, and so she smiled to make him feel better, reassure him that she's here to help. So busy trying to be someone different that she forgets to wonder how he knows where she lives.

'Hi.'

'Hi.' He didn't look at her, scuffing his feet into the snow.

She should ask where his family was. Where was his mother? Then remembered Ben and the relief she had felt when Tom had said they were going out, and she wanted to cry.

'You . . . you're okay?' Cecilia asked, trying not to think about her son.

Richard didn't answer for a moment, still studying his feet. Then he nodded. 'I wanted to see you. I'm sorry. I know you have kids of your own. I shouldn't . . . I just . . . I'm sorry. It's just that I really needed to talk to someone. My sister, she said I should talk to her, but I can't tell her . . . and my mum . . . she hasn't got out of bed. You know, since. I mean, it's just different with you.'

Cecilia felt her chest inflate.

He had wrapped his arms around himself,

shivering. There were tears in his eyes. 'They don't know, you see . . . about Dad. About what it was like. But you know, 'cos you were there. With Dad, I mean, and you knew him so I can talk to you.'

Cecilia rubbed her forehead, sudden feeling like she had been drinking. 'I . . . I guess, but you know, there were an awful lot of passengers that day. I probably didn't even see him.'

Richard looked up at her. Frowning. 'He wasn't a passenger. He was the pilot.'

Cecilia stared at him, the dark eyes, the dark hair, and now instead of the boy it's the father before her, and it's not now, it's ten days ago, and they haven't taken off yet, but they're going to, and then they will fall and the world around them will spin away.

'You're Oliver's son.'

CHAPTER 43

Freya: Monday 26 March, 8.38 p.m.

There was singing, a yawning wail tumbling off-key, the high notes morphing into a shriek. A thud against the sepia-toned wall. Freya sipped water-weak coffee. Trying to pretend this was all normal. No big deal. Her hands were shaking. The room was spartan: a table, four straight-backed chairs cushioned with a thin layer of listless grey foam. It smelled of disinfectant, the faint acid of vomit. The guy across the table smiled at her. He looked like a rugby player, had the thick build, close-cropped hair the colour of her grandmother's mahogany table. But his navy blue eyes were soft, looked like he was just waiting to understand. Freya smiled back, imagined a paintbrush in her hand, moving in the rounded shape of his cheekbones. Then she shook her head, suddenly remembering why she was there.

'I'm sorry, Maddie. I feel awful asking you.' The other detective stood just beyond the open door to the interview room, his voice low, almost vanishing in the singing, the distant sound of

306

shouting. He stood, was rocking, back, forth. Looked like he didn't even know he was doing it. The little boy slept heavily on his shoulder, cheek marked by the cables on his father's sweater, curls flopping into his eyes.

'Don't be stupid. I need all the practice I can get. We'll be upstairs when you're done. Come here, little man.'

The child stirred, just slightly, head lolling as his father handed him to the woman, the one who had brought her coffee, apologising that she couldn't find any decent biscuits. *People working nights, we get depressed. So we eat all the chocolate digestives.* Patting her stomach, the gentle curve of early pregnancy. A laugh like rain on treetops.

The father watched them leave, his hands on his hips, tired, defeated.

She hadn't gone to bed. Had stayed curled on the sofa, staring at the dark television screen. Replaying it, over and over again. The girl's face. The dead girl's face. The crumbled buildings, a casket for a downed plane. This was too much, was more than she had bargained for. That was the thing about the truth, though, wasn't it? It came as it was, raw and unvarnished. Didn't stop to consider what you could handle, what you wanted to hear. Part of her wanted to bury her head beneath the cushions, pretend that she didn't know anything. Pretend that her world was stable and perfect, just what it should be. In other words, be just like her mother.

She would talk to someone, share it. That would make it easier. She had even stood up, head swimming with lack of sleep, before she realised that there was no one. Her brother was too young, too raw with grief. There was her grandfather. She could talk to her grandfather. Had felt a soaring relief, then an immediate plunging as she thought of her grandmother. She had sunk back down to the sofa, finally falling asleep, sometime around dawn.

'You okay?' asked the detective.

It must have been in her face, the isolation, the sudden sparking of fear that she was in far deeper than she had ever meant to go. The rugby player watched her, features concerned. 'Can I get you anything?'

Freya shook her head, smiled. 'I'm okay. I'm okay.' If she kept saying it, she would start to believe it.

'Yeah?' He glanced up as the other man closed the door, dimming the wailing to a dull roar. 'Freya, this is DC Allison, Tom. I'm Dan. Dan Terrill.'

'Hi, I'm sorry about that.' The man with the little boy gave her a tired smile. He looked like a policeman, even though he didn't wear the uniform. He wore the build. Skinny. Upswept shoulders, like they were balancing the weight of the world on top of them, poker-player face, creased with lines of worry.

'That's okay. Your son?' Freya gestured to the closed door.

He nodded, pulling a chair out from beneath the table. 'I don't normally bring him to work.'

'How old is he?'

'Three.'

Then a splurge of guilt. Her determination, her stubbornness. Wasn't it all about her, when you came right down to it? Her need to know. And now that she knew, or thought that she knew, only now was she starting to understand the cost. To her family, who would buckle under the weight of all this truth. Even to these men, staying late to talk to her. 'I'm so sorry. It's late. I should have waited until tomorrow.'

'No, no.' The rugby player, Dan, smiled. He was handsome when he smiled. 'We're very glad you called. Besides,' a lopsided grin, 'there's nothing good on TV tonight.'

Freya smiled back, momentarily soothed. She looked at the skinny man, the one with the little boy, and felt something, tickling at the edge of her consciousness. 'I, I'm sorry. I know you, don't I? Weren't you at the memorial yesterday?'

The detective, Tom, nodded grimly. 'My wife. She was on board. Flight attendant.'

Freya felt her stomach drop, suddenly felt like a child playing Cluedo, confronted with a real murder. 'I'm so sorry.'

'No, no. She's . . . She made it. A broken arm. Some bruises. She was lucky.'

Then she realised. The woman with the chestnut hair. Richard's new friend. The proximity of

everything threw her. 'Oh, of course, my brother
. . .' Suddenly realised what she was saying, how
ridiculous it would sound. *My seventeen-year-old
brother has befriended your model wife.* 'My, ah, my
brother, he was there too. I mean, not there. He
didn't come in. He stayed outside, under the tree.'
She flushed. 'I'm sorry, I'm rambling.'

The detective frowned. 'Dark-haired boy? He was
wearing jeans?'

'That's him. He couldn't face coming in. It's
been a lot for him. For all of us.'

The two men nodded in unison, like they'd been
practising it, and then there was an awkward
silence.

'You said you thought your dad knew Libby?'
Dan asked, tone tentative.

'Yes. I think so.'

She could forget about it, pretend that she didn't
know. Wasn't that what their family did? After all,
she didn't know that she was right. She could be
wrong. She must be wrong.

'What makes you say that?' Dan leaned across
the desk, coaxing the words out of her.

'There was a picture, the two of them together.
I knew . . .' Freya pulled in a deep breath of
stale air. 'He had affairs. My mum, she has
always tried to pretend it wasn't happening . . .
I mean, she always did. But I knew, deep down. I
think she thought she was doing it for us.' Didn't
know why she was saying this, couldn't stop the
words from spilling out. 'Me and my brother.

But after this . . . I mean, you can't live like that, can you? Pretending all the time.' She shook her head, suddenly uncomfortable. This wasn't why she was here. 'I'm sorry, I, he just died, so it's a, a tough time, I guess.' She rubbed her eyes, was surprised to find them damp, suddenly.

'It's okay. Take your time.' Dan was watching her, and there was this look about him, like he understood, like he got it. And she wanted to blurt it all out, all of the stuff that was in there that had been hers and hers alone.

'Freya, your father's name . . .' Tom's fingers were twitching, like he was nervous.

'Oliver. Oliver Blake.'

'And what car did he drive?'

'A Mercedes, S-class. Navy blue.' An image sprung to her mind of the immaculate car, plunging her hands into the side pockets, the boot. That smell. 'I looked in it. After I found this picture of my father and this woman. I wanted to, I don't know, I guess I wanted to find out who she was. What had happened. And there was . . . there was this smell. It was, I don't know, like meat gone off, something rotten. And . . .' she looked down. Couldn't believe what it was that she was about to say, 'there were stains.' Shook her head. 'I'm sure it's nothing. It's nothing. I just . . .' A quick, uneasy laugh. 'I'm watching too many crime dramas.' The men glanced at each other; her stomach flipped. 'There was something else, in the boot. A sports bag. It had things in it. I guess, I

311

think he must have hidden them there, you know, so my mother wouldn't see. Phone bills, credit card receipts. I called one of the numbers. I assumed it was hers – the PCSO's – he rang it every day. But I got a man instead.'

The detectives started, staring at her, and she wondered what it was she had said.

'When was this?' Dan asked.

'Last night. Maybe around six, ten past.'

The two men glanced at each other, something transmitted that she didn't understand.

'Ah, Freya, you said there was a picture?' Tom asked.

'Yes. I have it. Do you . . .?'

'Please.'

Freya pulled her rucksack out from underneath the table, fingers shaking, head seeming to swim. 'I have the other papers too. Phone bills. Hotel receipts.' Pulled them free from the bag, slipping them on to the table. And there, at the bottom, the glove. Her mother's glove. She could leave that. That wouldn't matter. They wouldn't be interested in an odd glove.

'Everything okay?' asked Tom.

'Yeah, I . . .' She could forget about it. She could just forget. She reached back into the bag. 'I'm sure this isn't relevant. I mean, I don't know why I brought it.' She pulled the glove free, laying it out on the table in front of her.

It sat there. Seemed like it sucked up all of the

oxygen in the room. The quality of the air changed, charged now with electricity.

'Where did you get this?' Tom reached for it, hand hovering over it, not touching.

'The bag. It was in the bag with all of the papers and stuff. The one in the boot of my dad's Mercedes. I don't know where the other one is.'

The men were looking at each other. Seemed that she was missing something.

'I don't even know why he had it.'

'What do you mean?' asked Dan, gently.

'Well, the gloves. They're my mother's.'

CHAPTER 44

Tom: Monday 26 March, 10.38 p.m.

'Fuck.'

'Yeah.'

'I mean . . . fuck.' Dan sat forward in the chair, then a quick turn, glancing over his shoulder at the DS's office, the row of padded chairs, Ben's small figure huddled beneath his father's coat. 'Shit, sorry, mate.'

Tom smiled, weary, waved his apologies away. 'He's sleeping.'

'They're sure?' DI Maxwell leaned against the door frame.

'The air accident investigator said it'll take some time. Pilot suicide is a big conclusion. But the guy I spoke to said that he'd put his pension on it. Off the record, mind.'

'Jesus.' The DI scrubbed at his face. 'What a fucking mess.'

'Tell me.' Tom was drinking coffee, strong and stewed, sitting too long on the hot plate. He took a sip, grimacing. 'I've sent the glove to Forensics. We'll get Oliver Blake's toothbrush and a hairbrush, for comparison. I would also be very interested in talking to the wife.'

'The daughter's sure? That the gloves are her mother's? I mean, they're like those unisex ones, yeah?'

Tom shrugged. 'She says so. Says she bought them for her. I don't know. I mean, it's got a ring to it. The wife finds out her husband's been having an affair, goes after the mistress.'

'Woman scorned and all that crap,' offered Dan.

'Yeah.' Tom thought for a moment. 'The only problem I've got is, how the hell did she get Libby's body down to the riverbank? I mean, that was a fair walk and one hell of a climb down. So, unless this woman is built like a brick shit house . . .'

'Or . . .'

'Or,' finished Tom, 'she had help.'

The office was quiet, just the three of them left. *I can stay, if you need me to,* Maddie had offered, had stroked Ben's hair. *He's a poppet, Tom.* He had smiled, his heart clenching. *You go. It's late. Go home. You're sure? I'm sure. We'll be fine.* Had tucked his coat around his son, turning so that he wouldn't watch her walk away.

'Where's the daughter now?' asked the DI.

'She's downstairs. She's just freshening up. I said I'd give her a lift home.' Dan was looking at his desk as he spoke, moving papers around aimlessly.

Tom watched him. Smiling.

'I'll pick up Oliver Blake's hairbrush, toothbrush, that kind of thing. And I called the garage,' added

Dan. 'Tow truck is going to meet me at the house to collect Oliver Blake's car.'

The DI nodded. 'All right. Jesus. Right, good job, guys. I mean it. You worked your arses off. You've put the second glove into the lab on a quick turnaround, yeah? Let's wait and see what Forensics have for us and we'll take it from there. Go home. We'll pick this up again in the morning.'

'Cheers, boss.'

Dan watched the DI leave. Then sighed, shook his head. 'Jesus.'

'Yeah.' Tom looked down at his coffee. 'So, ah, you're giving her a lift home?'

'Yeah, well, you know. She came on the bus. And, you know, what with it being so late and the service will be rubbish . . .' He was flushing, cheeks turning pink. Then he looked up. 'Oh, piss off.'

Tom grinned. 'No. I hear you. I mean, the buses. They're shit.' A pause. 'She seems nice, mate.'

Dan didn't look at him. Just nodded. 'Yeah. She does. Must have been through hell.' He sighed. 'And it's about to get worse, poor bugger. So, how are things at home?'

Tom took another sip of the coffee. Really did taste like shit. He didn't answer for a moment, thinking about Jim staring at his dead daughter, about Ben, looking to his father to tell him the right way to live. Thinking about their home, stuffed with so much silence that you could barely breathe.

'It's rubbish, mate.'

Dan pursed his lips. Nodded slowly. 'Yeah. I figured.'

'We're a mess. We don't speak. Hardly look at one another.'

'Since the crash?'

'Since forever.'

'Oh.' Dan was watching him now. 'You never said.'

'I know.' Tom smiled. Didn't really feel like it. 'Didn't know what to say.'

'Then why . . .'

'Why have I stayed?'

'Yeah. Ben?'

'Partly. Partly because . . . it's just what you do, isn't it? When you're married.'

'Not for a lot of guys. A lot of guys would be long gone. Most, probably.'

'Yeah, well . . . I didn't want to be like that.'

'Your dad?'

Tom almost laughed. 'Jesus, Dr Phil.'

'I'm saying, is all. I know you two've got issues.'

'You could say.'

Dan shook his head. 'So what are you going to do?'

Tom leaned back against the chair, not looking at Dan, staring at a spot somewhere above his head where the windows are dark and the snow has stopped and somewhere in amongst all the blackness he can see stars. 'It's got to end, mate.'

Glanced back over his shoulder, at his sleeping son. 'For him and for her. It's got to end.'

'Yeah.' Dan nodded slowly, thoughtful.

They didn't say anything for long, quiet moments, because what do you say after something like that? Dan was watching him, waiting for something more. But there wasn't anything. Tom was spent.

Finally he pushed himself up, digging his elbows into the desk. 'There's one thing I don't get.'

'What's that?' asked Dan

'Who the hell set fire to the house?'

CHAPTER 45

Cecilia: Tuesday 27 March, 12.55 a.m.

Cecilia was sitting on the sofa, legs crossed, heeled boots resting on wooden floorboards. An encyclopedia salesman in a customer's home. The television was on, even though she wasn't watching it: flashing lights that looked like fire. They weren't home yet, Ben and Tom. She wondered distantly where they were. Wondered if she should call. But she didn't. Because it wasn't what they did and it wasn't the way they were and old habits die hard. So instead she sat, waited, even though she wasn't really sure what it was she was waiting for.

She had stood in the snow earlier, staring at Richard, feeling like the world had turned upon itself. Had she known that he was Oliver's son? Should she have known? Was there a protocol as to what you did next? Ring his mother perhaps. He had mentioned a sister . . . but he was standing in the snow, shaking with cold, so she had pulled him into the house. Made him a cup of tea.

'Did you speak to him? My dad.'

'I, um . . .' Cecilia hadn't looked at him, had concentrated on pouring the boiling water into the cup, paying more attention than she would have normally. 'Yes. I guess.'

'What did he say?' His fingers had gripped the kitchen counter; he looked like he was afraid he would fall down without it.

'Nothing.' She had turned away from him, pulling milk from the fridge. 'I just, I mean, you know, just the usual. We didn't *talk* talk.' She poured the milk slowly, keeping her eyes averted so that he wouldn't see that she was lying.

'So he seemed all right to you. He wasn't . . . I mean, you weren't worried?'

How to tell the boy dripping melted snow on her kitchen floor that she couldn't have been worried because she had barely noticed his father? Had known Oliver too long, had learned to look beyond his charm and his patter. How did you tell someone that you weren't worried because, in truth, you hadn't cared? Because you were running away from your son and that was all you would ever care about again.

'No.' She had handed him the tea. 'I wasn't worried.'

Cecilia didn't hear the car pulling into the drive, the key in the lock. Just the front door swinging open, her husband cradling her son, sagging under the weight of a dead sleep. Tom glanced at her, but if he was surprised to see her sitting there on her own, he didn't let on. He was looking at her, and Cecilia felt a turn in her stomach. The sense of something changed. Ben gave a tiny harrumph, small hands clutching at his father's coat. Cecilia watched them, and there was something, unsaid words waiting.

Tom sighed. Sounded like an old man. 'I'll be back in a minute.'

Cecilia nodded, watching as he turned. Footsteps creaking on the stairs.

Richard had cried. After the tea had gone cold, sitting untouched on the kitchen table. Had leaned on his hands and sobbed. She had stroked his back. Thinking again that this was so wrong. That she could do this for someone else's child but not for her own. Thinking that there was something so wrong with her.

He had cried until he had nothing left in him. Then he had pushed himself to his feet, movements abrupt.

'I have to go.'

'Well.' Cecilia had stood too, pulled by the intensity in him, that look like he's decided something she can't even begin to fathom. 'Let me run you home.'

He hadn't looked at her. Shook his head. 'I have a car.' Had stopped, then had looked up at her. 'Thank you.'

Then he was gone.

She had watched him walk down the drive. Had

tried not to think too hard about the lie she had told.

Thought instead about her hand on his back. The ease with which strangers cried on her. The fact that her own son barely seemed to know her. Was it possible that she was two people? One strong and brave and kind, when she was out there amongst those she barely knew. And the other weak and afraid and distant, when she was in here with her family, the ones best equipped to hurt her. A part of her wanted to run. Her eyes looked around for the keys, mind running through what she would need, what she would take. But of course everything she would take she had taken. And it had fallen from the sky, just like she had.

She had stood there at the window, looking out at the snow. Thinking of Maisie. Frail and little and tough. Facing down what life had to throw. Not turning from it, pretending. An inimitable hope. Then, when all hope was lost, quiet, unyielding acceptance. The high-pitched trilling had startled her, her mobile phone vibrating harsh against the wooden cabinet, and she had stared at it, wondering who in the hell would be calling her.

Number withheld. Her heart had beaten a little faster. Her brain had no idea why.

'Hello.' Cecilia's voice came out as a rasp, one she didn't recognise.

'Oh hi. Is that Mrs Allison?'

Was she? Was that who she was? Wasn't it only a minute ago that she was Cecilia Williams, most popular girl in her sixth form? Now *she* had been a fun girl. Young, exciting and excited. Whatever happened to her?

'I . . . yes.'

'This is Yvonne, from Morriston Hospital? Maisie's nurse.'

'Oh.' Fear gripped her stomach. *Please no. Please don't say it.*

'You left your number the first time you came. Maisie, she—'

'Is she dead?' The words blurted out of Cecilia, a sob buried within them.

'What? No. No. God, I'm sorry. No. It's just that she wondered if you could bring some stuff in for her. Her daughter's coming tomorrow, and she says she'd like to look . . . ah . . . I think "less like death" is the way she phrased it. She said if you're coming in to see her, would you bring her some lipstick and a hairbrush.'

'Lipstick,' repeated Cecilia faintly.

'Pink, if you have it.'

'Pink. I . . . sure. Yes. Okay.' Cecilia turned, sinking on to the sofa, her head in her hands. 'Of course.'

Her heart beating in her mouth. She had said goodbye. Hung up. Stared into space. And suddenly knew, more clearly than she could remember knowing anything, that she couldn't pretend any more. She couldn't keep hiding, hoping that if she kept her eyes closed for long enough then the past would vanish, become just a dream she once had.

The creaking floorboards came from a lifetime away, closer, closer. She didn't look up as Tom came down the stairs. An amorphous vision in her periphery. She waited as he walked into the living room, sinking down on to the sofa next to her.

'I can't do this any more.'

It took her a moment to work out whose words they had been. Hers or his. Which one of them had finally said it, ripping the plaster off.

He was looking at her.

'I'm sorry, Cecilia. But we can't go on. I'm not happy. And I know you're not happy.'

She was watching his lips move. Felt a flush flooding through her. Tears sparking in her eyes. Realised that it was gratitude she was feeling. She didn't say anything, couldn't speak. Just nodded.

'I think, for Ben's sake, we need to call it a day. I . . . I don't know what your thoughts are about the house, and about . . .'

'I'll go.' She didn't want him to say it, didn't want to have to hear herself admit that it wasn't her that Ben needed, that it wasn't her who should stay. 'It's okay.'

'I'm sorry.'

Cecilia didn't say anything for a moment. Then reached out, took his hand. 'It was never right, was it? For you either?'

'No.'

'I'm sorry.'

'No, Cecilia. It's not your fault. It's . . . it's us. We were never meant to be here. If not for . . .'

'Ben.'

'Ben.' Tom hung his head. 'I wanted to try. I so wanted to try. Give him a proper family.'

'I know. But it's . . .'

'. . . pretending.'

'Yeah.' Tears were spilling down her cheeks. 'This way. It'll be better.'

'I guess.' He squeezed her fingers. 'I wish it could have been different. I really, really do.'

'Me too.'

They sat there for a long, long time. And then Cecilia leaned forward, and kissed Tom on the lips. A kiss that seemed to last longer than their entire marriage.

'Thank you.' She was crying now, openly, and when she pulled back she realised that so was he.

'You don't have to . . . I mean, there's no hurry.'

'No. I'll go now. I'll come back for my stuff.' Cecilia stood, picking up her handbag, her coat, her keys. 'Tell Ben . . .' Her voice cracked, and she let it. 'Tell him that I love him very much. Okay?'

She didn't wait for Tom's response, but turned on her heel and walked out of her life.

She made it to the car. Was sitting in the driver's

seat, letting the tears fall, when her mobile phone began to ring again. She reached for it without thinking, never stopping to wonder if it was Tom asking her back. Knowing that it wasn't.

Richard.

Her finger moved to the answer button.

Outside, a few stray flakes of snow fell.

CHAPTER 46

Freya: Tuesday 27 March, 12.55 a.m.

Dan drove steadily, taking his time on the quiet midnight motorway. They had sat for a while, hadn't said much. Freya risked a glance at him. He was, she thought again, good-looking. Strong in a kind way. Then she looked back out of the window, pretending to study the banked-up snow, headlights hitting it, making diamonds of it.

'So, you're doing a PhD?' Dan glanced sideways at her.

Freya smiled. 'Yes. In psychology.'

'God. That's impressive.'

She laughed. 'Yeah. You think that. Until you get in there. Then you realise that what you've become is a crazy person who works in a lab and has no connection to reality, and that after three years or four years, however long it takes, you'll be so over-qualified you'll be pretty much unemployable.'

'But you keep going?' He was smiling wryly.

Freya shrugged. 'I know. I'm stubborn. Can't bear to give up.'

You need a boyfriend, sis.

Did she? Could that be true? How was it possible that she could have moved through her life, all twenty-three years of it, and never had this most fundamental of relationships? There had been men, of course there had. She wasn't a nun. But the moments had been fleeting at best. A few dates here. A month or so there. And it was, she had to admit, always the same. It was always her who ran. Once it got past a certain point, when it wasn't just about the fun of it any more, she would suddenly get this feeling, her skin crawling with impatience. Would feel like she couldn't breathe, couldn't move. Would have to go.

She stared out of the window, into the snow, thought of the men she had hurt. It's not you. It's me. And they were always perfectly pleasant guys. It was true. It was her. Because after a while, once the thrill had died down and the excitement began to fade, they all began to look like her father.

'So, have you been a police officer long?'

Dan shrugged, a pause as he worked it out. 'Nearly ten years. It's a good job. The guys are great.'

'I imagine it can be tough, though.'

'Yeah. Yeah. CID can be, especially. Long hours. But it's worse for those with families. I'm lucky like that. The hours don't really matter to me.' Said in a tone that suggested he didn't think he was very lucky at all. 'How, um, I mean, this thing with your dad. It must be really hard on you. You know, and your family.'

They were coming close now, only a mile or so to go till the exit. The snow was light here, only patches of slush remaining.

'Yes. It has been. For my mother the most. And my brother.'

'And you?'

And me? Suddenly Freya felt a heat behind her eyes. 'Yes. I suppose. For me too.'

Then they were sliding up the off ramp, and slowing at the traffic lights, tyres splashing in puddles of melted snow.

'The tow truck is a couple of minutes behind us. It won't take long. We'll just pop your dad's car on it, get it out of your hair.'

Freya nodded, strangely grateful that he hadn't used the words. *See if there has been a dead body in there.* Snuck another glance at him. Thinking that he looked nothing like her father.

'Okay.'

But it wasn't okay, was it? Because this couldn't possibly be her life.

Then they were rounding the corner. Into the quiet street where the snow had all but vanished, melting away, revealing its secrets. And there, where her father's Mercedes should have been, was the empty drive, slush outlining the bare space, chalk around a corpse.

CHAPTER 47

Tom: Tuesday 27 March, 8.09 a.m.

Tom shrugged his coat off, slinging it on to the back of the desk chair. He didn't sit though, not for a moment, standing looking over the deserted Swansea streets. The magistrates' court was still closed for now, would spring to life later. The doorway, usually littered with the guilty and the innocent alike, blowing dark smoke into the busy street, now locked up tight, floor-to-ceiling windows bouncing sunlight on to the rapidly melting snow. The temperatures were starting to rise, a full-blown thaw beginning. It wouldn't be long before all the snow had melted away.

The CID office was empty. Desks littered with papers, chairs pushed back, all waiting. Something knotted in his stomach. Guilt. He shouldn't have come in today. Should have stayed with his son. He hadn't told Ben that his mother had left, had banked on him not noticing, had dressed him and given him breakfast. *I'm sorry, buddy, but I've got to go into work for a couple of hours. Not long, I*

330

promise. You okay going to see Grandma? Ben had shaken his head, cheeks billowing with Coco Pops, chin stained a chocolate brown. *I go with you, Daddy. I see Maddie.* A smile, a feeling like his heart would break. *Not today, kiddo.*

Tom slid into the chair, pain lancing through his shoulder. They needed a holiday. Just the two of them. They would go somewhere that Ben would enjoy. Maybe Florida. Once this was done. He glanced at his watch, wondered what Jim was doing now. Whether he had slept, with the bleeping of machines, the nurses checking him every hour. They would go on holiday, but first this had to be done. Jim had asked him to keep him informed, tell him what he found. He deserved to know this. Wouldn't bring his daughter back, but still, the truth can set you free. Glanced at his watch again, even though it was seconds since he'd done it the last time. Once he had done this, once he was sure, he'd drive down there, tell him face to face.

Pulled the phone towards him, even though it was early. Punched in a number on the card taped to the phone. Listened as the phone connected. Started to ring. Allowed himself to wonder, just for a moment, where Cecilia had gone last night. Then pushing it away because he had other things to deal with, and, ultimately, what did it matter to him any more? He was almost startled when the ringing stopped, a voice on the other end, sing-song, and far too bright for a morning like this.

'Hello, Forensic Sciences, Gillian speaking.'

'Hi, Gillian. It's DC Tom Allison from South Wales Police.'

'Hello, Tom. How are you on this lovely morning?'

'I'm fine. Look, I know it's early . . .'

'No, no, we're all done. I finished it off myself this morning.'

'What have we got?'

'We had a look at the glove. The one you so kindly provided us with. We found a small area of blood in between the thumb and index finger.'

'And?'

'The blood is a match to that of Libby Hanover.'

'Shit.'

'Indeed. We also looked for DNA, skin cells and that kind of thing, inside the glove. Now, your very handsome partner so kindly brought in Oliver Blake's hairbrush. I understand that his daughter volunteered it? We compared the DNA that we found inside the glove to that lifted from Mr Blake's hairbrush. They were a match.'

'So the gloves were worn by Oliver Blake? What does that mean? We got him?'

'Not exactly.'

There were footsteps just outside, a heavy tread, the door swinging open. Dan stopped when he saw him, a frown, mouth shaping words. *You okay?* Tom nodded quickly. 'Sorry, say again?'

'I said, not exactly. Things are a little more complicated than we were expecting. Now, like I said, the blood on the glove was Libby's, the DNA

332

inside the glove was that of Oliver Blake. But the PM also threw up skin cells under her nails which the pathologist concluded were likely to have come from her attacker.'

'Okay?'

'Those skin cells belonged to someone else.'

'You've got to be fucking kidding me.' Tom closed his eyes, could feel himself sliding down in the chair, could feel Dan's eyes on him, wanted to throw the phone, just pick it up, lob the whole thing through the mirrored glass window and go home, back where he should be, with his son.

'Calm, Detective. Breathe. I haven't got to the really interesting bit yet, and if you're not a good boy, you won't get to hear the real headlines.'

'What's that?'

'Well now, the skin cells that were found under Libby's fingernails, the DNA isn't a match to that of Oliver Blake. It is, however, pretty close.'

'What does pretty close mean?'

'Well, let me tell you, we can do some pretty fancy stuff here. I mean, I am an expert, you know.'

'Impressive,' Tom mumbled.

'Isn't it? Anyway, we had a look at something called short tandem repeats on the Y chromosome. I won't bore you with the details.'

'Too late.'

'Oh, Tom. You wound me. But despite that, I am willing to give you a little present. Call it a goodwill gesture. What our testing has shown is that whilst the skin cells don't come from Oliver Blake, they do come from someone to whom he was very closely related. Someone male. A son, perhaps.'

CHAPTER 48

Tom: Tuesday 27 March, 9.20 a.m.

The phone rang, and rang, and rang. Tom gritted his teeth, hand pressing against the dashboard as Dan took a bend hard, engine whirring from the pressure. Pulled the phone from his ear, glancing at the display, hoping that he had dialled the wrong number, that he had called the house instead of her mobile, and of course she wouldn't be there. *Cecilia mobile.*

'You okay?'

'Been better.'

'What's . . .?'

'It's over. She's gone.'

Dan looked across at him. 'Shit, mate. I'm sorry. What happened?'

Tom didn't look at him, stared at the road ahead. 'We talked. Decided it was for the best.' He gestured to the phone. 'And now I'm chasing her again. The kid, Richard Blake? I saw him at the memorial service. Didn't know it was him at the time. But then Freya mentioned it and I put two and two together. He was staring at

335

Cecilia. And there was something . . . I found footprints in the garden, under our kitchen window in the snow. I think it was him. I think he was watching Cecilia.'

There was silence, Dan processing this. 'You think . . .'

'I think that a murderer was watching my wife.' Forgetting for a moment that she's not his wife any more. 'And I think that now I can't find her.'

Dan glanced across at him. 'Try her again.'

Pushing buttons, car skewing on slick roads. It could just be that she wasn't speaking to him, didn't want to answer. She was probably sitting somewhere, maybe in some hotel, probably nowhere near Richard Blake, staring at her phone, Tom's name on the caller ID, letting it ring. She couldn't know that he wasn't begging her to come home.

'Anything?'

'Nothing.'

'Fuck.'

'Yeah.'

'You don't think he would have . . .?'

'I don't know.'

'No. No. Best not to think the worst. No point, really.'

What was the worst? That he'd killed before. That he'd already dragged one lifeless body to a snow-bound riverbank, dumping it before returning to his life. That this boy had been watching his wife. That he couldn't find her.

Breathe. Breathe. 'Look, I'm probably getting carried away. It's probably nothing.'

'Yeah. Probably.' Dan wasn't looking at him. 'I put out an observation request on the Mercedes. We'll find him.'

'Yeah.'

'Try her again.'

The phone rang and rang.

Dan braked sharply, banking the kerb as though he'd never driven before. The driveway was empty, the windows of the large double-fronted house staring blankly out at them.

Tom slipped his seat belt off, climbing from the car, pushing the door closed behind him. Rapid steps down the drive. Pushed his thumb hard against the doorbell. There was a shape, coalescing behind the stained glass. He could feel himself tensing, fingers flexing, tight from the cold. Dan's bulk beside him. The door pulling open, a breeze of warm air.

Freya started when she saw them, gaze falling to Dan. A tentative smile. Then a new emotion, crowding in on top of the old, the realisation that this isn't a social call. Her shoulders pull themselves in, bracing herself for what's to come.

'Freya.' Dan's voice was softer than Tom was used to hearing it, apologetic almost. 'Your brother, Richard, is he here?'

'No.' She frowned, looked confused. 'Why?'

'We . . . we need to find him.'

She stood there for a moment, studying them,

and then a new shadow crosses her face. She sways, like a boxer who has taken too many hits, buckling from the final blow. Dan stepped forward, reaching for her arms.

'No. I . . . no. That's ridiculous.' She let out a laugh, more of a squawk. 'For God's sake. That's absurd. He's a kid.'

'Freya. I need you to listen to me. I am so sorry, and I know you've been through so much. But we *have* to find him.'

Looking at Dan, small hands clinging to his thick wrists. Like she will fall down without them.

Then, slowly, face creased in pain, she righted herself.

'He didn't do this. He wouldn't do this. I . . . Look, I think I know where he might be. I'll take you to him and he can tell you. You're wrong. Let's . . . let's just go, and you'll see that you're wrong.'

CHAPTER 49

Freya: Tuesday 27 March, 10.00 a.m.

They were wrong. That was all there was to it. There had been some mistake. And whatever the forensic evidence said, whatever the DNA said, there would be some explanation. Because this was her baby brother. The little boy she had carried around the house, cradling like a doll, had caught up in her arms when he took his first steps, and defended when the mean kids picked on him in school. There was a space in her head for a father who could cause death, sow destruction with the force of his own self-involvement. There was even room, if she worked really hard and twisted it and turned it, for a mother who lashes out because she's been hurt so many times and because she can't stand for her life to be like this and because she's so, so angry.

But not this.

She couldn't fit this. This one didn't make sense.

They would find him, and they would talk to him, and he would explain and then the detectives would understand.

The other one, Tom, he was driving now, steering them gut-churningly fast around mountain roads. Dan kept glancing over his shoulder, trying to meet her eye. Freya looked out of the window, tried to ignore the tears that simply would not stop falling.

Couldn't believe it. Wouldn't believe it. Because if she did, and if this was true, then she had been just as blind, just as wilfully self-deceiving as the family that she had judged so harshly.

Tom slowed down as they hit Talgarth, easing the car through the narrow streets. And there was the Mercedes, parked at a dog-leg angle, the front tyres riding the pavement in front of the church, a swathe through the snow, its rear bisecting the carriageway. Sunlight glinted from it, dazzling.

The detective stopped the car, braking too hard so that their bodies lunged against the seat belts. Freya pushed the door and it swung open, almost sideswiping a Ford Ka. She slammed the door shut, taking off at a run. The village was stirring. Voices, laughter, coming from somewhere she couldn't identify. The smell of bread baking, cinammon and honey. Smoke curling from chimneys. Her winter boots slipping in the slush. She ducked down a side street, in through the wrought-iron gate. The churchyard was still, deathly quiet.

The church was locked up, porch barred against the people who would defile a house of God. Freya stopped, pulled up sharp. For a moment didn't know where to go. Had been so sure. She spun on the spot, looking at the gravestones, the over-hanging trees were he had hidden before. But there was no one. Just her, the detectives following close in her wake.

She had to find him. She had to find him. Because if she found him then he could explain. And it would be something perfectly reason-able and logical and Dan's face would lift with relief, and they could go back to where they were, which, bad as that had been, still remained infin-itely better than this.

Her gaze rolled across the yew trees and the houses, climbing up to the mountain. Then she was running again, pushing past Dan, slipping, sliding. Along the pavement, on to winding roads still quilted in snow, overhung by bare dancing branches.

The police tape remained. The ruined building, the charred metal, layered with snow. And her brother kneeling on the bitter cold ground, his head bowed forward. For a heart-chilling second, Freya thought that he was dead.

'Richard!'

But there was movement, a stirring, and then she heard something else, the sound of sobbing.

'Richard.'

She reached him, her hand gripping his shoulder. Ducked down beside him, where she could see his lip trembling, round tears rolling down his cheeks.

'Richard? Honey. What is it? Richard? I need you to tell me what happened.'

There was a sound behind her, the quick crunching of footsteps on snow, and she glanced back, even though she knew without seeing. She held out her hand, her palm out, and Dan slowed, stretching his arm to slow his partner.

'Richard?' She sank to her knees, the cold gnawing through her jeans, put her arm around her brother. 'I need you to tell me the truth.'

CHAPTER 50

Richard: Tuesday 27 March, 10.05 a.m.

Richard was sinking into the snow, the cold clawing at him, promising to swallow him whole. Didn't mind that, though. At least then it would be over. Looked at his sister, swimming in and out of focus. Knew that he shouldn't say it. Should do what his father had told him to do and just keep his mouth shut. But she's looking at him, really looking, right into his eyes, and her hand is clutching his, and it's like a promise, that she can pull him back over this cliff edge that he is clinging to.

'I didn't mean it.' His words were broken up, part swallowed by the sobs, and he sucked in a few quick gasping breaths, still grasping his sister's hand.

'What, honey? Didn't mean what?'

'I'm . . .' Breathing hard, then goes at the words with a run, the only way he can get them out. 'Frey, I'm not, am I? Please say I'm not.' He had pulled her closer, without realising he was doing it, so that his head almost rests on her shoulder. He can smell the coconut shampoo she uses, that scent that is just her.

'I don't understand, Rich.'

He closed his eyes, nestling in so that her hair grazed his face. 'Please tell me I'm not a monster, Frey.'

He had watched Libby through the bright-lit window, the way he had a hundred times before. Lithe, swaying like she's dancing to her own private tune, her chestnut hair tied up in a low knot, grazing the nape of her neck, white pressed shirt, black trousers. He watched her, glancing at the clock, leaning out of view, rising again, hands full of plates, opening a cupboard, stacking the plates on to shelves. It was snowing heavily, thick, torpid flakes that snuck their way into his collar, melting, trickling ice-cold water between his shoulder blades. He had stood in the shadow of the fence, where he had stood so many nights before, just watching.

It was the car that had done it, his R-reg Ford Fiesta, formidably old and yet new to him. He had passed his test less than a week before, the car a present from his parents – something to get him on his way. But the Fiesta had shuddered to a halt on narrow country lanes. Less than a mile from Cardiff airport. He didn't have his phone with him, had left it on his bed that morning. Had sat there for a while wondering what it was that he should do. Then he had seen the wing lights of a plane, low overhead, gliding in for a landing. He would go to the airport. His father should be back now, and if he wasn't, he shouldn't be long. He would go to the airport and wait for him. It had been late, around nine o'clock, but it was a late summer evening, sky just shifting to sepia. It would be a pleasant walk. He had set off, tucking into the hedges when cars came by, thinking about his father, surprised to see him, a look of pleasure, that he can show off his son. Perhaps he'll suggest they go for a drink. They'd never done that. Maybe he'd take him on to his plane, let him sit in the pilot's seat.

He had got to the airport, was pushing his way through a middle-aged tour group with their roll-along suitcases, their harried expressions, when he saw his father. He was wearing his pilot's uniform, a smile lighter than he had ever seen before. He was holding her hand. Richard had stopped, pulled up sharp in amongst the tutting and sighing tourists.

She was young, not much older than Richard himself. She was pretty and slender and had a face made for smiling.

He had stood, as they walked right by him. As they slipped into the car park. As his father pulled her in, kissing her.

Had felt the anger clawing at the base of his skull, tasting something in his mouth, green and bitter. Had wanted to run after them, drag the girl away from his father, say to her, *You think he's so*

345

great? He's married. He has kids. And he's done this before. Loads of times.

He had followed his father, the next time he left the house throwing out some ill-thought-out, unlikely excuse. Hadn't been able to stop himself. Had driven his car, the one he had had repaired himself, never telling anyone that there was anything wrong with it, hanging back on the M4, his father's Mercedes only just in sight, towards Swansea and the setting sun. Had followed him to her house.

After that he just couldn't seem to stop. He didn't know why. But even when his father wasn't there, he would go. Just to see. Found the back entrance, the shadows by the fence that fell just so. She was attractive in a careless kind of way. He would dream about her, looking at him the way she looked at his father. After a while he searched out her number, taking it from his father's phone while he showered. Had distant thoughts of talking to her. But when the time came, he couldn't. It was enough to hear her voice, though, that lightly trilling 'hello', said like she really wanted to hear from you. Like she was pleased that you had called. So he, had picked up a cheap mobile from the supermarket, a pay-as-you-go, had tried to tell himself that there was nothing wrong in that, that the subterfuge didn't turn it into something sordid and unpleasant. And had called. Again. And again.

He knew it wasn't normal. He knew it wasn't

right. But then, what his father was doing wasn't right either. So how much worse could this be? Really? And he was lonely. He was so bloody lonely. He had friends, of course, if you could call them that. Guys that he had gone to school with, that he still saw now in college. They would hang out. Have a laugh. But he couldn't talk to them. Couldn't talk to anyone. Had tried occasionally to talk to his mother. But she could never listen, her head always seemingly so full of his father, of where he was, what he was doing. It was like she was obsessed with him, like he was all she wanted, even above her own kids.

He had got angry with her one day, after another failed attempt at a conversation. Had snapped. Throwing out something about his father's girlfriend. He had even told her about the lockbox, the picture, the receipts, found after many hours of searching. Had done it so that she would have to listen. Had seen her face, her world tumbling out from under her. Felt terrible after. But still, he had reasoned to himself, at least things would change now. His mother would deal with it. She would yell at his father and his father would stop and then there wouldn't be this anxiety, this cloud hanging over their family all of the damn time, and maybe one of them would listen when he spoke. But instead there was nothing, just a choking ball of silence.

So he had gone back to his father's girlfriend. Watching. Wondering what the hell it was she had that could so efficiently capture his father's attention, while he never could.

Libby had been sitting at the kitchen table, pulling on her work shoes. The light dancing off them. She would leave soon. He would wait until she was gone, then he would slip away. Just like he always did.

But then the fence behind him shook. Richard started, heart thumping.

The black and white cat dropped soundlessly on to the thick snow, stopped, looking up at him questioningly. He pressed back into the fence. Then it turned, trotting along the path, to the patio doors and the bright light of the kitchen. A miaow, plaintive and unearthly.

She stopped what she was doing, she looked up, squinting to see into the darkness beyond the snow. A smile, pushing herself to her feet, reaching to the kitchen counter for a key, twisting it in the lock, pulling the door open.

'Hey Charlie boy. Come on in.' Reached down, scrubbing the cat behind the ears, smiling so brightly. 'You want some food, mister?'

Turned back into the kitchen, the cat dancing and winding around her legs, almost tripping her, and she laughed a sparkling laugh.

The door hanging open.

He wasn't going to go anywhere, wasn't going to move. But the door was open, it was beckoning him, like she wanted him to go in, and without knowing what he was doing he had felt his feet unstick from the wells of snow, carry him forward. She wasn't looking at him, her back was turned, and he walked towards the light, pulled, the warmth from the kitchen caressing him, and he was so cold. Stepping inside.

He didn't know what he was expecting, hadn't thought that far ahead.

She spun, shoulders spiking, and the look on her face wasn't the one he'd been seeing in his dreams. It was fear instead.

'Who are you?'

He just stood there, and it seemed that his mouth had been stoppered up. Because he knows her so well, how can it be possible that she doesn't even know his name? So he stood there, dripping melting snow on to her kitchen floor, his mouth opening and closing uselessly, until finally he managed to squeeze out 'Richard' like that will answer everything.

'Get out.' Her voice was all hard edges, eyes flashing. Her hands at her sides, knotted into fists, and it was all so far from where he'd imagined it.

So he raised his hands. Meant to show her that there was nothing there, no weapon, that he's not a danger to her, so that she'll calm down and she'll listen to him, and then they'll talk and then it will all be all right. But he must have done it wrong, moved too fast, because instead of calming down she flew at him, her nails catching his cheek, grating the flesh with a stinging pain. Her narrow hands gripping his wrist, twisting it around so that

349

it throbs, and he can feel himself being pulled down.

And he pulled away, because now he was frightened and now he wanted to run. So he yanked his arm backwards with all his might, and even though she was strong, she couldn't hold on to him. Letting go. Stumbled backwards, an 'oh' of surprise, and Richard felt a wash of relief, half turning towards the still open door.

Then there was a thud, bone on granite.

Afterwards it was the sound that would replay, over and over in his head. Afterwards he wouldn't be able to remember how long he had stood there, how long it was before he sank to his knees, gripping her by the shoulders, begging her to wake. But she didn't. She just stared at him, eyes flecked with the horror.

He would remember that he cried, sobbing, wrenching tears, for the girl lying dead on the floor, for what he had done.

And he would remember the sound of the key, grinding in the lock. The squeal of the front door. Slow, uncertain footsteps.

'Lib?'

He had been sitting on the floor, curled up beside the girl, almost touching her but not quite. Had heard his father's voice as if from a long way away.

'Lib? Are you . . .'

Then he was standing at the kitchen door, staring at the girl, at his son.

'Dad.' Richard remembered reaching out to

him, pleading. 'It was an accident. I didn't mean to . . .'

His father wasn't looking at him, was looking at his girlfriend. Strands of hair had unwound themselves from her bun, falling into her eyes. His father crouched, reaching out a shaking hand, brushing the hair aside, touching the softness of her cheek. Then, in a strangled voice that Richard had never heard from him before, 'She's dead.'

'I didn't mean to, Dad. Honest. I was just . . . She went for me, and I was just trying to push her off . . .'

He didn't look at Richard, growled, 'Shut up.'

Then he stood up and was gone.

Richard wouldn't remember how long he was alone, left with the consequences of his actions. Looking back, it would seem to have been a lifetime. Then there were footsteps again, but from the other direction this time, and his father coming in, hair white with snow.

'Come on.'

'Where?'

He still wasn't looking at Richard, was still staring at the girl. 'We have to move her.' His voice poured liquid hatred.

'I . . .'

'You want to go to prison? You want to be known as a murderer?'

Couldn't speak, shook his head.

'Then fucking move.'

He crouched again, over his girlfriend. Richard

351

pushed himself up, too afraid to do anything else, and reached out a tentative hand towards her.

'No. Don't you fucking touch her.'

His father, pushing the hair back behind her ear, slipped his hands underneath her, lifting her, a sleeping child. Her head lolled on to his chest, she's so tired. Leaving behind a dark smear of blood. Pushed himself up slowly. Crying. He turned, walking with her out into the night, pulling Richard along behind him. He had moved his Mercedes, had pulled it around into the car park, positioned it close to the gate, boot open. He laid her down, so gently, Snow White in her glass coffin. Stood there for a moment, staring, then, without looking at his son, 'Get in.'

They drove in silence, and, although it couldn't have been far, the trip took them a lifetime. Pulling in to a copse of trees, hidden from the road, turning off the lights, turning off the engine. His father picking her up like she was no weight at all, cradling her, they walk through the driving snow, along the cycle path above the iced river, walking and walking and walking, and then they stop.

'What are we doing, Dad?'

In a far-off voice, 'She likes it here.'

He pushed his way through undergrowth, balancing on the precipitous bank, seems inevitable that he will fall, that the tragedy of their night will be compounded further. Richard standing on the bank, waiting. Then his father stopped, laying her down, like he was putting her to bed, tucking snow under her head as a pillow, under-growth as the blanket. He stooped and kissed her on the lips.

Richard turned, looking along the empty path into the blizzard.

Then he was back and they were walking again and his father still wasn't looking at him and, although he wanted him to, Richard didn't blame him. They climbed back into the car, his father leaning forward so that his head was resting on the steering wheel.

'Dad? I'm so sorry . . .' Richard was reaching out, his fingertips, blue with cold, brushing the soft cashmere of his father's jumper.

'Don't.' His father pushed himself up, turning, finally looking at him, but it's with something like hatred. 'Don't. We're going back. We're going to clean the house. We're going to hide it so that you don't go to prison for the rest of your worthless little life.'

'I . . .' Richard was crying now, hard, heavy tears. 'I'm so sorry, Dad.'

His father had turned the key, starting the engine.

Richard pushed himself back, looking up at Freya, realising for the first time that there were other people there, men that he couldn't place. But he wasn't looking at them, he was looking at his sister, and she was looking at him, and she looked frightened and there were tears in her eyes, and now he is frightened too, because he can feel her loosening the grip on his hand, so he grips her tighter.

'He never spoke to me again, Frey. I think he hated me.' Clinging on to her fingers, pushing his face into the nape of her neck. 'You still love me, Frey? Don't you?'

CHAPTER 51

Tom: Tuesday 27 March, 10.47 a.m.

Freya cradled him, a small boy with a grazed knee. Looking up at Dan, at Tom, eyes pleading, *just one more minute, just one more minute*. And so they wait, even though time is pressing so heavily, and there is something resting like a stone in Tom's stomach. She rocked the boy back, forth. She was crying, silent tears streaking her cheeks, staring into the wreckage of her father's crashed plane. Tom watched them, but it isn't them he sees, but himself cradling Ben. Wondering what he has done to him, what the consequences of that will be. Have I taught him to be blind? Have I taught him not to face up to things because it is easier? Is it already too late?

Then Freya leaned back, half sitting in the piled-up snow, and unravelled her arms from around her brother. She looked at him, studying him like she was seeing him for the first time, then up at Tom.

Tom stepped forward. 'Richard Blake, you are under arrest for the murder of Libby Hanover.'

He could see Libby's body in the snow. Jim, a broken man with his head rested on the mortuary glass. 'You do not have to say anything, but it may harm your defence if you do not mention when questioned something which you later rely on in court. Anything you do say may be used in evidence.' It felt like a rosary, a balm to wash away sin. That in spite of all that he has done wrong, there is this that he can give to a family and say, *I did my best.* 'Stand up for me please, Richard.'

The young man looked at him, as if he was seeing him from a very long way away, and Tom could feel his muscles tense, waiting. Then, as if he was a thousand years old, Richard pushed himself to his feet, hands held out, palms down, head sunk low. Tom clasped cold metal around his wrists, fingers brushing bare iced skin. Thinking of Libby on a mortuary slab, of smoke so thick it steals the breath from your chest, a pulsing heat that presses down on you, threatening to devour you whole.

'Did you set fire to the house, Richard?'

The boy looked up, glazed, confused almost. 'I . . .' Looking at his sister, and she looks afraid again, as if she's wondering just how much more there is to come. 'I'm sorry. I was just . . . I was so scared. It was a mistake. Please. It was a mistake. I didn't mean to kill her. I didn't want to. And I didn't know how to fix it, and Dad was gone, so I thought, if the house wasn't there any more, they wouldn't want to arrest me . . .'

'So you set fire to it?'

He paused for a long moment, then a quick nod. 'I put petrol in the letter box.' Then his voice dropped to a whisper. 'I didn't know that her father was in there. I heard it on the news. After. That's why I came here, I just, I didn't know where to go, and Dad, he always knows what has to be done, but he's . . . I'm so sorry. I didn't mean to hurt anyone.'

Tom stared at him, this man-child, so heavy with what he has done, so weighted down by it, and yet for him the answers are so simple. *I did it because I didn't want to think about it.* Thinks of his marriage, knowing that he is somewhere that he shouldn't be, and yet willing to push it away, do whatever he had to, just so he wouldn't have to think about it.

'Richard.' His voice was softer than he had expected it to be. 'Where's Cecilia?'

'Cecilia?'

'Cecilia Williams. She's my wife.' Saw him pull back, a wash of recognition crossing his features. 'You remember me? From the memorial? From the kitchen, the night you were standing in my garden, watching me and my family. Just like you did with Libby.' Now there was something else, something building inside, the anger and the fear. 'What have you done with Cecilia, Richard? The same as you did to Libby?'

Freya was crying openly now, and she had reached out a hand, clinging on to Dan as though without him she would fall. Looking from her brother to Tom.

'I don't know . . .'

'What do you mean, you don't know? You don't know what you did with her?'

'No, I, I didn't do anything. I saw her last night. And then, I called her, late, but I couldn't reach her, she wasn't answering.' Gestured to the metal fragments, the burn marks on the ground. 'I didn't speak to her, honest I didn't.'

Wanting to rail back and punch him. Just because it'll make it easier. But Tom was looking into his eyes, and saw it sitting there. He was telling the truth.

CHAPTER 52

Cecilia: Wednesday 28 March, 10.22 a.m.

Cecilia walked, high above the crashing waves. The rocks tumbled away beside her, a precipitous fall into white foam pierced by jagged edges. A cold wind swept in from the sea, wrapping itself around her and tugging at her clothes, her face. There were few other walkers. Too early, too cold. But Cecilia didn't mind, the quiet suited her. Just her and the seagulls that circled overhead.

Thought about Tom, his phone call yesterday, his voice quick, fearful.

'Are you okay?'

'What? Yes. I . . . why?'

A long, static-filled silence. She could hear his breathing, slowly steadying. 'I'm sorry. It's . . . it's nothing. It's okay. I just, I wanted to check, and I couldn't get hold of you.'

'I'm sorry. I was at the hospital. Visiting Maisie. I left my phone in the car. You sure everything's okay?'

'Yeah. Yeah. It's okay.'

'Look,' Cecilia had taken a deep breath, 'I was wondering . . .'

'Yeah?'

'Tomorrow. Would it be all right if I visit? To see Ben?'

Tom had paused. She thought she could hear him smile. 'Yes. Of course it is. Look, I was going to do him a party. You know, he didn't get one for his birthday. Just my mum, a couple of the neighbours. Will you come for that?'

Cecilia had pulled in a deep breath, steadied herself. 'I . . . I'll try.'

A rough cawing broke out above her. She tucked her hands into her pockets, tilting her head upwards. The seagull spun, gliding, then plunging downwards, faster, faster. Like it was falling. But then, just at the last second, as it hovered inches above the white foam, it pulled up, climbing again. Not falling then. Flying.

She had been to the hospital, way before visiting hours. Had held her head up, pretended that she belonged. Had stood for a moment watching Maisie eating porridge, spooning it to her mouth with slow, awkward movements. Then Maisie had become aware of her standing there, had looked up with a smile that had lifted Cecilia six inches off the ground.

'I brought your lipstick.'

Maisie had set down her spoon, leaning back against the pillows. 'Well. Now, you shouldn't have come so early. It could have waited.'

Cecilia smiled. 'Didn't want you looking like death when your daughter gets here.'

She had held out the lipstick and Maisie had reached, grasping her hand tightly. 'You. You're a good girl. Do you know that?'

Tears had sprung into Cecilia's eyes. She shook her head, not trusting herself to speak.

'No. Now you listen to me, young lady. Without you, I wouldn't be here. You kept me alive out in that field. I know you think I'm wrong.' Maisie was watching her, gaze knowing. 'But it's true. I know people. I can always tell. And whatever it is you think about yourself, you're one of the good ones. You mark my words, my lovely, things will come right.' She had squeezed Cecilia's fingers tightly.

The tears had spilled down Cecilia's cheeks. She leaned in, kissing Maisie on the cheek, allowing her to brush away the tears with awkward fingers. Maisie didn't ask why she was crying, and Cecilia didn't tell her that she had spent the night in the Marriott. Had ordered room service, had taken a bath. And had cried and cried and cried. For all that had passed. For all that would never be.

Cecilia watched the gull. It was carrying something in its beak now, a prize for its daring. Watched it climb, climb, until it vanished into the sunlight. She turned, looked out over the waves, the wind scouring at her cheeks until they burned.

She couldn't even remember why she had gone

361

into the cockpit now, some last-minute errand before the passengers boarded.

'You, ah, you got a minute?' Oliver had been facing away from her, had been sitting in the pilot's seat, punching in numbers. For a moment, she hadn't been sure that he was talking to her, had glanced over her shoulder at the co-pilot, whatever the hell his name was. But he had gone, had slipped through the door into the main cabin, muttering something about using the head before the chaos began.

Oliver had glanced back at her, following her gaze. 'Guy's a prick. Won't last long here.'

'Yeah.' She hadn't wanted to talk, had wanted to do her job and go back to her seat. She hadn't looked at him.

'I, ah, shit.' He'd let out a sound, a half-laugh, half-sob. 'Shit, I've had a rough day.'

'Yeah?' He looked grey, like he hadn't slept in months. Cecilia had pulled her papers together, glancing up at the snow. Not at him, though. Looking anywhere but at him.

'You, ah, you ever done anything bad?'

That had caught her attention, gluing her to the floor. Her heart had begun to thump. 'What?'

'I, fuck, what was I . . . oh, there it is.' He was still typing in numbers, moving dials. 'I don't know. I just, ah, you ever just wish that you could go to sleep and never wake up again?'

She hadn't been able to speak, the words clogging her throat, wondering how it was possible that he could know so much. Had felt him watching her, and it was like he was pleading with her for something, only she didn't know what. Hanging there, waiting to see which way life would go. Then the door had swung open, the co-pilot squeezing his way back into the cockpit, a wave of voices getting closer, and now she had an excuse, a reason to run away. She hadn't looked back. Had just pasted on a happy smile. Had left knowing that he was still watching her.

Another seagull wheeled overhead, diving on thermals. Or maybe it was the same one. How did you tell? Cecilia leaned her head back, tilting so that she almost fell, watched it until she felt dizzy. It sounded like a newborn baby, crying.

CHAPTER 53

Jim: Wednesday 28 March, 11.03 a.m.

'Did you see him? When you came in? That bloke across the way there. You know the one, grey hair, bit paunchy. The one sleeping. Well, he's that bloke. You know, was in that fire. His daughter was that girl, that police officer they found dead.'

'Mum. Shhh.'

'No, well, I'm saying. Did you see him?'

Jim stared at the curtains pulled tight around the bed on the opposite wall. Could feel their gaze through the thin fabric. Wished like hell that he was anywhere else. Had tried to leave, had told the doctor that he'd had enough, he was fine, that they could just remove these damned drips and these beeping bloody machines and let him go home where he belonged. He had meant it too, at the time. And then Esther had looked at him, locked him in a spotlight stare. *You're staying. No, I'm not. I need to come home. Jim, I'm telling you now, you are staying.* She had folded her arms across her chest, had pulled herself up, a Napoleon in

364

tennis shoes. *I've lost enough.* Her voice had fractured, a crack running right through the heart of it. *I am not losing you too. You are staying until they tell you that you are ready to come home. Now that's an end of it.*

'Yes, I saw him.' The second voice was low, a whisper. The woman's daughter at least attempting to be discreet. But honestly, they were hidden by fabric. 'Keep your voice down . . .'

'Oh, he's asleep. Well, I tell you. There's a lot of coming and going. They had someone here, late last night. I mean, it's not on, it's really not on. There was me, trying to get some sleep, and they're like chatting and all.'

'Right, well . . .'

'No, but it turns out they found him. You know, the one who did it. That's what the police came here to tell him.'

Jim stared at the curtains. You beg for answers. You tell them, and yourself, that you cannot live another day without them. You have to know. You have to unravel it, pulling at the thread until the entire pattern is laid bare, and then you can understand why it is that this has happened to you. He knew this. Had spent thirty years chasing those answers for everyone else, because they were that important. They mattered.

And then you get your answer.

Tom had arrived late, after the lights had gone off, the television silenced. Jim hadn't been asleep, had been struggling lately, not keen to close his

365

eyes. Kept feeling the flames lapping at his skin, the smoke pressing down on him. He had considered reading, had a Ludlum, page corner folded down, but couldn't seem to bring himself to do that either. So he had lain there. Waiting.

At first, when he heard Tom's voice, he wondered if he had fallen asleep after all. But there was no heat, no fire burning his skin. He had pushed himself up, glancing around the darkened ward, deep-throated rumble snores washing their way from the bed in the corner, the elderly man with pneumonia. The lights were bright over the nurses' station. And there stood Tom.

He had known then. Had felt the knowledge of it plump inside his stomach. You wait for the answers, because you believe, right down in the guts of you, that the answers will make everything better.

Tom had turned, seen him. Had raised a hand in greeting, gestured to the nurse, words that Jim couldn't hear. The nurse, the one with the short hair, cut to make her look like a man, glanced over her shoulder, had sighed audibly.

Jim had pushed himself up, pain racing along his side, down into his pelvis. Tried to shift the elephant on his chest. Was breathing like he had run a damn marathon. But he had wanted to be sitting up for this.

Tom had walked quietly, glancing around at the other beds, the patients sleeping, or at the very least, pretending to.

'Hey.'

'Hey,' Jim echoed.

'How are you feeling?' Tom had slipped into the chair, fingers clawing at the fabric on his knees.

Jim shrugged. 'You didn't come to ask me that.'

'No.'

'Well?'

Tom had lifted his head then, his gaze settling on Jim. 'I have news.'

'You got him?'

Tom had looked at him, framed the words carefully, picking his way across fractured ice. 'We got him.'

Jim had expected happiness, had expected the moment to come with a flush of relief, satisfaction at the very least. But instead, his heart had pounded in his head, he could taste bitter iron in the back of his throat.

'Who?' The word seemed to stick, coming out as a croak.

Tom had spoken slowly, his voice soft. Had talked about the boy, for that was all he was, about his father. About the relationship that Libby had been having, the one that she had kept a secret even from Jim, about the phone calls, and the boy standing hidden in the shadows beyond her kitchen window.

'I don't believe that he meant to harm her. But that is no consolation.'

Jim wasn't looking at him, had gone back to studying the patterns on the cardboard-stiff blanket. You pray for answers, and you think they will make everything all right. But when you get the answers, you realise that they are merely a beautifully wrapped box that is empty inside. Because no matter what, she is still dead.

Then Jim had cried.

'Awful thing, mind. Awful. He doesn't like to talk about it. I did try.'

'Mum!'

'No, well, he's not well, is he. Not feeling very chatty. He was in a fire, you know.'

There were footsteps, out in the hall, and Jim shifted his gaze, anything to distract from the inane twittering. Was hoping that it would be Esther. He had rung her, after Tom had gone. Had told her what he had said. Had held the phone, useless, as she cried. Then the steps rounded the corner. Ethan looked like he hadn't slept, was wearing cargo pants, a sweater, two days' worth of stubble. He glanced up, giving Jim a water-weak smile, and Jim felt a flash of irritation, and then a spill of something else, guilt, bile rising in his throat.

Staring at his son, now two years old again, shrieking, 'Uppa, Daddy!', always so happy to see him, a laugh that would light up your world.

When did it change? When did it go from that to this? They say the teenage years are the hardest. Was it then? His son striking out, becoming a person that Jim didn't recognise, and Jim not man enough to cope with it. Or was it simply that Libby came along, and was so much more like him, so much easier to understand, that he got lazy, just stopped trying with Ethan, allowing him to vanish into his sister's shadow?

Ethan wasn't looking at him. Or rather was, but from under lowered lids, like he was afraid to face him head on, like he didn't know what to say to his father, in case the words he chose would be the thing that would annoy him, set him off.

Jim wanted to cry again.

'You all right, boy?'

Ethan paused, taken aback. 'Yeah, I . . . Well, you know. Mum, Isabelle's with her. She's doing okay. She's having a little sleep. Said she'll be along later.'

'Good. That's good.'

Ethan pulled out the chair, lowered himself into it, a quick glance at the curtained bed across the way. They were talking about *EastEnders* now.

'Dad. I . . . Can I ask you something?'

Thinking of the first time he had ridden a bike, baby-round hands gripping the handlebars like they are all that lies between him and the end of the world, knees pumping. 'Daddy, I'm doing it. I'm doing it, Daddy.'

'Of course, Ethan.'

'Did you think it was me?'

Jim stopped, stared at his son. Ethan was plucking at the blanket.

'We had that argument, me and Libby, before she . . . Did you? Did you think I killed her?' A tear slid down Ethan's cheek.

Did he? Did it ever cross his mind?

'No,' said Jim. 'Never.' He grabbed hold of Ethan's hand, held on for dear life. 'You are my son. I know you. I know I'm tough.' His voice was giving, bowing under the pressure of the words. 'But you . . . you and your mum. You're all I've got, boy.'

Jim felt Ethan's hand close around his own.

CHAPTER 54

Tom: Wednesday 28 March, 1.32 p.m.

Tom rolled the Blu Tack between his fingers, back and forth, feeling it soften with his body heat. There was music playing, a tinny bass from the radio in the kitchen. He reached up, tugging softly at the banner, pushing the putty on to the plastic, the plastic on to the wall. HAPPY BIRTHDAY, BEN!! Ben would be home soon. Tom glanced at the clock, another half-hour or so. In another hour the guests would start arriving – his mum, some of the kids from playgroup, a neighbour or two. And Cecilia. He pulled in a breath. If she came. She had said that she would try, but . . . He wouldn't tell Ben. Wouldn't mention it, just in case.

'What the hell is wrong with these things?' Dan studied the balloon in his hand, frowning. 'I'm telling you, mate, you got a dud batch.'

'They're not dud. You just can't blow them up.' Tom slid from the stepladder, looked up at the banner. Crooked. Damn. 'Surprises the shit out of me. What with you being so full of hot air and

371

all.' He moved the ladder over, one step, two, and climbed up it.

'Funny. You're funny.' Dan pulled at the red latex. 'Who's got Ben, then?'

Tom tugged the banner straight, leaned back, eyed the line, then pushed his thumb into the putty. 'My mum. They'll be back in a bit.'

'Oh, I was wondering, you know, if he was with Cecilia.'

The house smelt different. That was what he had noticed when he had woken this morning. That there was no trailing musk of her perfume, nothing left behind to mark her presence. He had gone to the spare bedroom, her bedroom, had stood in the doorway and stared at the empty bed, the skeletal wardrobe. There was nothing, no one big thing that marked out the change. She hadn't taken the television, the sofas. The fridge was still where it was supposed to be. In essence the house was as it had ever been. But still there was the smell.

'No. I invited her to the party. I thought it would be good. You know, for Ben.'

Dan nodded, blowing hard into the balloon, his face flushing as the latex expanded.

Tom climbed down the ladder. 'How's Freya?'

A pause as Dan finished exhaling, then the grating squeak of the latex being tied. Dan shrugged, studying the tiny knot between his thick fingers. 'About as good as you would expect, I suppose. Her mother's a wreck, apparently. The brother was in magistrates' this morning. Crown next week.'

'So you've talked?'

'Yeah.' Still wasn't looking at Tom, face flushing darker. 'I called her just to, y'know, see how she was doing. Last night. We talked for an hour or so.'

'So, you think . . .'

Dan leaned over, slipping another balloon from the packet. 'I don't know. It's not a good time for her really, is it? I'm guessing dating is probably the farthest thing from her mind.'

'But you like her?'

'Bloody hell, Mother, yes. Yes, I like her a lot.'

Tom grinned. 'Good.'

'And Cecilia?'

She had called him, late last night. The phone had lit up, puncturing the darkness of the empty bedroom, and for a moment his heart had stood still in his chest. Because the house smelt different. And even though what there had been was so thin, surely that was better than the emptiness that its absence had left behind. It would be so easy, to slip back, just close his eyes. Pretend. He could do that. He wanted to do that, wanted everything to be back as it was, familiar and spiky and incomplete.

'Hello?'

'Hi.'

'Hey.'

'I . . .' It sounded like Cecilia had been crying. 'I'm sorry. I know it's late.'

'It's okay. I wasn't asleep.'

'Oh. Okay. I just . . . I wanted to tell you, I needed to say, I'm sorry.'

'For what?'

He could hear her breath, thought it sounded like ocean waves. 'I never gave you a chance. You are a good man. I know you are. And I never gave you a chance to be a good man with me. I'm sorry.'

'It's okay. It wasn't just you.'

'No, I . . .'

'Cecilia, it was me too,' said Tom. 'They weren't just your mistakes. They were mine too.' He stared into the darkness, and thought how much easier it would be, to step back.

CHAPTER 55

Cecilia: Wednesday 28 March, 2.45 p.m.

She drove slowly, steadily, along the M4. The snow was all but gone now, just the odd white patch turning the surrounding fields into an iceberg sea. She wondered if the party had started yet.

She had sat on the king-size hotel bed, her legs pulled up tight to her, so that the bed beyond seemed vast. Had needed to hear Tom's voice. In a way that she wasn't sure she had ever felt before.

'We're going to be okay,' said Tom. 'You and me and Ben. We had to make a change. Things just weren't working, for any of us.'

'No.' She had cradled her knees, had stared out of the window at the starlit sky beyond. 'I want . . . Tom, I want to do the right thing. For Ben. This time, I want to do what's right.'

He sighed heavily. 'Me too. But what we've had, where we've been, that hasn't been it.'

'No.' Cecilia plucked at the quilt threads weaving

their way across her feet. 'I hope you find happiness, Tom.'

There was a long silence, and for an uneven moment it had seemed that the world could be about to spin again, throwing them backwards. Then, 'You too, Cecilia.'

Cecilia indicated, pulling around a Mini travelling tentatively along the inside lane. She would have to find an apartment, a house. Something with two bedrooms. So Ben could visit. Her heart took a leap into her throat. Perhaps she would try to get somewhere near the sea. He would like that. In the summer they could play in the waves.

Then she thought about the other baby, the way she always did.

She pushed her foot down a little harder on the accelerator, passing motorway junctions. She couldn't forget. In truth, didn't want to. But there was nothing she could do for that first child of hers. And there was one who remained. Perhaps it wasn't too late for her to do something for him. You just had to keep on trying. An ambulance passed her, flying in the opposite direction, sirens blazing, and she could feel the flames, the screaming of the plane as it tore itself apart around her. She kept going.

Breathing. In, out. In, out.

Indicated, took the turning. Worked her way around the roundabout, slow through the country lanes. A quick glance at the clock on the dash-board.

She steered the car into her street. Their street. Pulled up outside the house.

Breathe. Just breathe.

There was a parcel on the seat behind her, wrapped in gaudy orange paper. A Mickey Mouse farmyard. She had gone to the shop, picked it out herself. Had handed the cashier the money, told her shyly that it was for her son. For his birthday. She reached over, hefted it with her good arm.

There were voices from inside the house, tinkling laughter. She stopped on the path. They were in the living room: Tom, the couple from number 43, Dan from work. And Ben. His father had put him in the shirt and sweater set, the one that he wore any time they went somewhere nice.

She stood there on the path. Watching. Ben was opening a present, tugging at the paper, his mouth an O of delight, and she felt her heart skip. But then there it was again, the sense of ghosts crowding in on her. An almost child on flimsy paper. A sharp pain. The sense of falling through the sky.

Cecilia's hands began to shake. She could leave the present. She could put it on the doorstep and go. She had only said that she would try to come. She hadn't said anything definite. She could turn and walk away and get in the car and drive to somewhere the ghosts wouldn't follow her.

But they did, didn't they? Wherever she drove to, wherever she went, they came too.

You just had to keep on trying.

She stepped forward and pressed the doorbell.